MERMIN™

BOOK FOUR: INTO ATLANTIS

MERMIN

PETE

TOBY

CLAIRE

PENNY

RANDY

BENNI

MAK

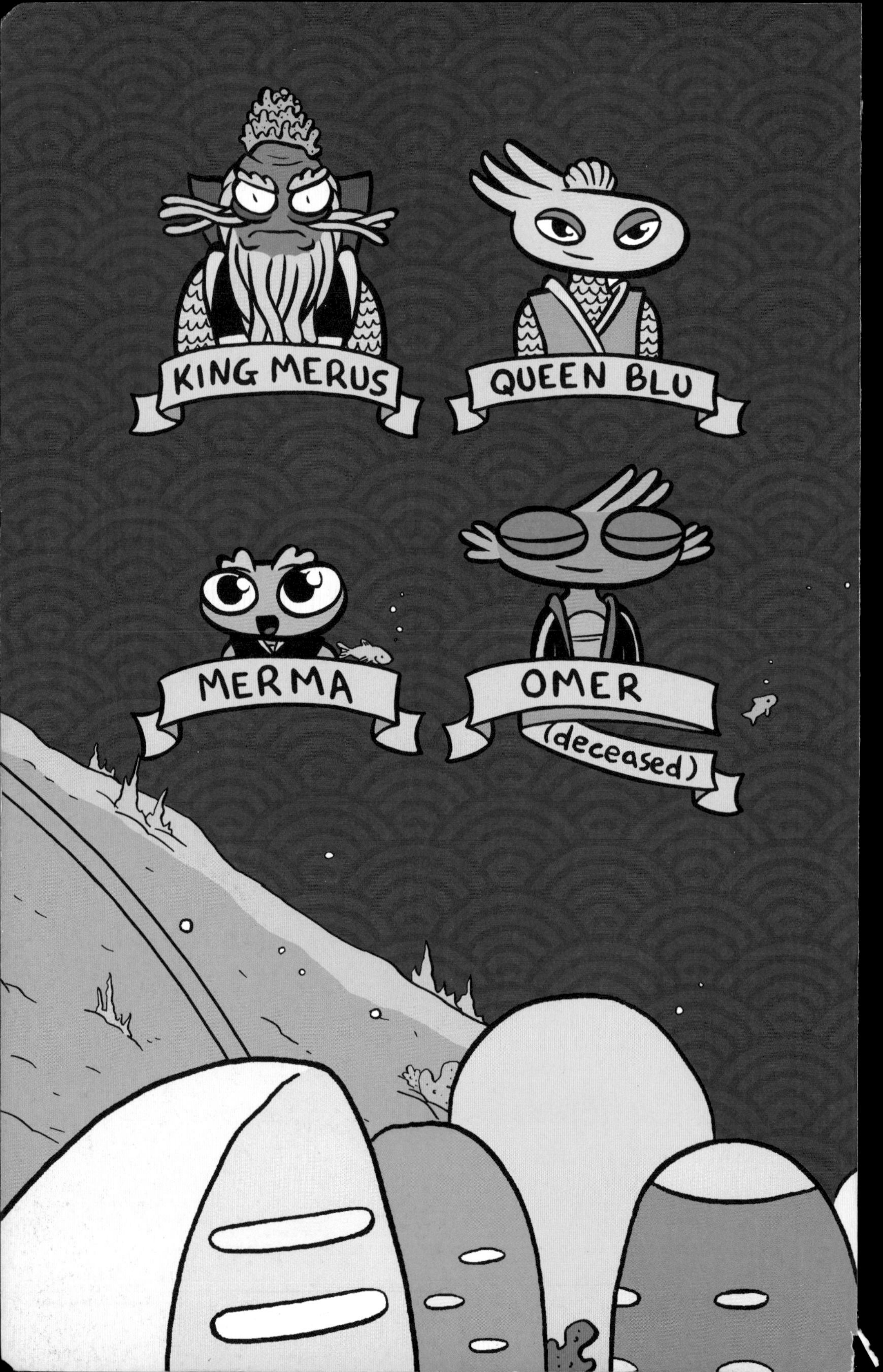
KING MERUS
QUEEN BLU
MERMA
OMER
(deceased)

MERMIN™

BOOK FOUR: INTO ATLANTIS

Written and illustrated by
Joey Weiser

Colored by
Joey Weiser and **Michele Chidester**

Edited by
Robin Herrera

Designed by
Keith Wood
with
Hilary Thompson

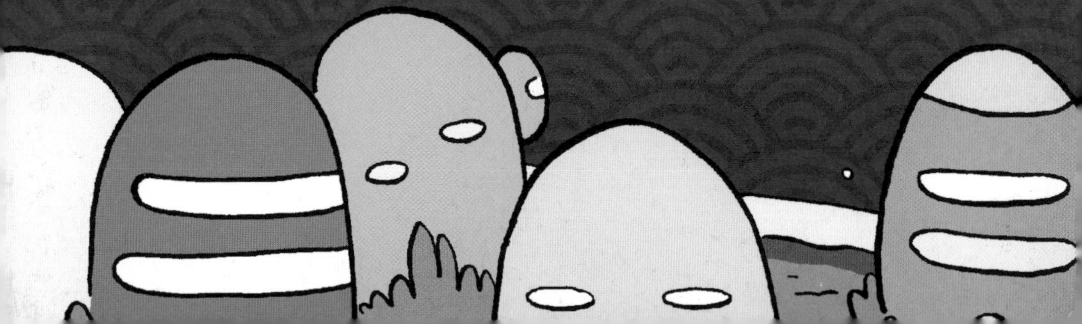

Published by Oni Press, Inc.

founder & chief financial officer, **Joe Nozemack**

publisher, **James Lucas Jones**

v.p. of creative & business development, **Charlie Chu**

director of operations, **Brad Rooks**

marketing manager, **Rachel Reed**

publicity manager, **Melissa Meszaros MacFadyen**

director of design & production, **Troy Look**

graphic designer, **Hilary Thompson**

junior graphic designer, **Kate Z. Stone**

digital prepress lead, **Angie Knowles**

executive editor, **Ari Yarwood**

senior editor, **Robin Herrera**

associate editor, **Desiree Wilson**

administrative assistant, **Alissa Sallah**

logistics associate, **Jung Lee**

ONI PRESS

onipress.com
facebook.com/onipress
twitter.com/onipress
onipress.tumblr.com
instagram.com/onipress
tragic-planet.com

First Edition: February 2018

ISBN 978-1-62010-467-5
eISBN 978-1-62010-259-6

Library of Congress Control Number: 2012953664

CHAPTER ONE

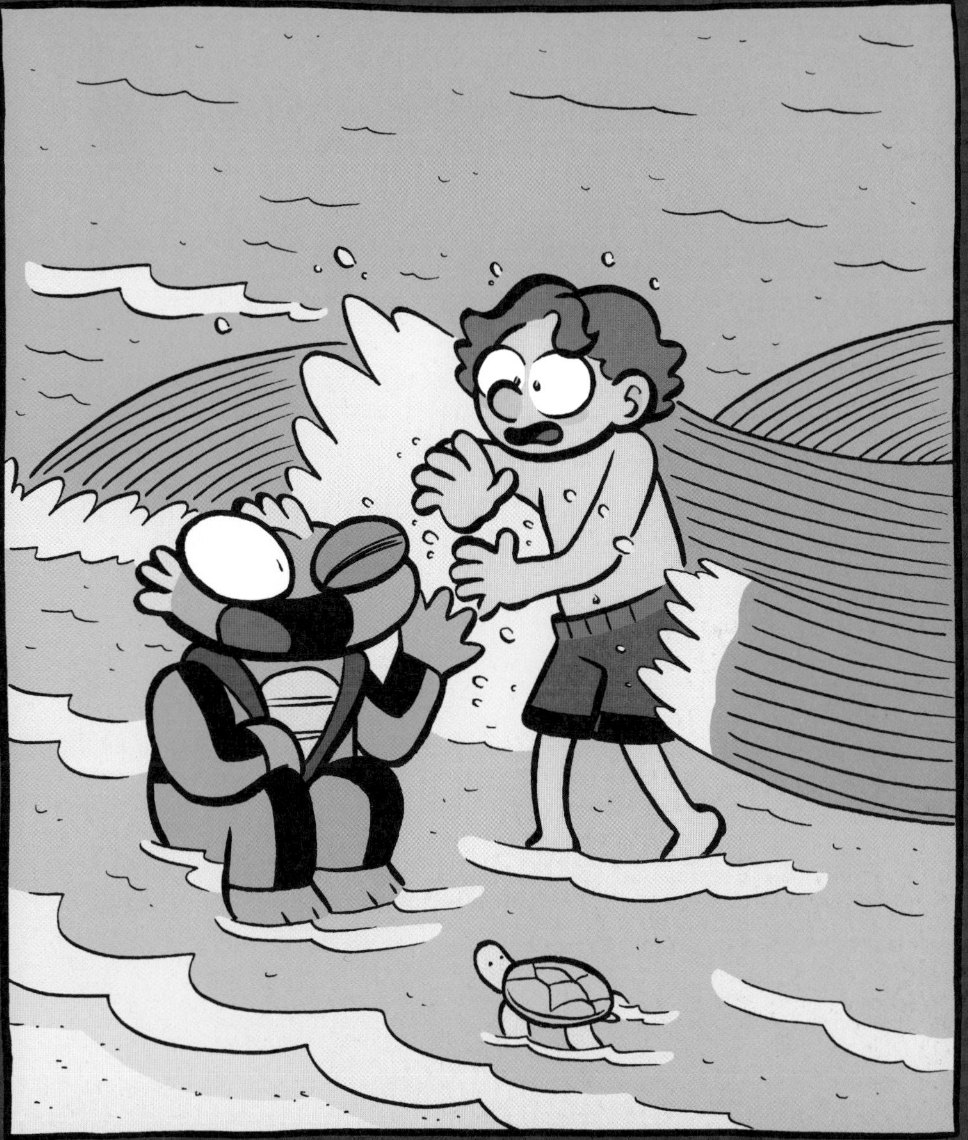

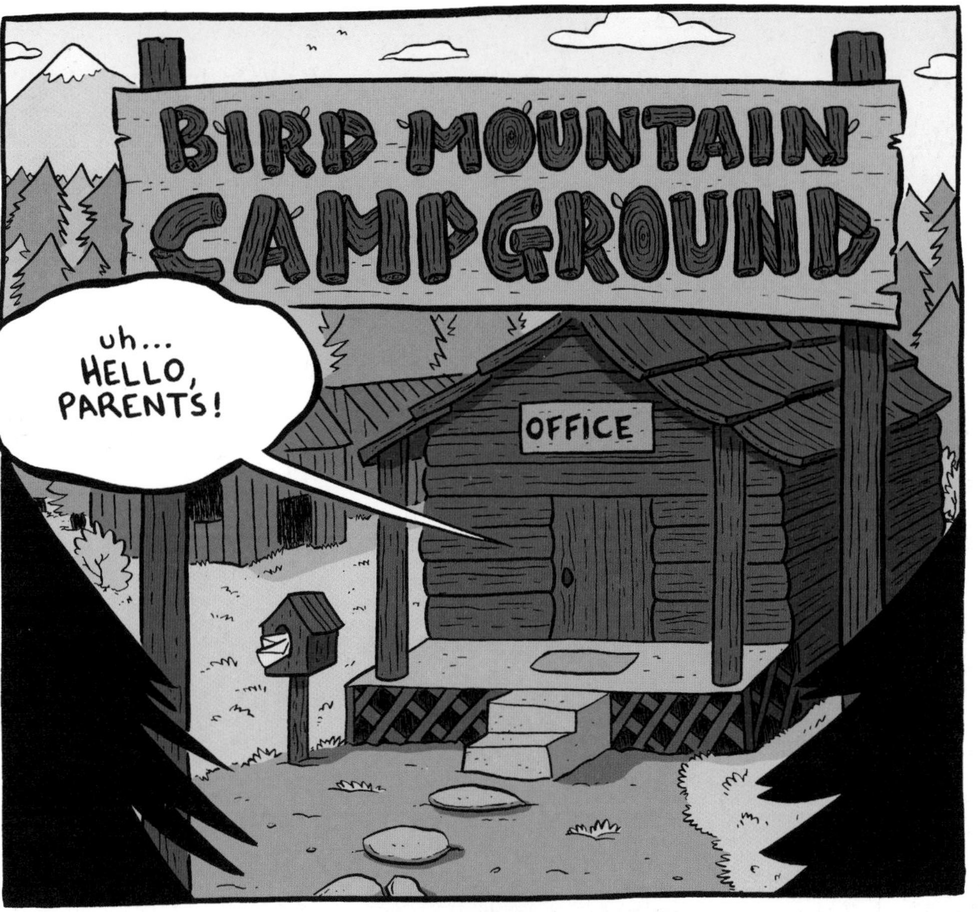
BIRD MOUNTAIN CAMPGROUND
OFFICE
uh... HELLO, PARENTS!

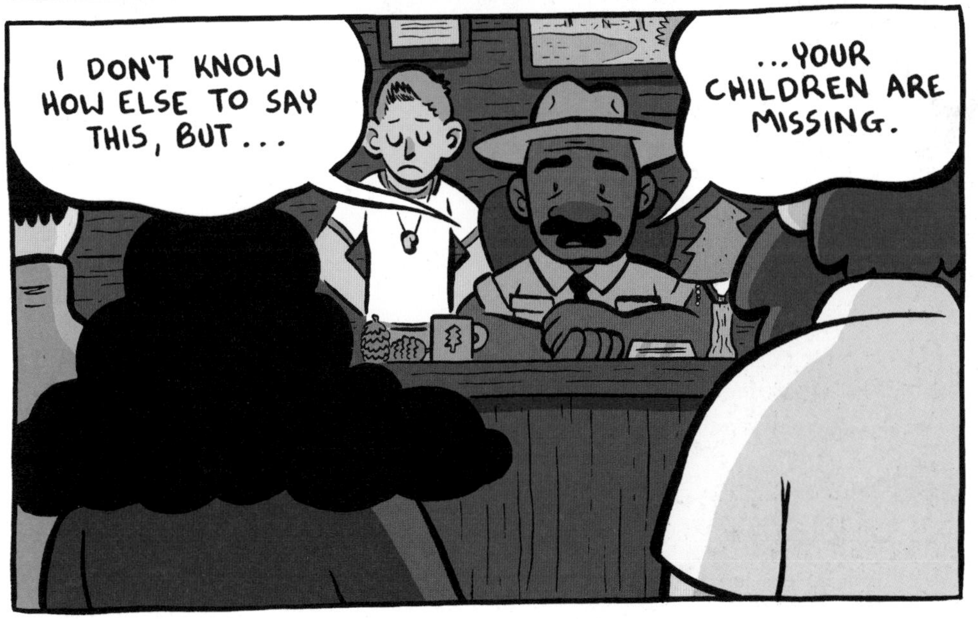
I DON'T KNOW HOW ELSE TO SAY THIS, BUT . . .
...YOUR CHILDREN ARE MISSING.

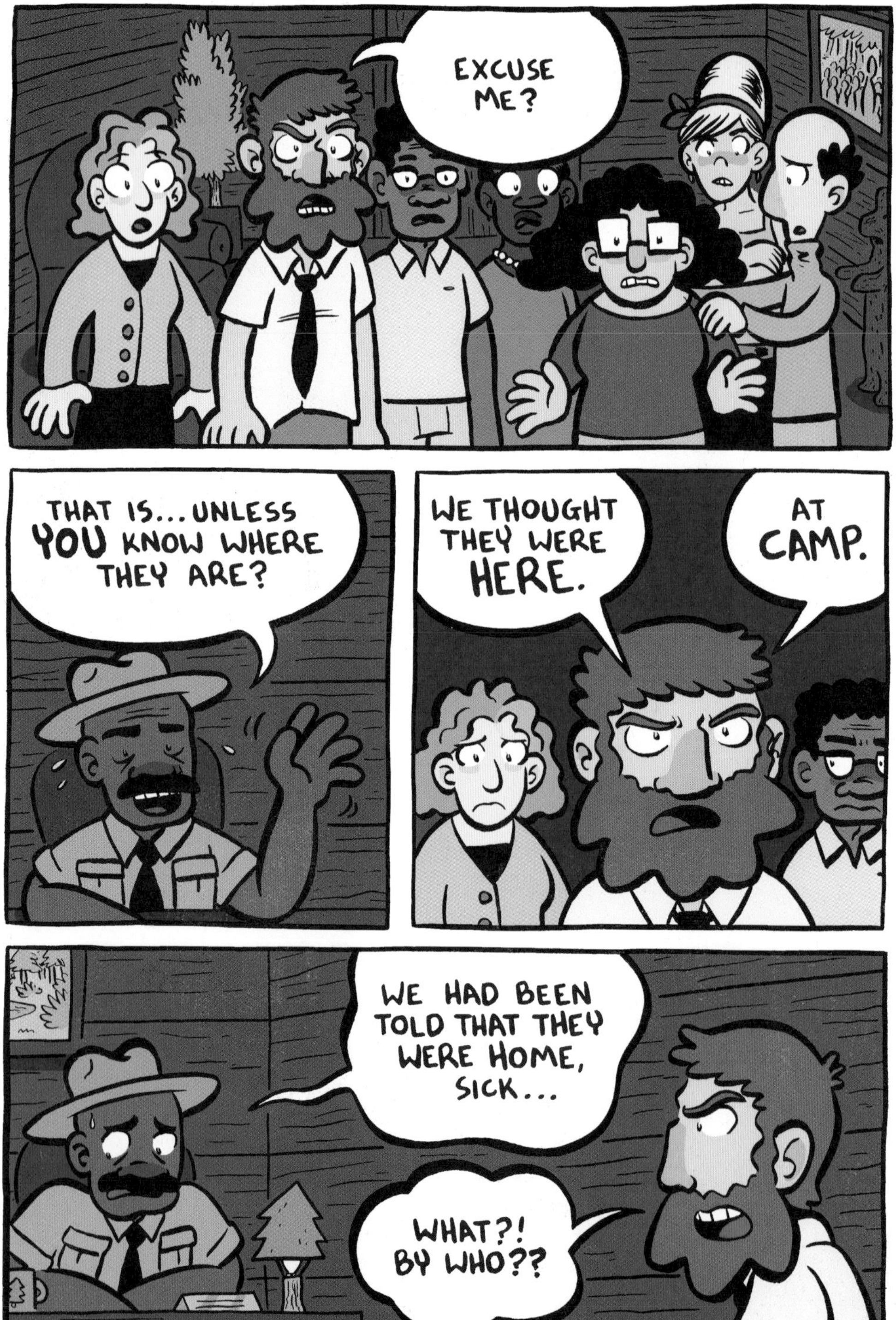
EXCUSE ME?
THAT IS... UNLESS YOU KNOW WHERE THEY ARE?
WE THOUGHT THEY WERE HERE.
AT CAMP.
WE HAD BEEN TOLD THAT THEY WERE HOME, SICK...
WHAT?! BY WHO??

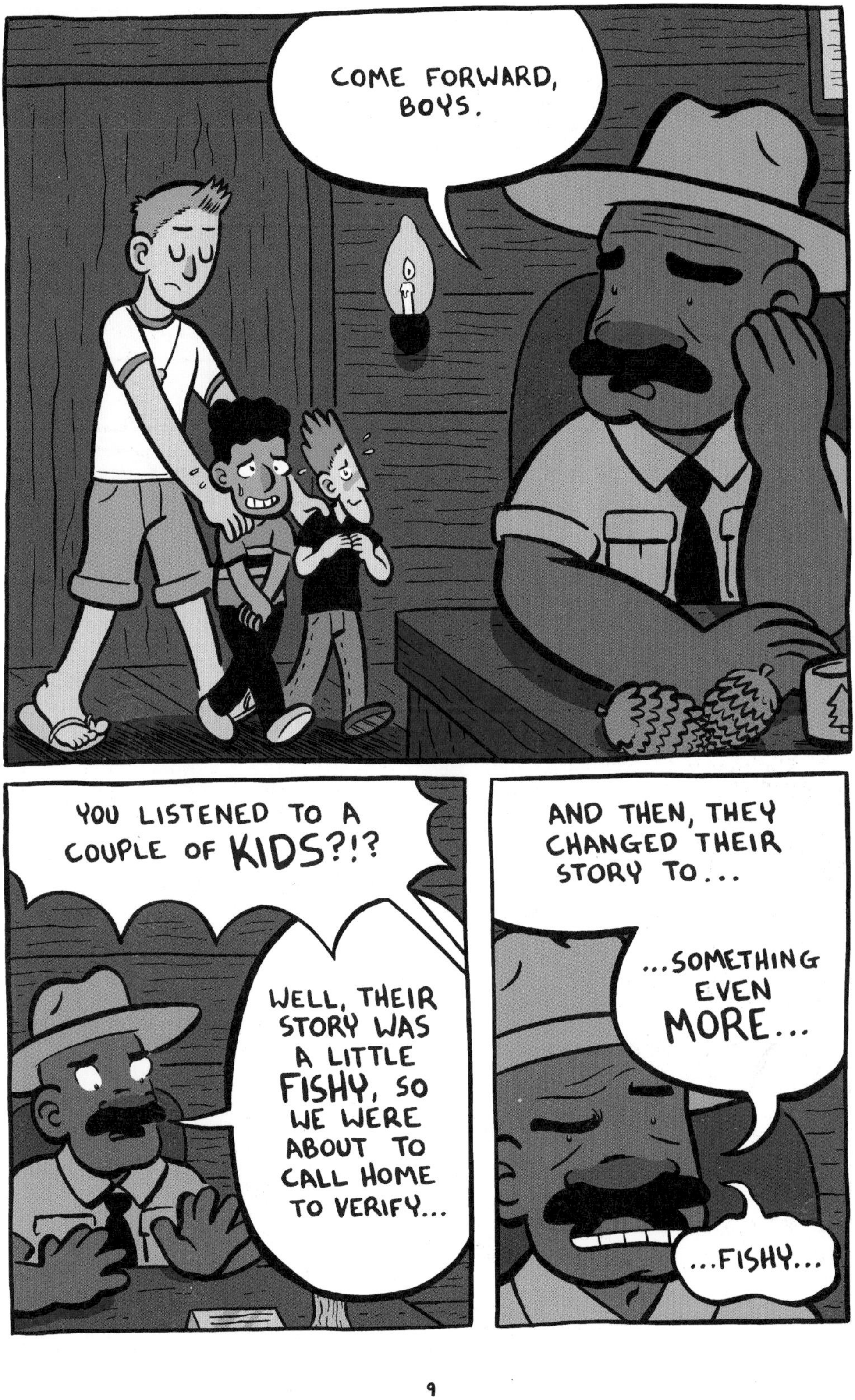
COME FORWARD, BOYS.
YOU LISTENED TO A COUPLE OF KIDS?!?
WELL, THEIR STORY WAS A LITTLE FISHY, SO WE WERE ABOUT TO CALL HOME TO VERIFY...
AND THEN, THEY CHANGED THEIR STORY TO...
...SOMETHING EVEN MORE...
...FISHY...

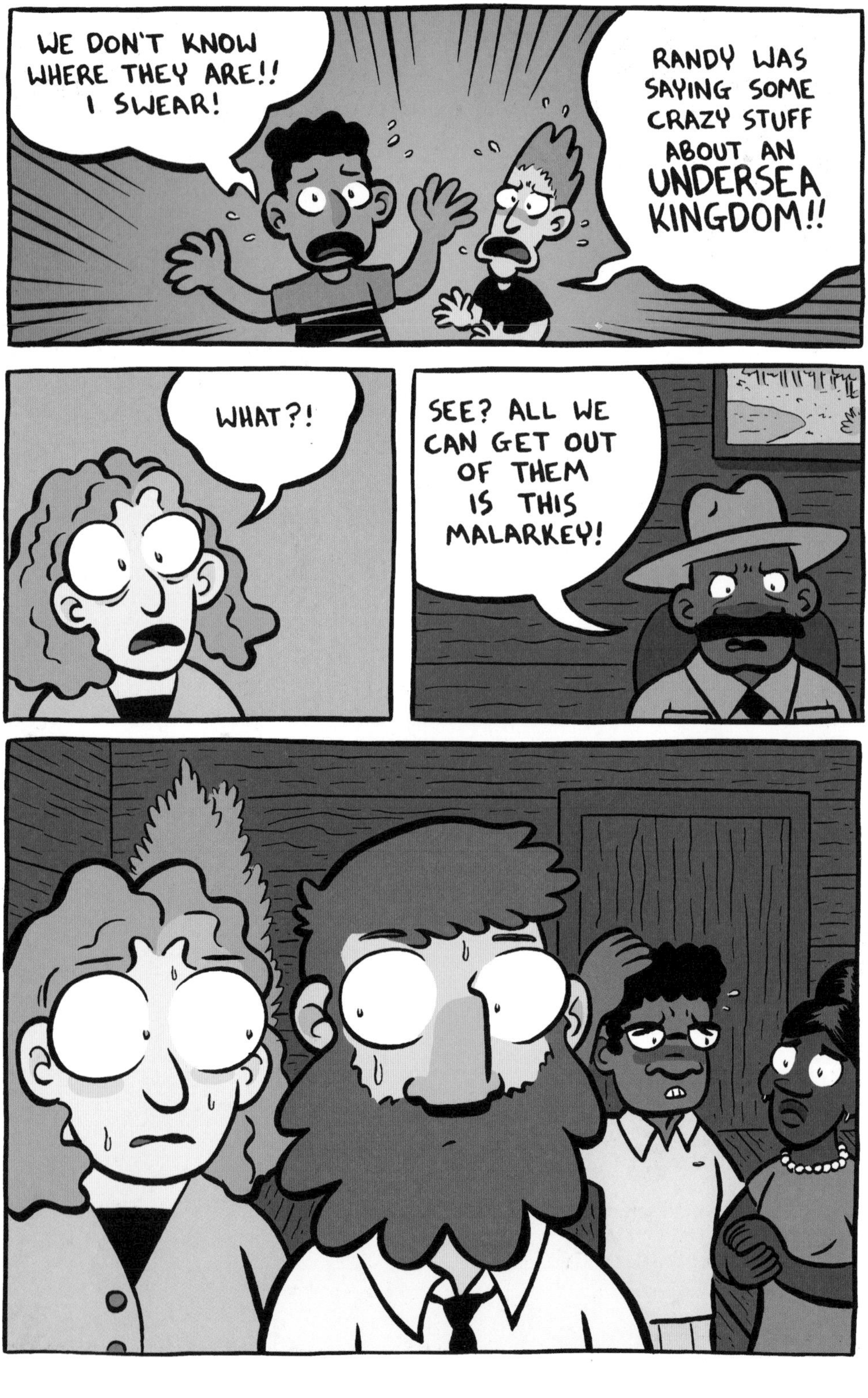
WE DON'T KNOW WHERE THEY ARE!! I SWEAR!
RANDY WAS SAYING SOME CRAZY STUFF ABOUT AN UNDERSEA KINGDOM!!
WHAT?!
SEE? ALL WE CAN GET OUT OF THEM IS THIS MALARKEY!

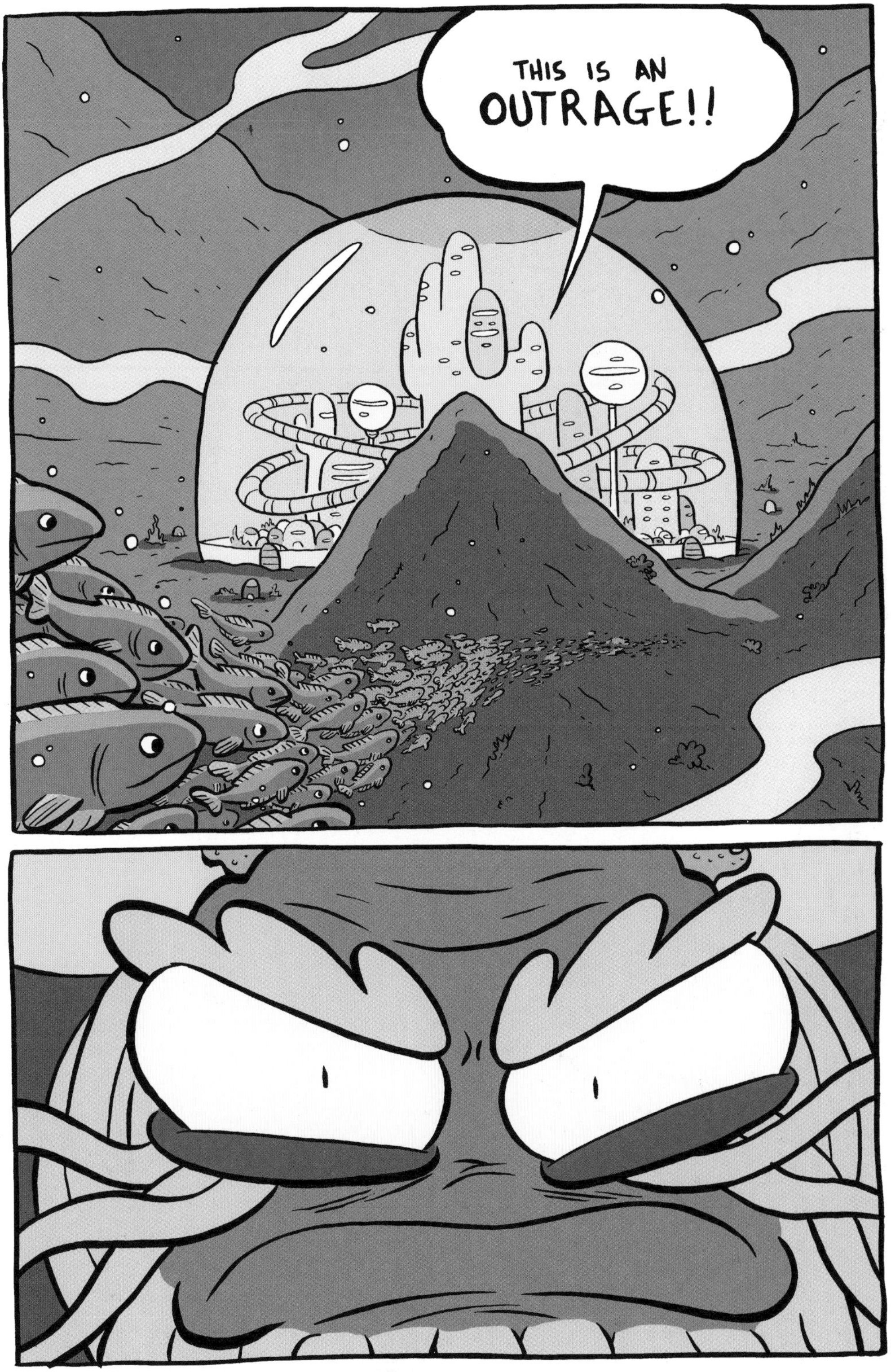
THIS IS AN OUTRAGE!!

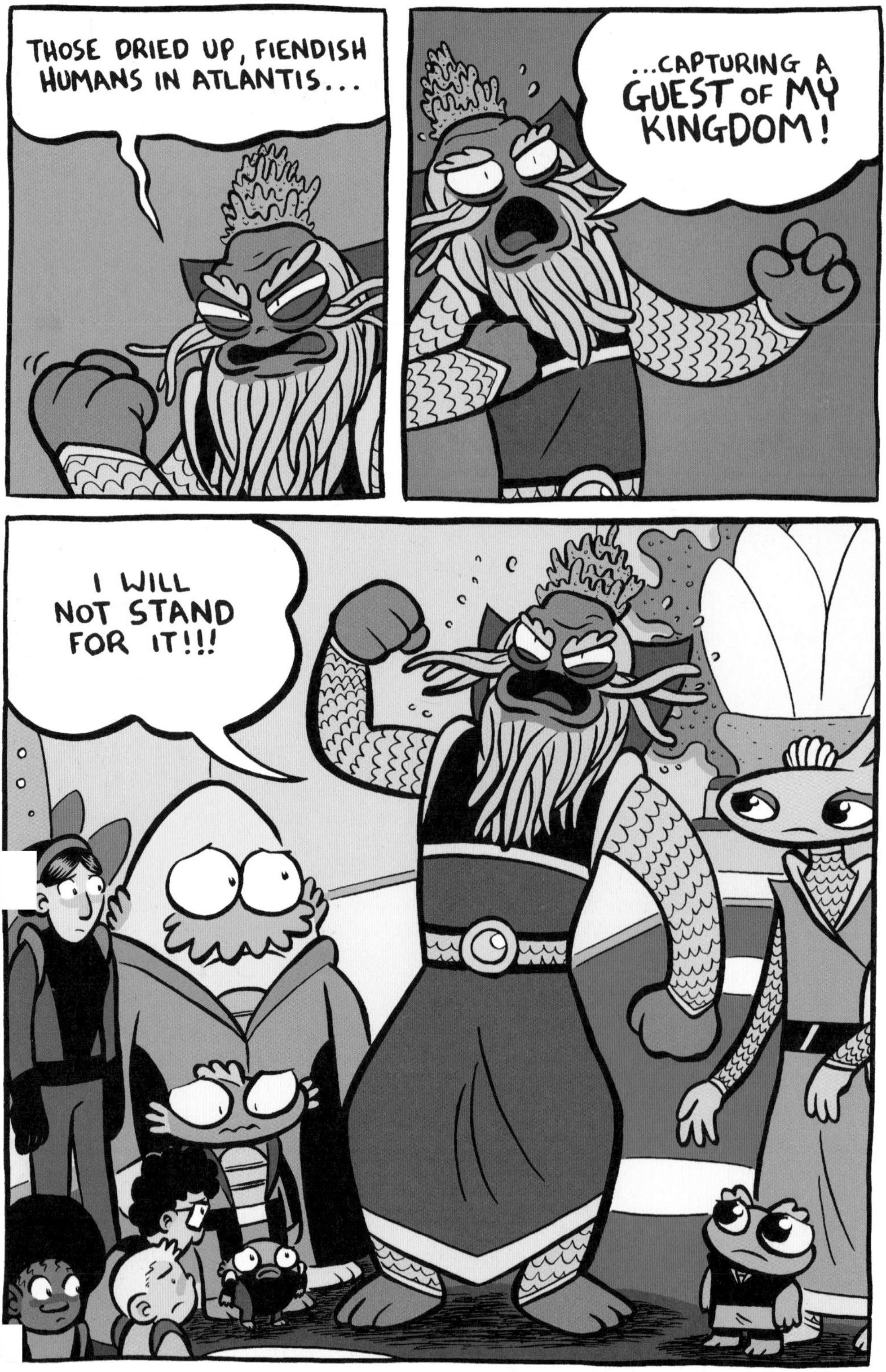
THOSE DRIED UP, FIENDISH HUMANS IN ATLANTIS...
...CAPTURING A GUEST OF MY KINGDOM!
I WILL NOT STAND FOR IT!!!

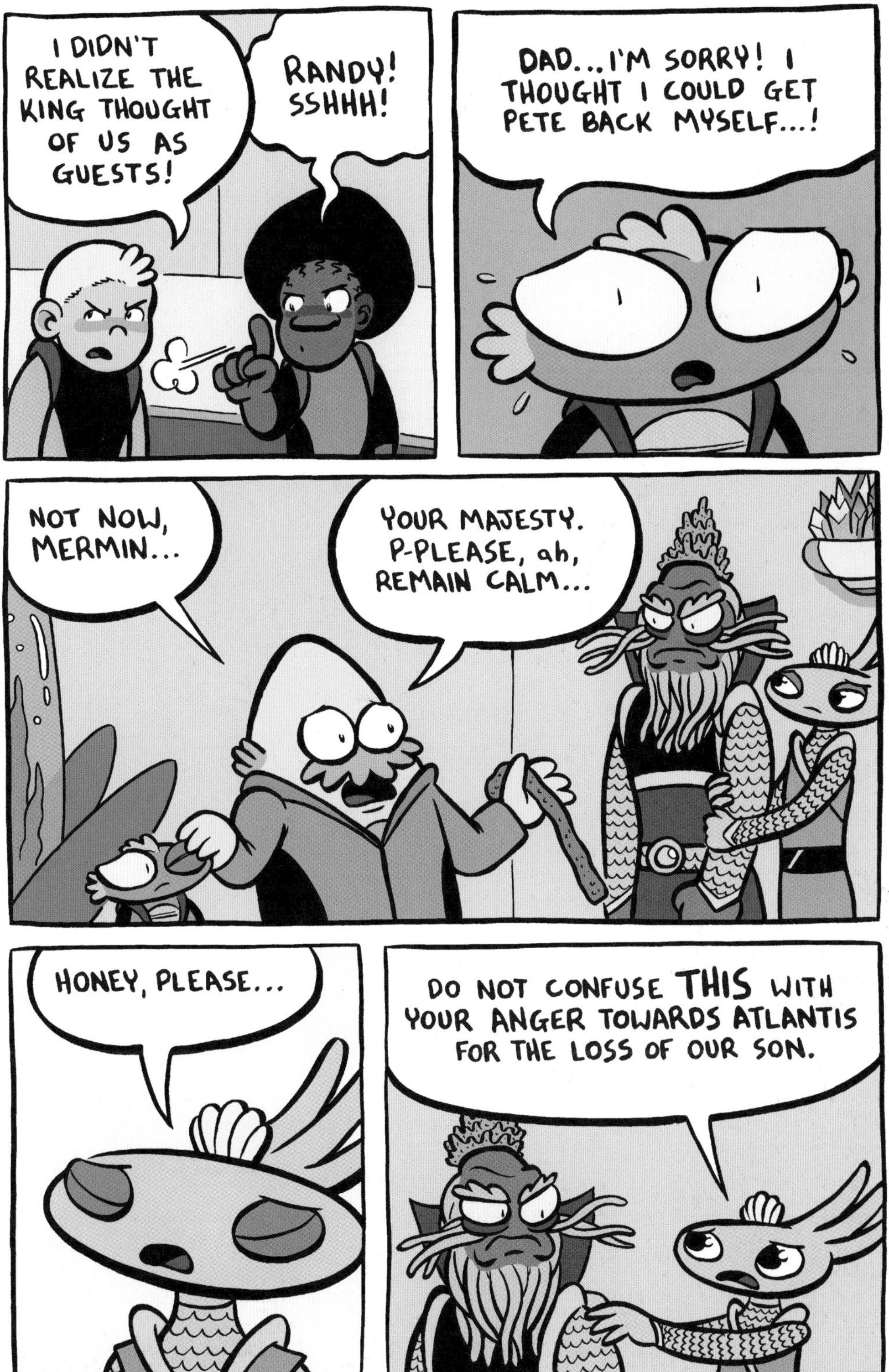
I DIDN'T REALIZE THE KING THOUGHT OF US AS GUESTS!
RANDY! SSHHH!
DAD...I'M SORRY! I THOUGHT I COULD GET PETE BACK MYSELF...!
NOT NOW, MERMIN...
YOUR MAJESTY. P-PLEASE, ah, REMAIN CALM...
HONEY, PLEASE...
DO NOT CONFUSE THIS WITH YOUR ANGER TOWARDS ATLANTIS FOR THE LOSS OF OUR SON.

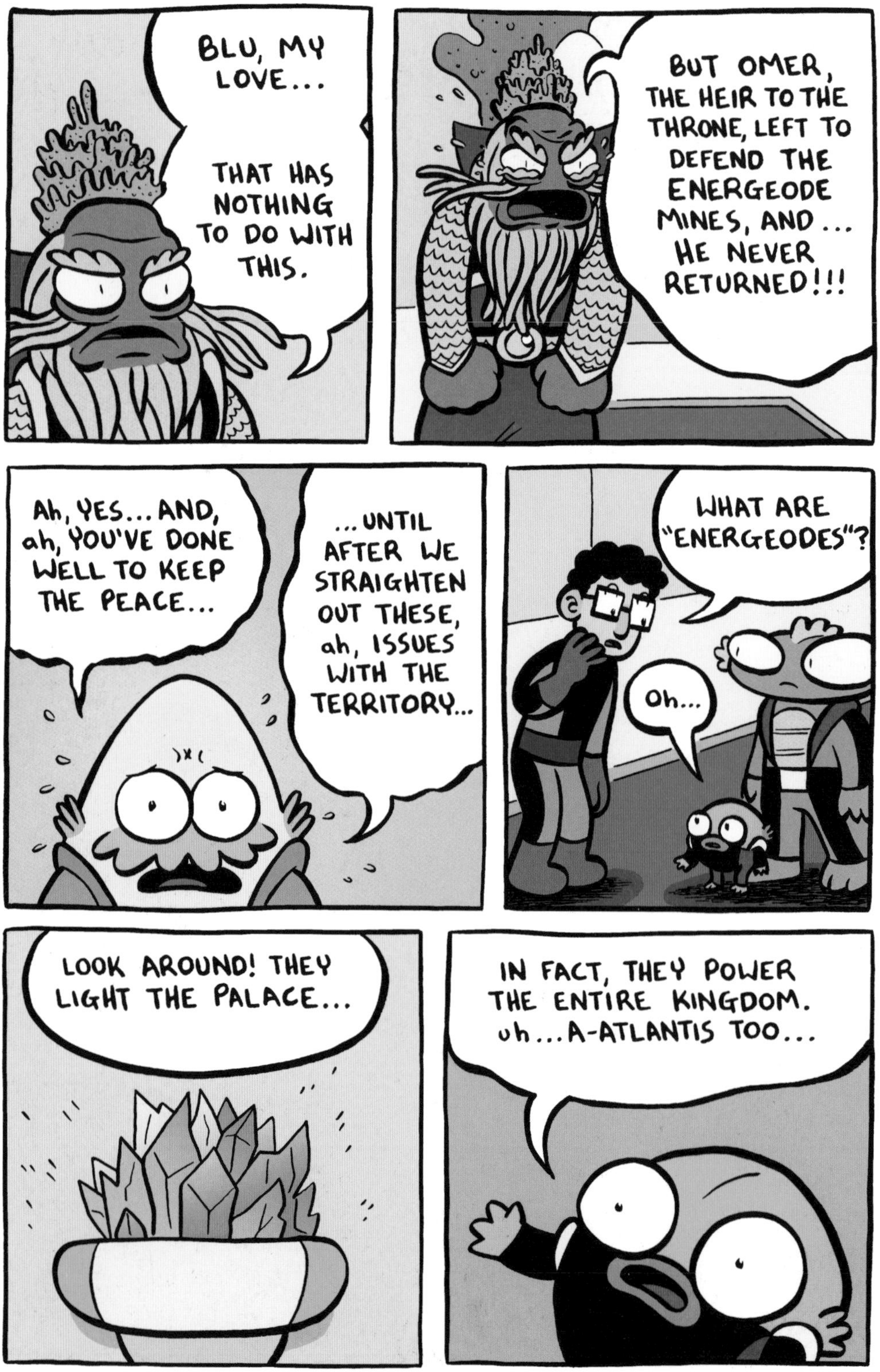
BLU, MY LOVE...
THAT HAS NOTHING TO DO WITH THIS.
BUT OMER, THE HEIR TO THE THRONE, LEFT TO DEFEND THE ENERGEODE MINES, AND... HE NEVER RETURNED!!!
Ah, YES... AND, ah, YOU'VE DONE WELL TO KEEP THE PEACE...
...UNTIL AFTER WE STRAIGHTEN OUT THESE, ah, ISSUES WITH THE TERRITORY...
WHAT ARE "ENERGEODES"?
Oh...
LOOK AROUND! THEY LIGHT THE PALACE...
IN FACT, THEY POWER THE ENTIRE KINGDOM. uh... A-ATLANTIS TOO...

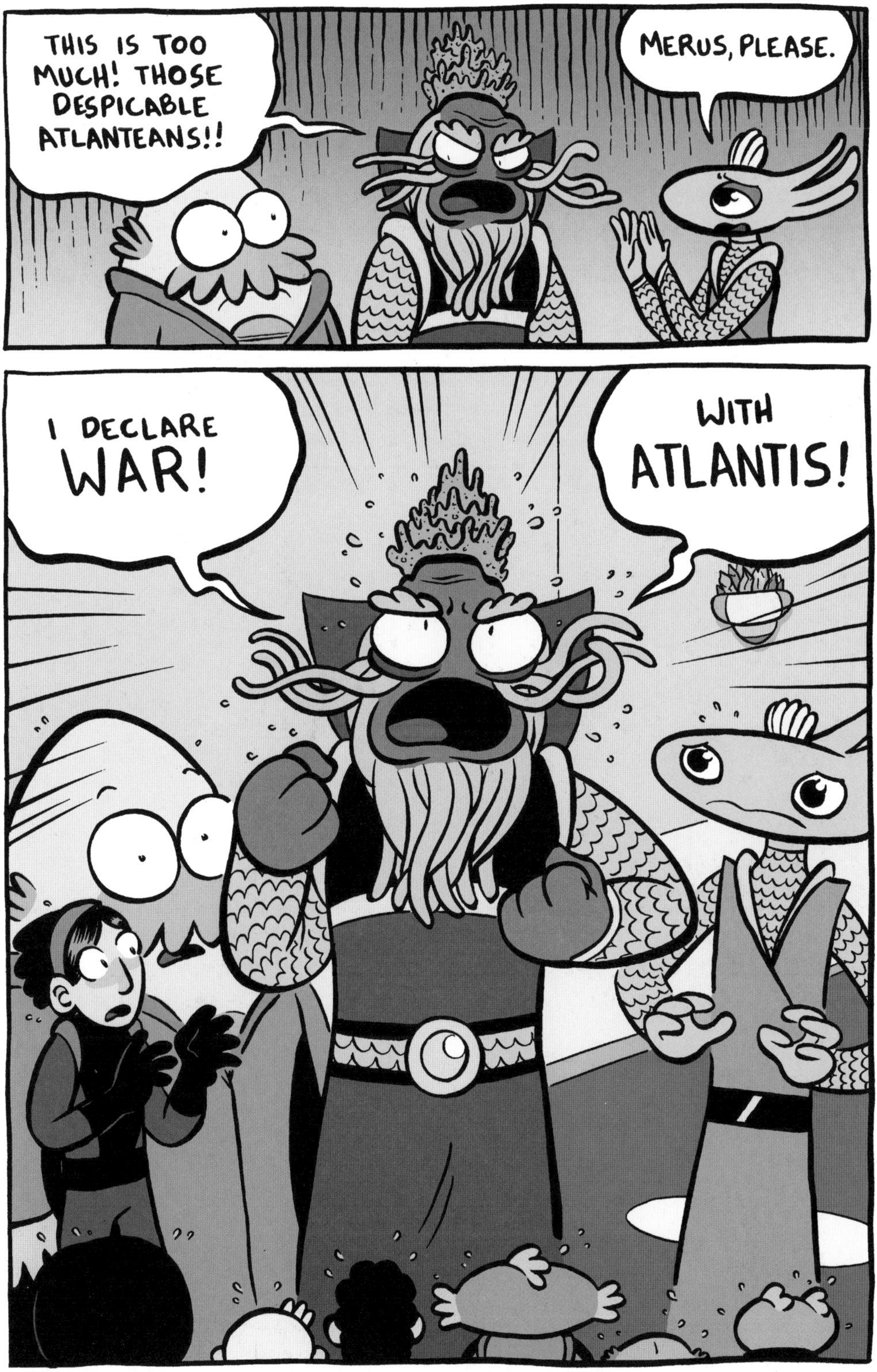
THIS IS TOO MUCH! THOSE DESPICABLE ATLANTEANS!!
MERUS, PLEASE.
I DECLARE WAR!
WITH ATLANTIS!

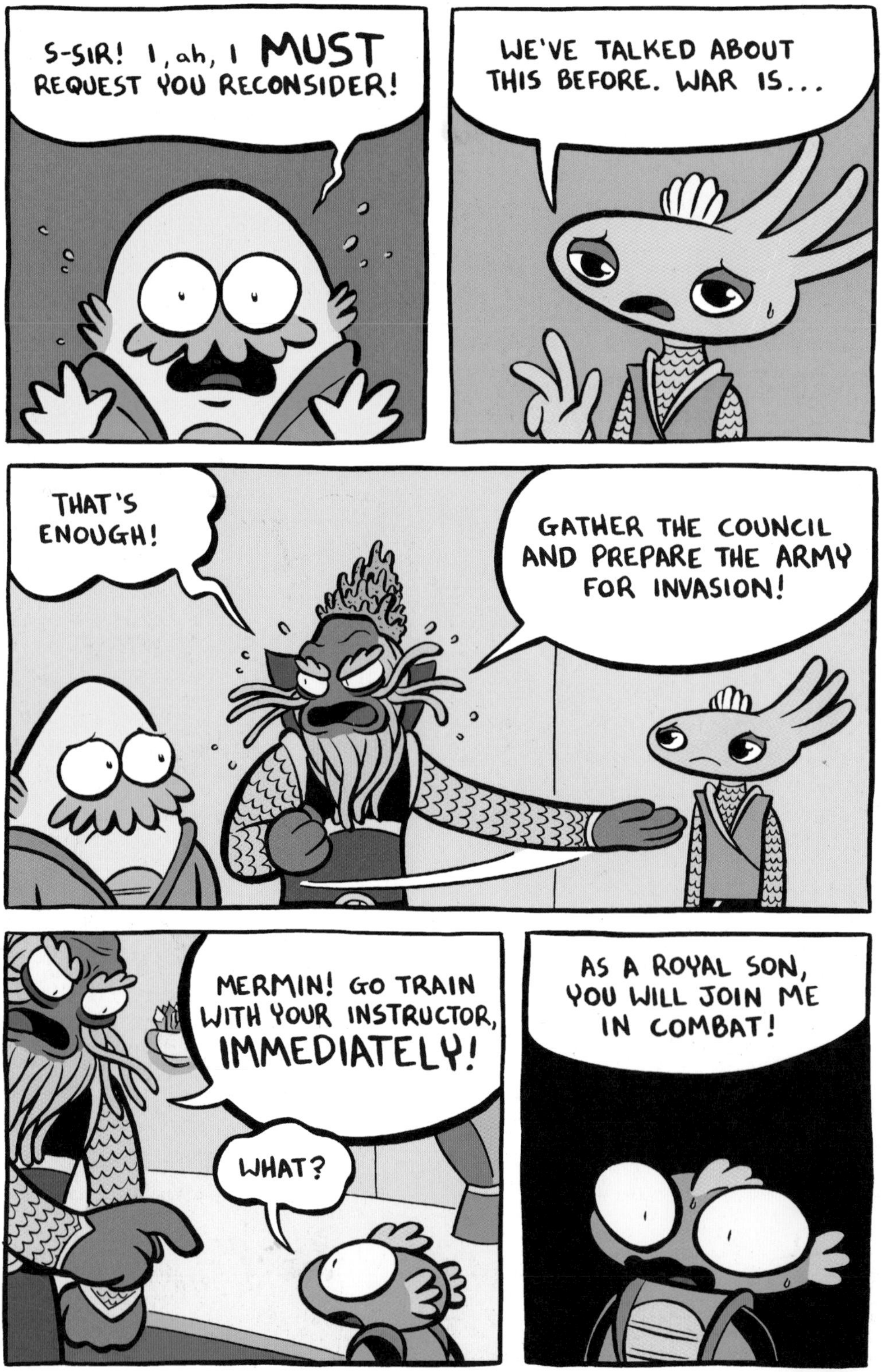
S-SIR! I, ah, I MUST REQUEST YOU RECONSIDER!
WE'VE TALKED ABOUT THIS BEFORE. WAR IS...
THAT'S ENOUGH!
GATHER THE COUNCIL AND PREPARE THE ARMY FOR INVASION!
MERMIN! GO TRAIN WITH YOUR INSTRUCTOR, IMMEDIATELY!
WHAT?
AS A ROYAL SON, YOU WILL JOIN ME IN COMBAT!

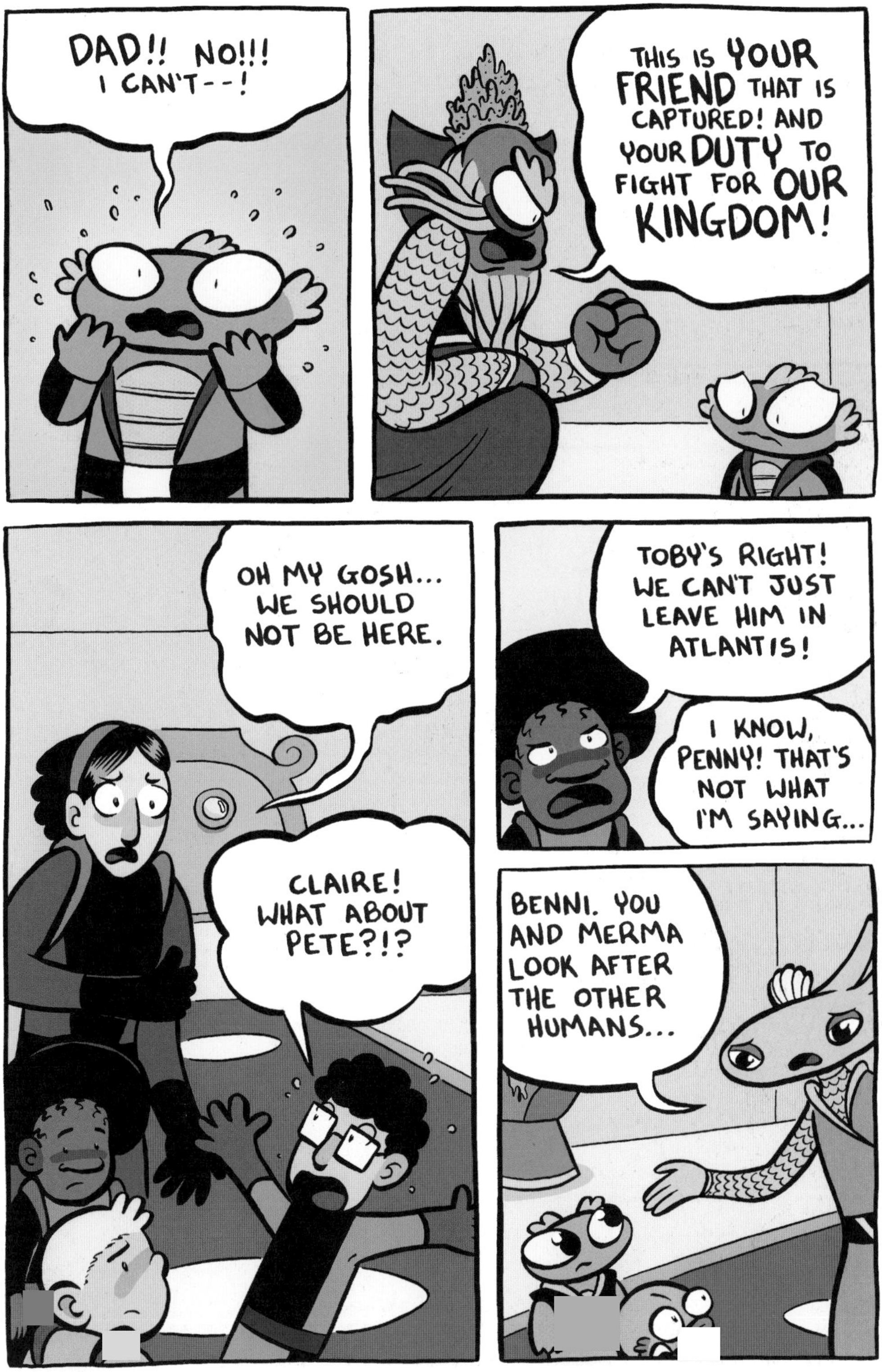
DAD!! NO!!! I CAN'T--!
THIS IS YOUR FRIEND THAT IS CAPTURED! AND YOUR DUTY TO FIGHT FOR OUR KINGDOM!
OH MY GOSH... WE SHOULD NOT BE HERE.
CLAIRE! WHAT ABOUT PETE?!?
TOBY'S RIGHT! WE CAN'T JUST LEAVE HIM IN ATLANTIS!
I KNOW, PENNY! THAT'S NOT WHAT I'M SAYING...
BENNI. YOU AND MERMA LOOK AFTER THE OTHER HUMANS...

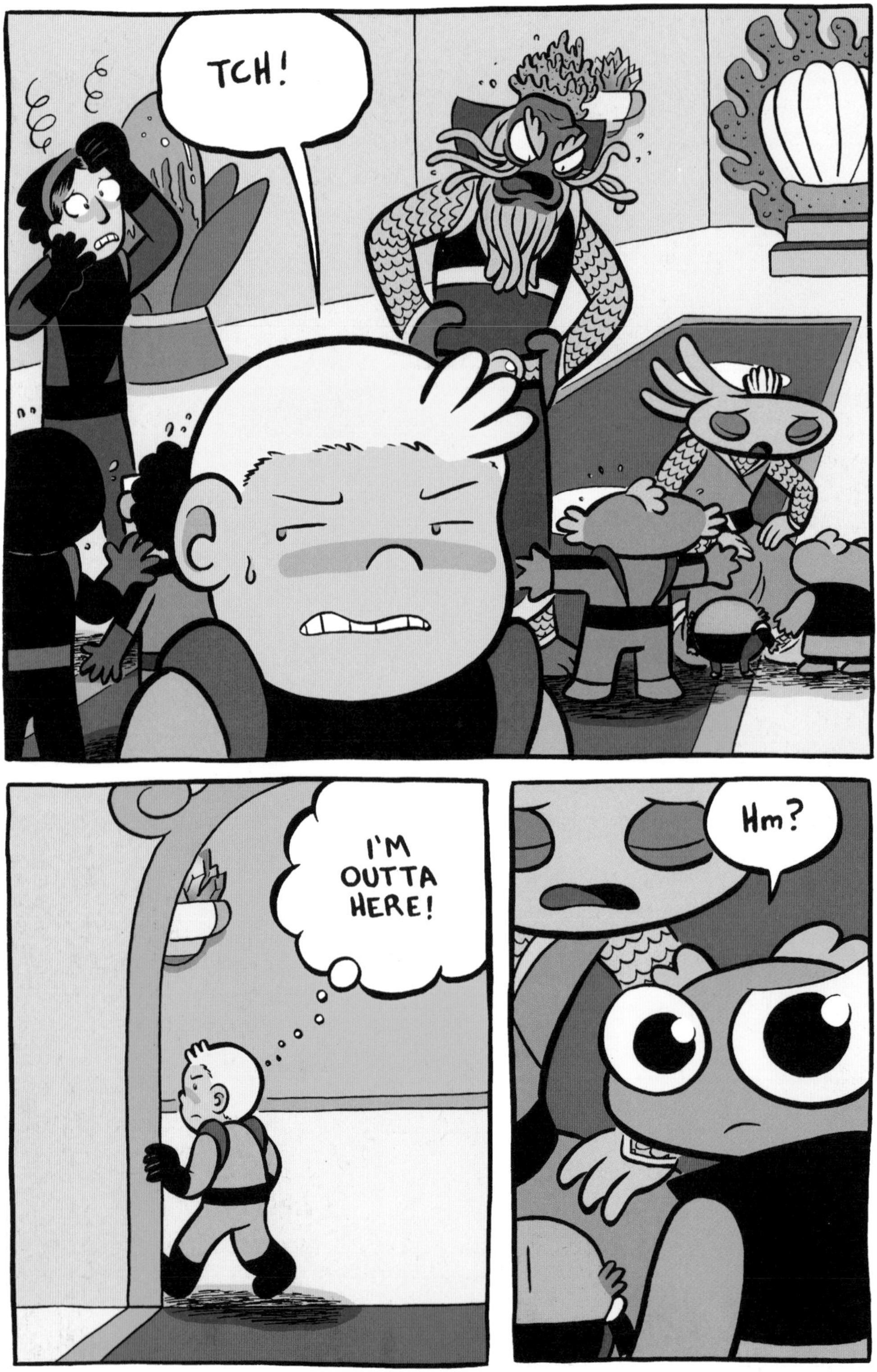
TCH!
I'M OUTTA HERE!
Hm?

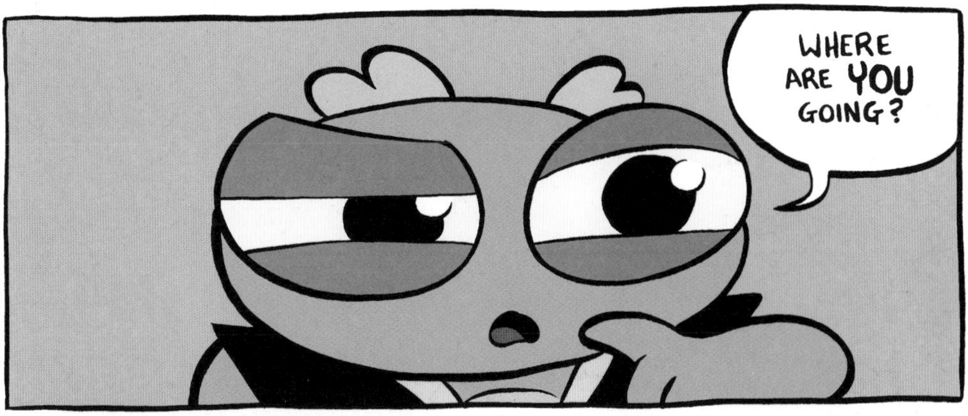
WHERE ARE YOU GOING?
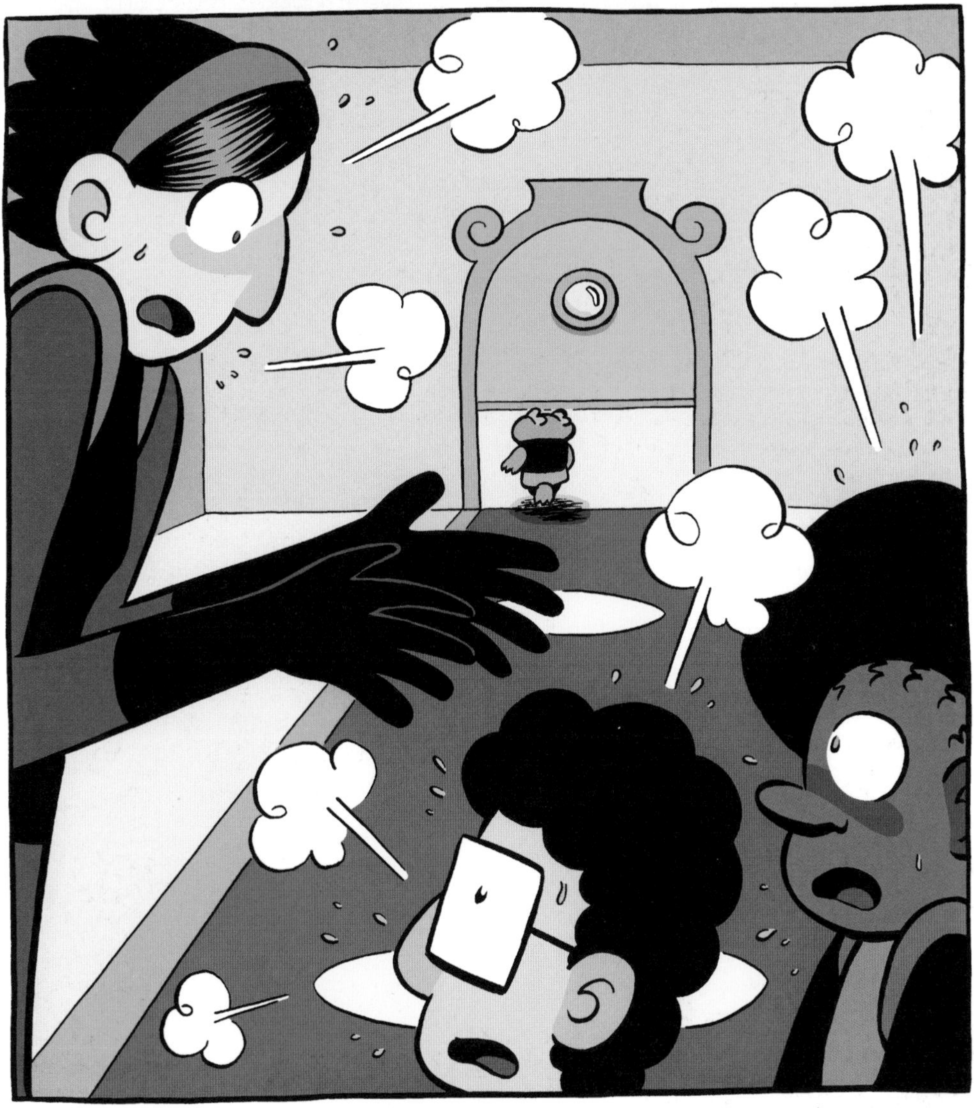

CHAPTER TWO

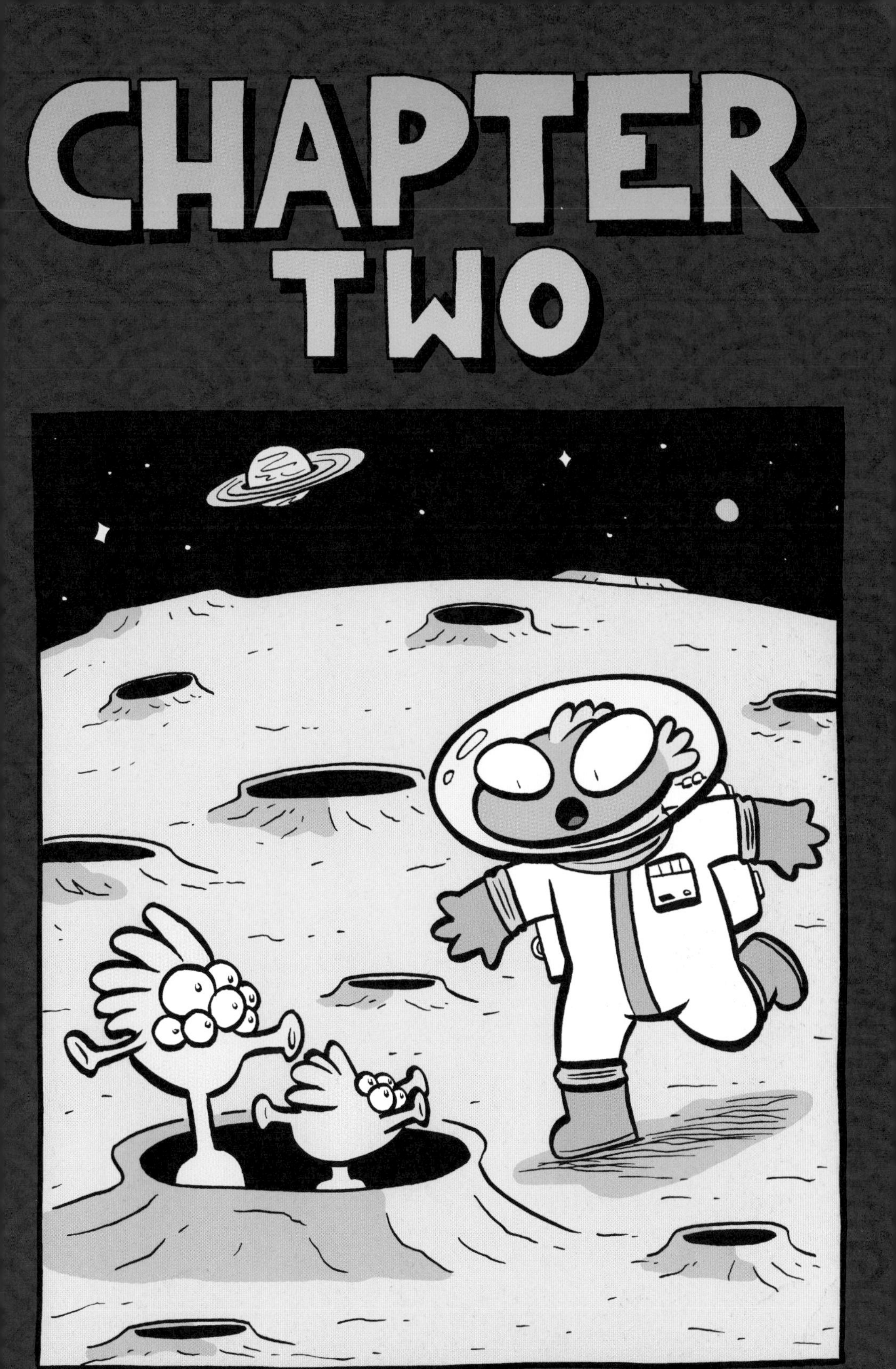

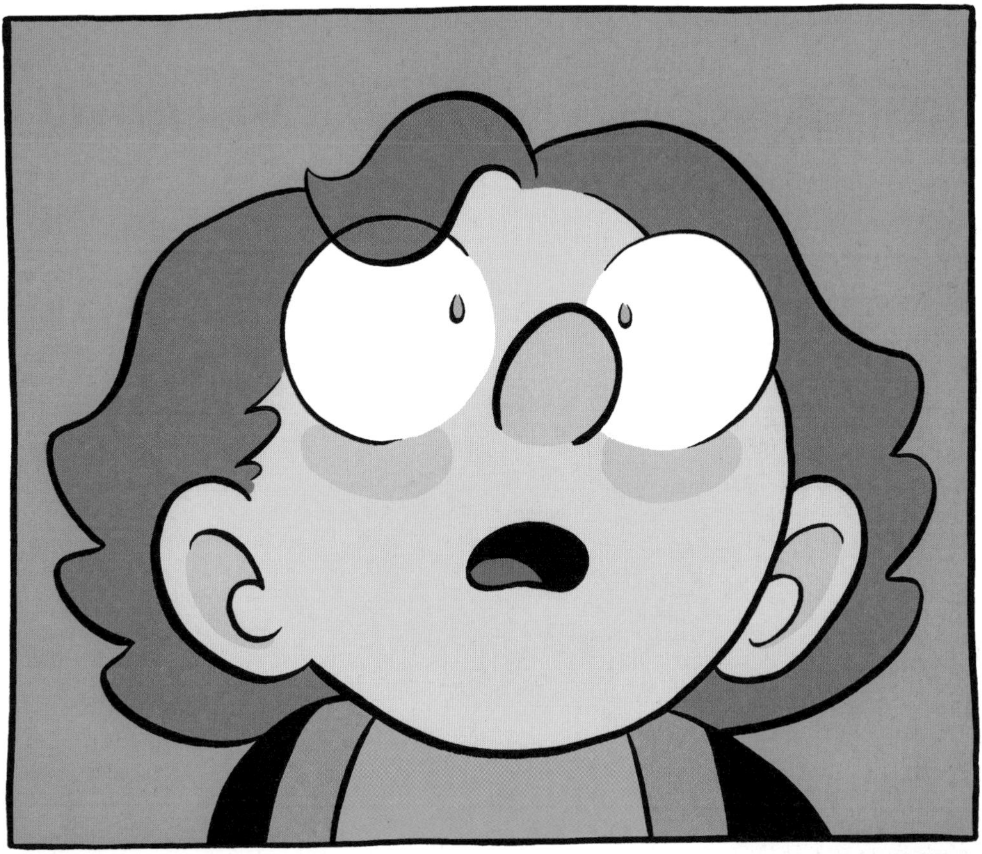

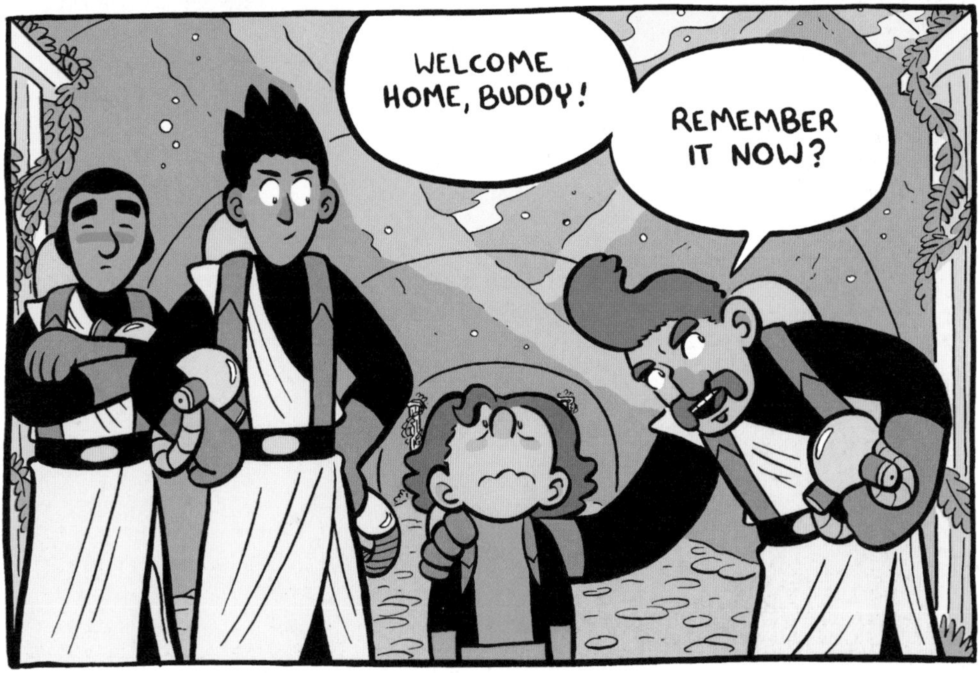
WELCOME HOME, BUDDY!
REMEMBER IT NOW?

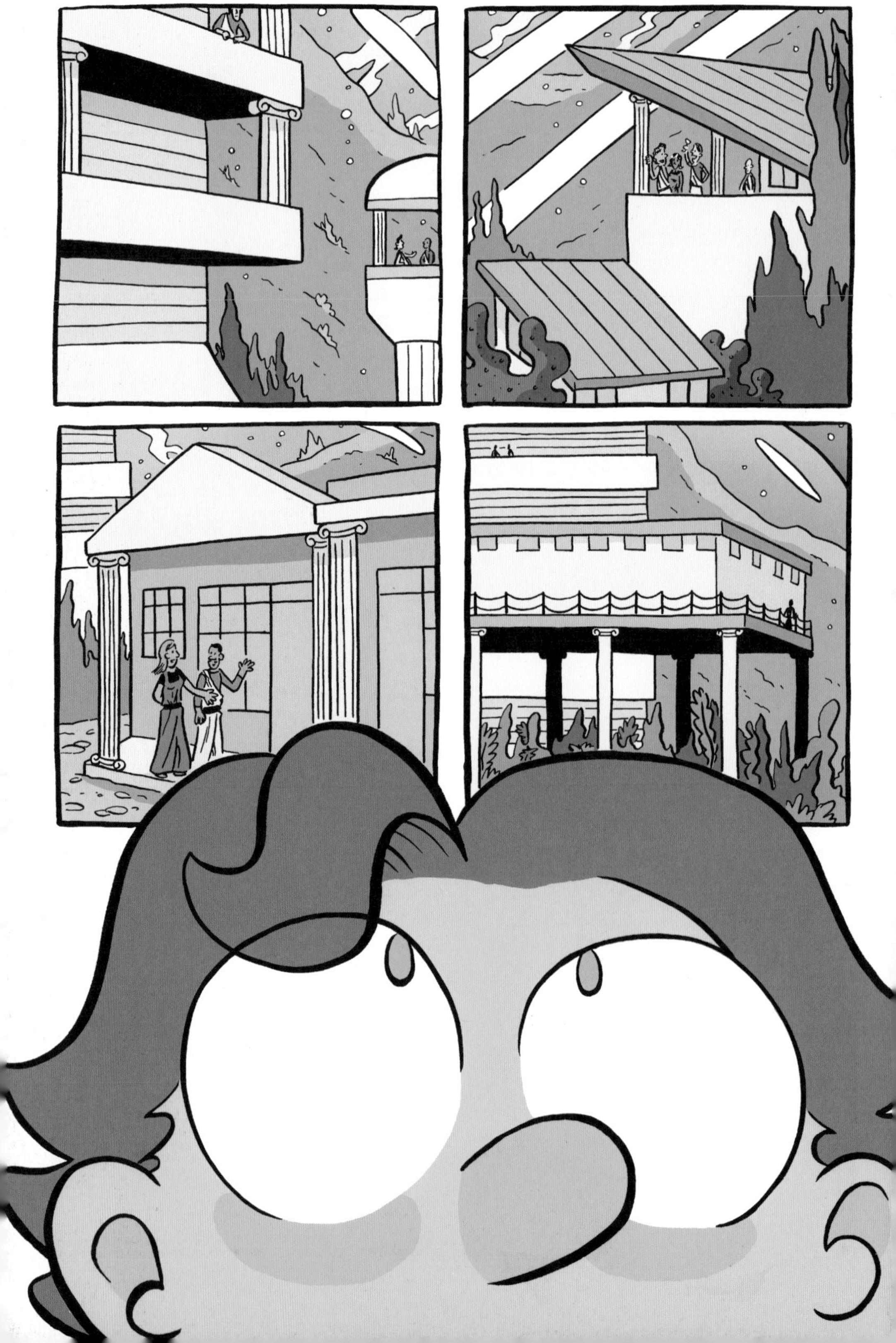

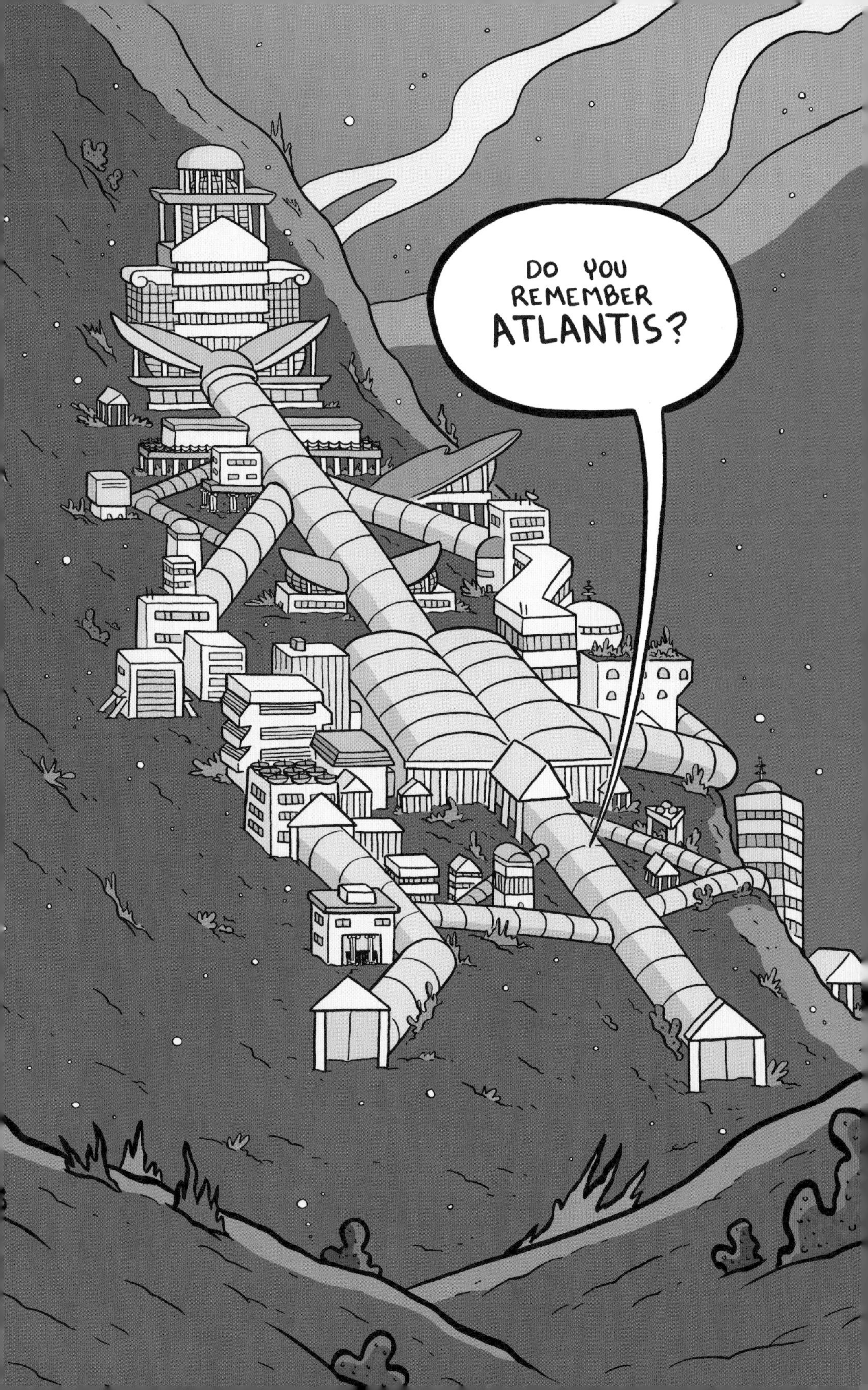
DO YOU REMEMBER ATLANTIS?

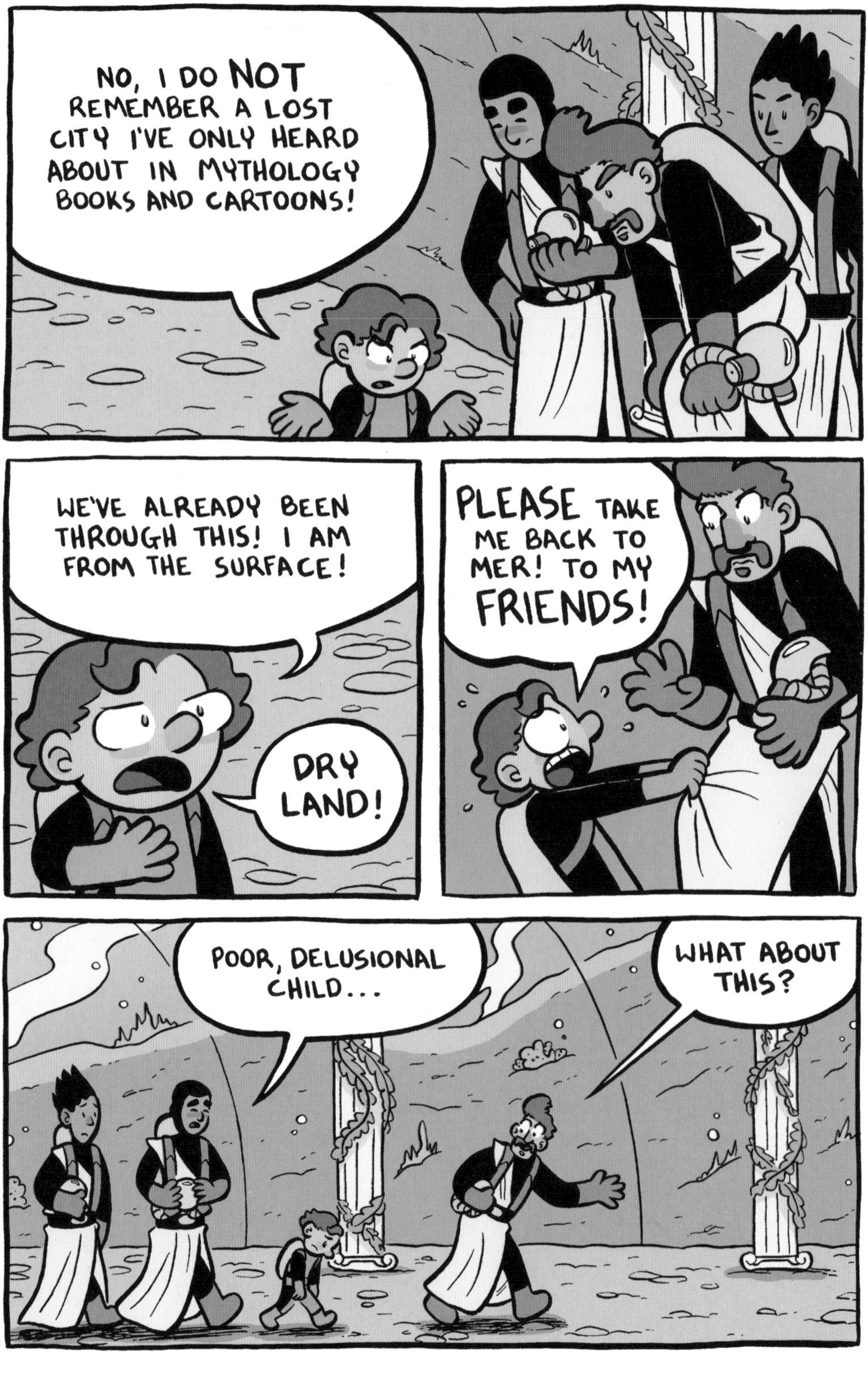
NO, I DO NOT REMEMBER A LOST CITY I'VE ONLY HEARD ABOUT IN MYTHOLOGY BOOKS AND CARTOONS!
WE'VE ALREADY BEEN THROUGH THIS! I AM FROM THE SURFACE!
DRY LAND!
PLEASE TAKE ME BACK TO MER! TO MY FRIENDS!
POOR, DELUSIONAL CHILD...
WHAT ABOUT THIS?

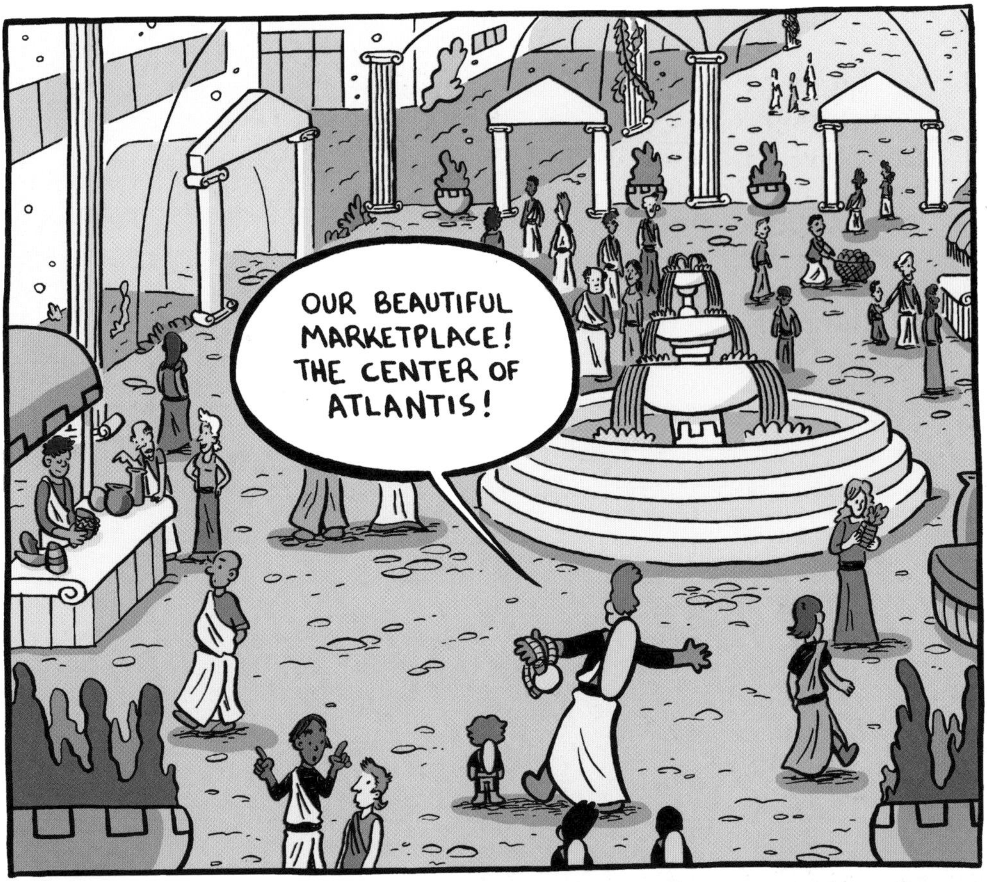
OUR BEAUTIFUL MARKETPLACE! THE CENTER OF ATLANTIS!

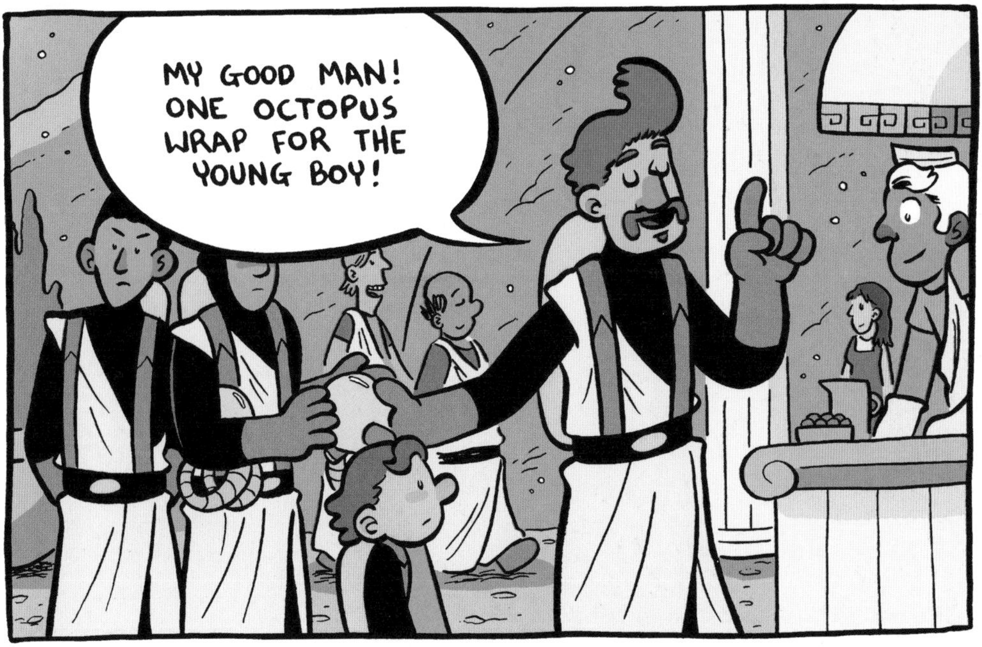
MY GOOD MAN! ONE OCTOPUS WRAP FOR THE YOUNG BOY!

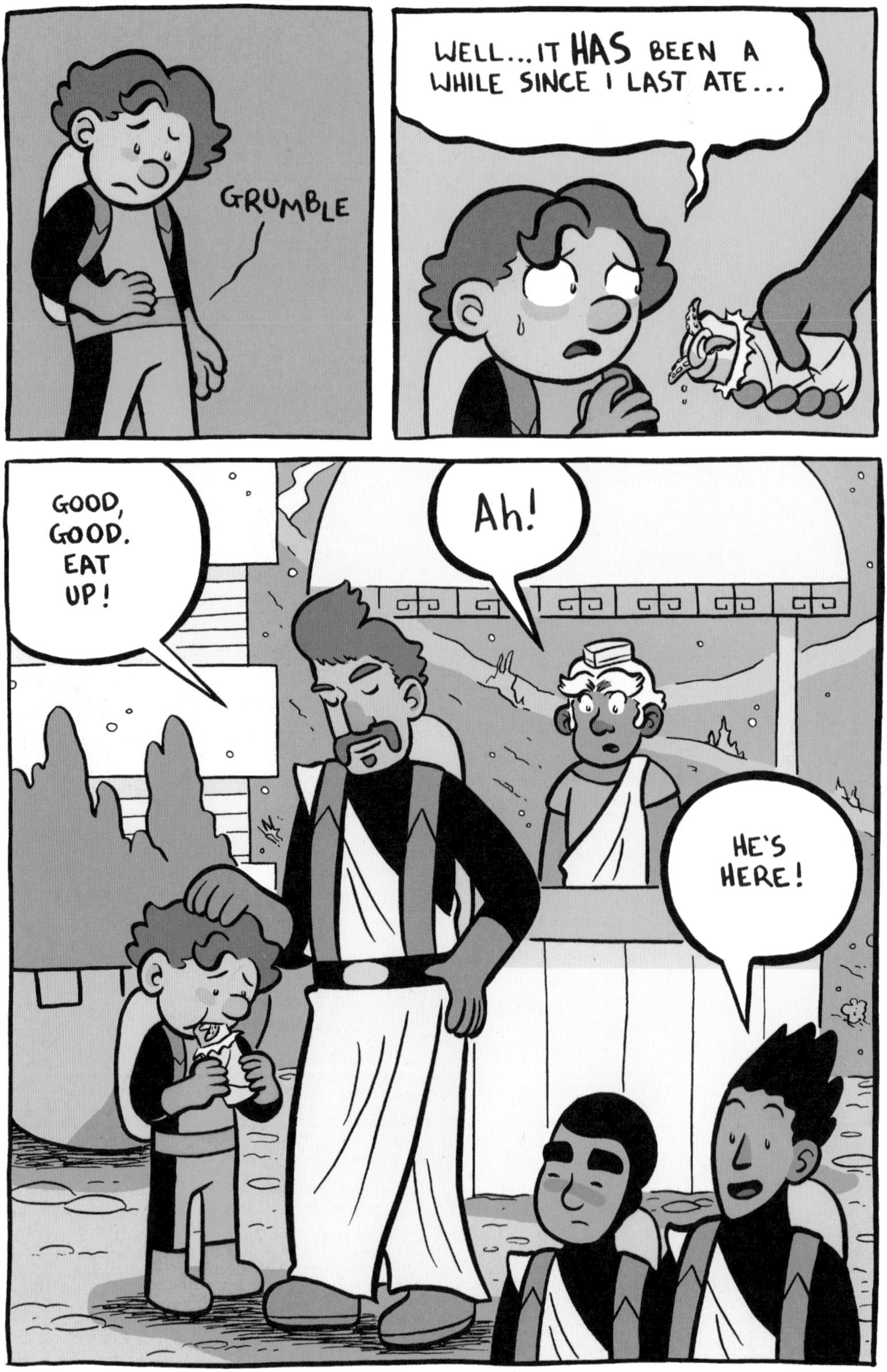
GRUMBLE
WELL... IT HAS BEEN A WHILE SINCE I LAST ATE...
GOOD, GOOD. EAT UP!
Ah!
HE'S HERE!

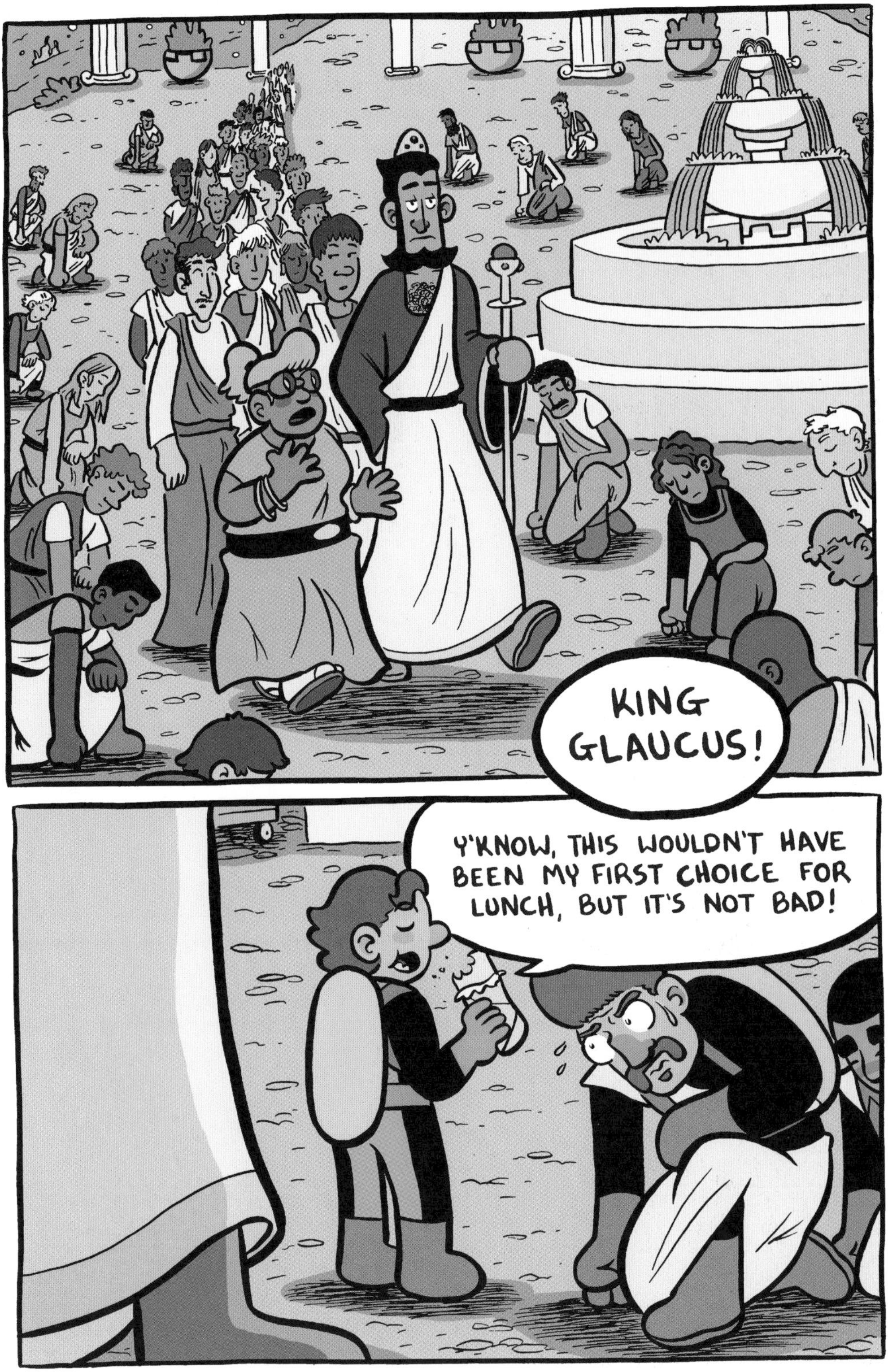
KING GLAUCUS!
Y'KNOW, THIS WOULDN'T HAVE BEEN MY FIRST CHOICE FOR LUNCH, BUT IT'S NOT BAD!

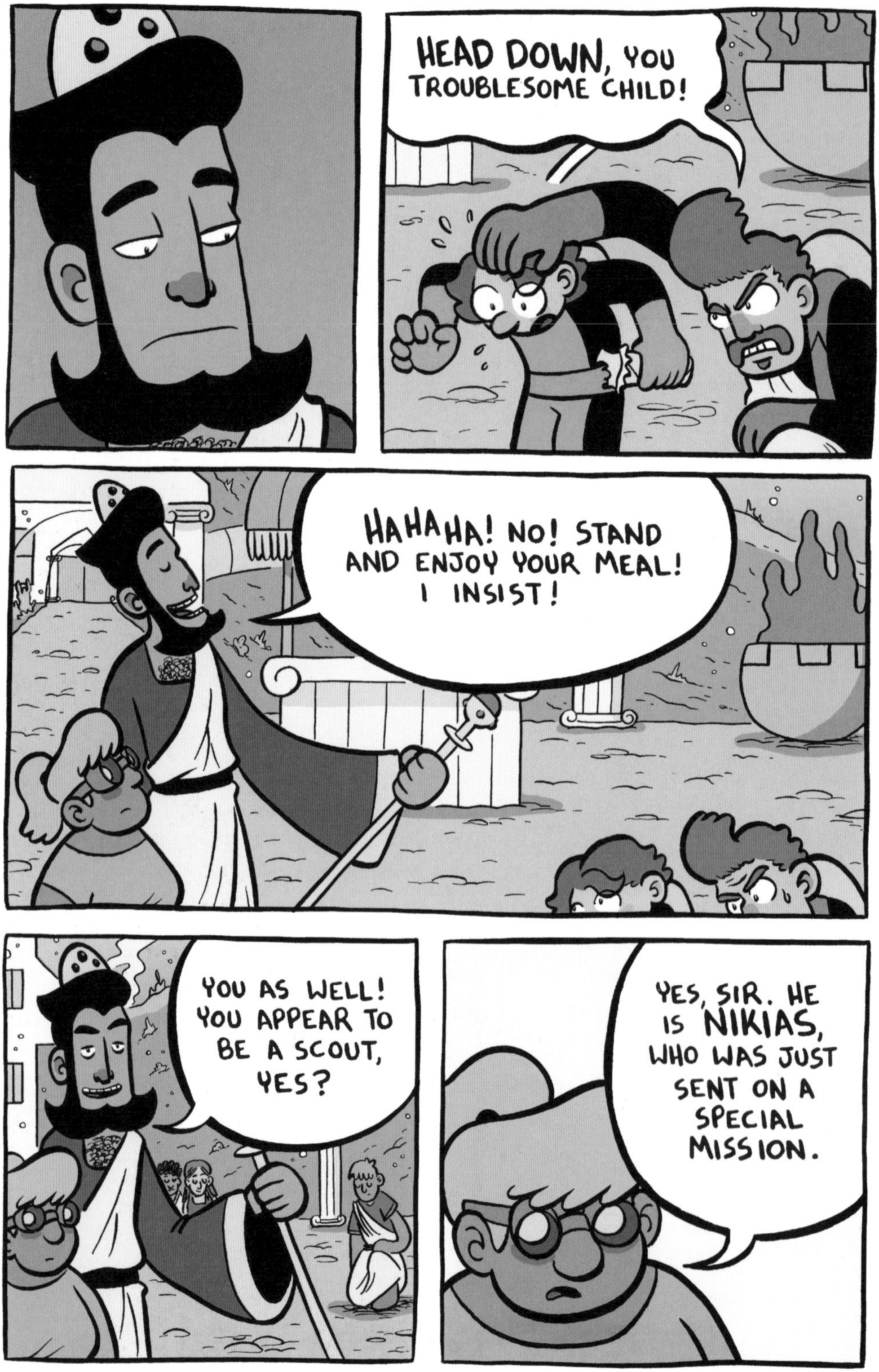
HEAD DOWN, YOU TROUBLESOME CHILD!
HAHAHAHA! NO! STAND AND ENJOY YOUR MEAL! I INSIST!
YOU AS WELL! YOU APPEAR TO BE A SCOUT, YES?
YES, SIR. HE IS NIKIAS, WHO WAS JUST SENT ON A SPECIAL MISSION.

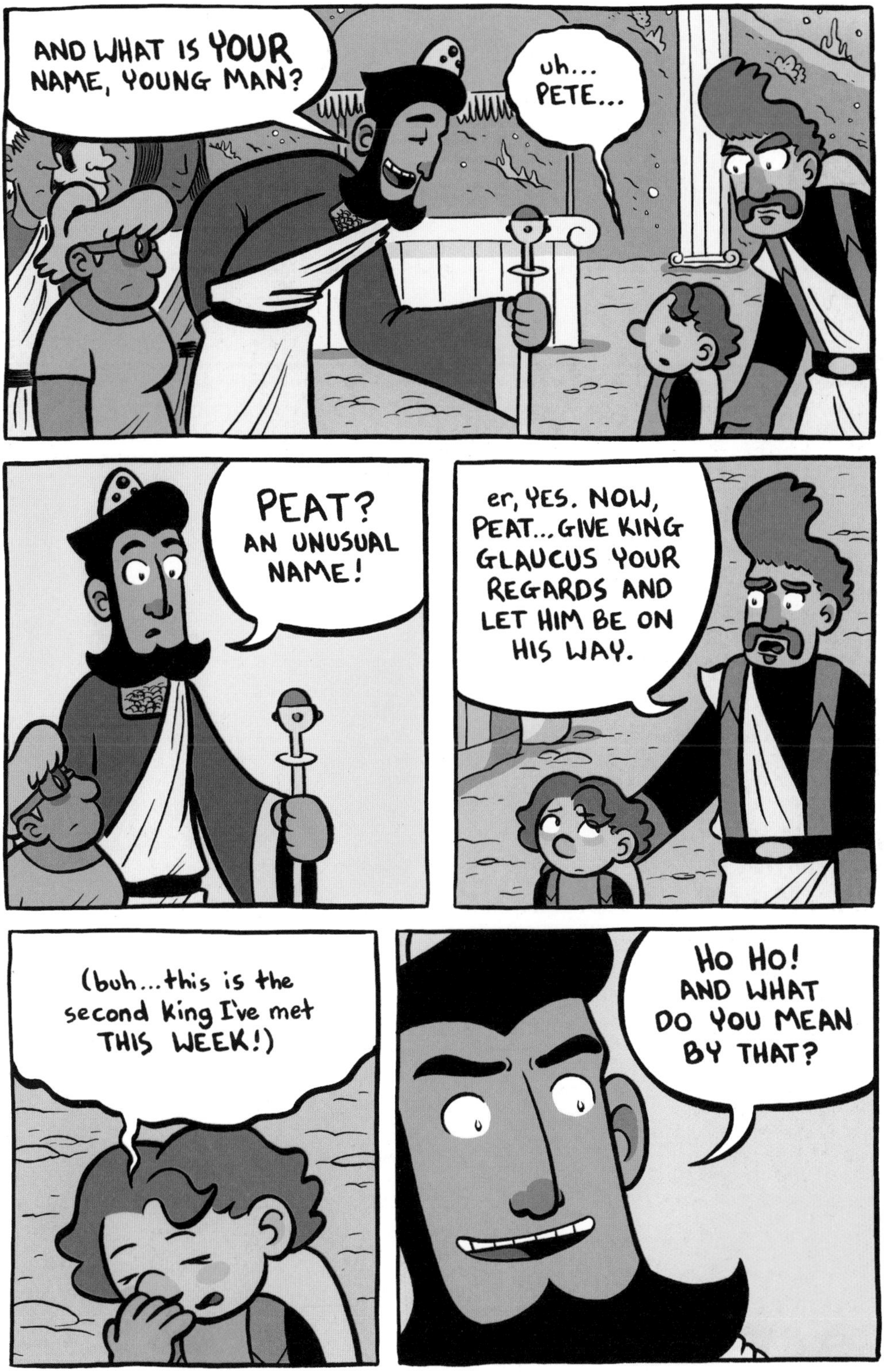
AND WHAT IS YOUR NAME, YOUNG MAN?
uh... PETE...
PEAT? AN UNUSUAL NAME!
er, YES. NOW, PEAT... GIVE KING GLAUCUS YOUR REGARDS AND LET HIM BE ON HIS WAY.
(buh... this is the second king I've met THIS WEEK!)
HO HO! AND WHAT DO YOU MEAN BY THAT?

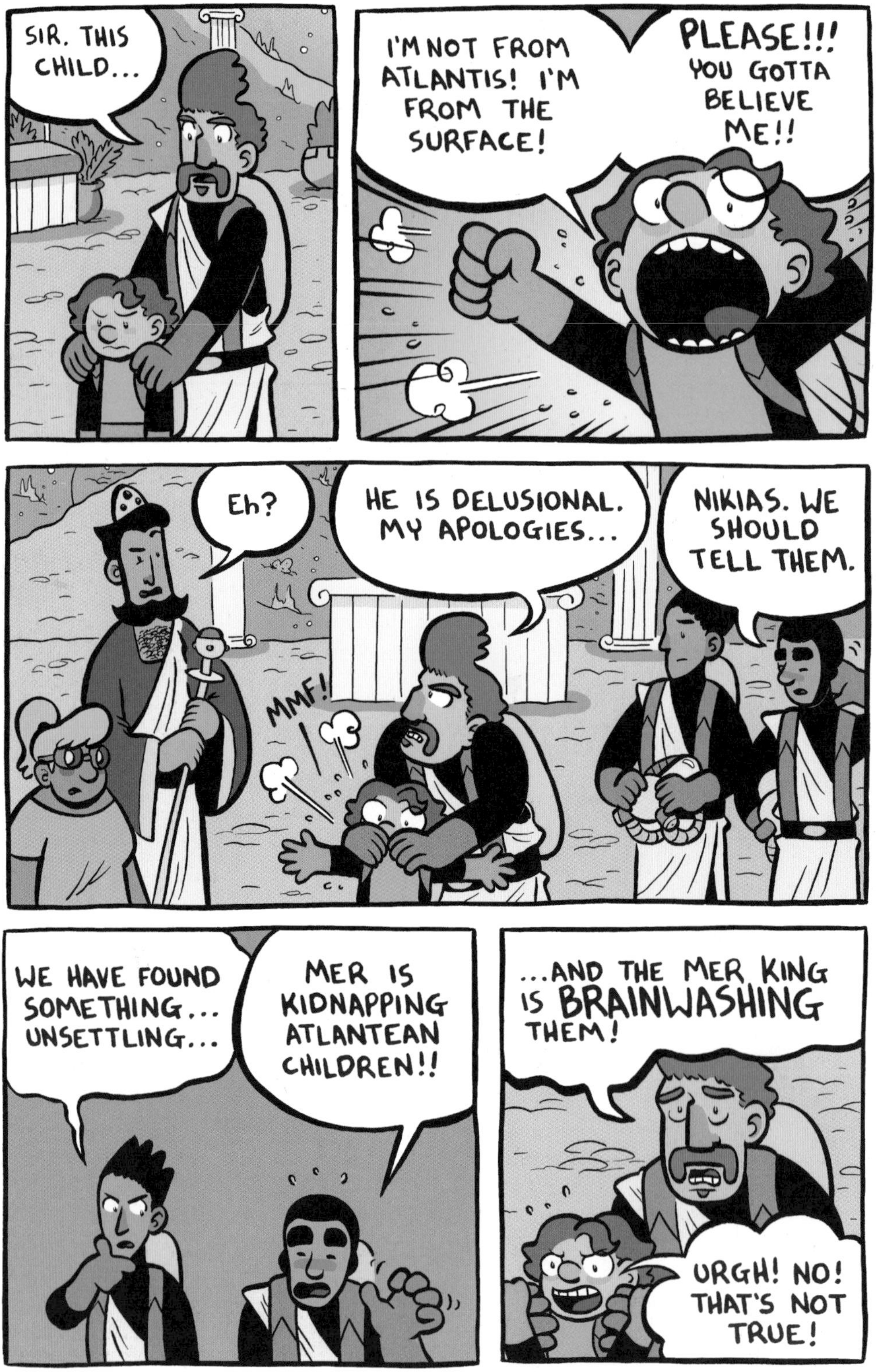
SIR. THIS CHILD...
I'M NOT FROM ATLANTIS! I'M FROM THE SURFACE!
PLEASE!!! YOU GOTTA BELIEVE ME!!
Eh?
HE IS DELUSIONAL. MY APOLOGIES...
MMF!
NIKIAS. WE SHOULD TELL THEM.
WE HAVE FOUND SOMETHING... UNSETTLING...
MER IS KIDNAPPING ATLANTEAN CHILDREN!!
...AND THE MER KING IS BRAINWASHING THEM!
URGH! NO! THAT'S NOT TRUE!

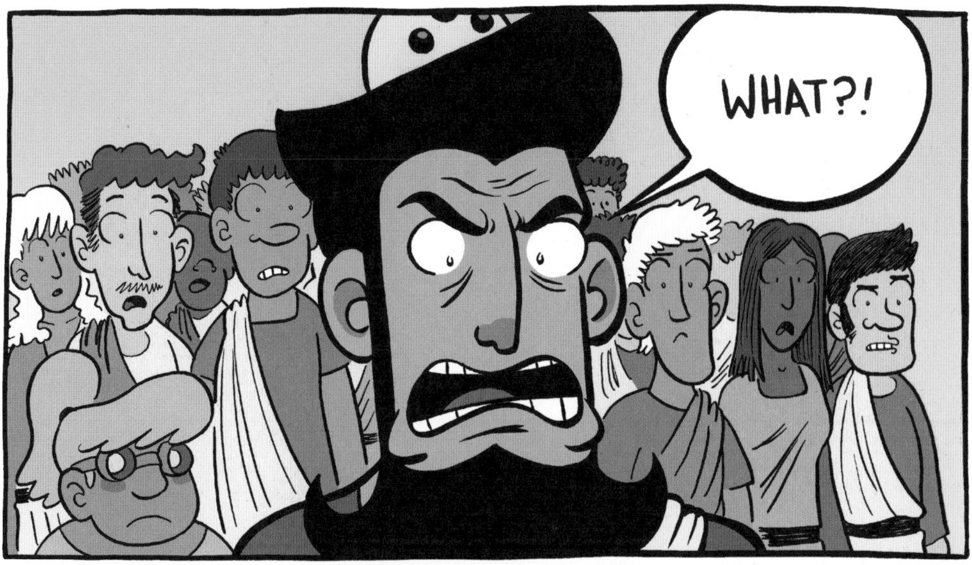
WHAT?!

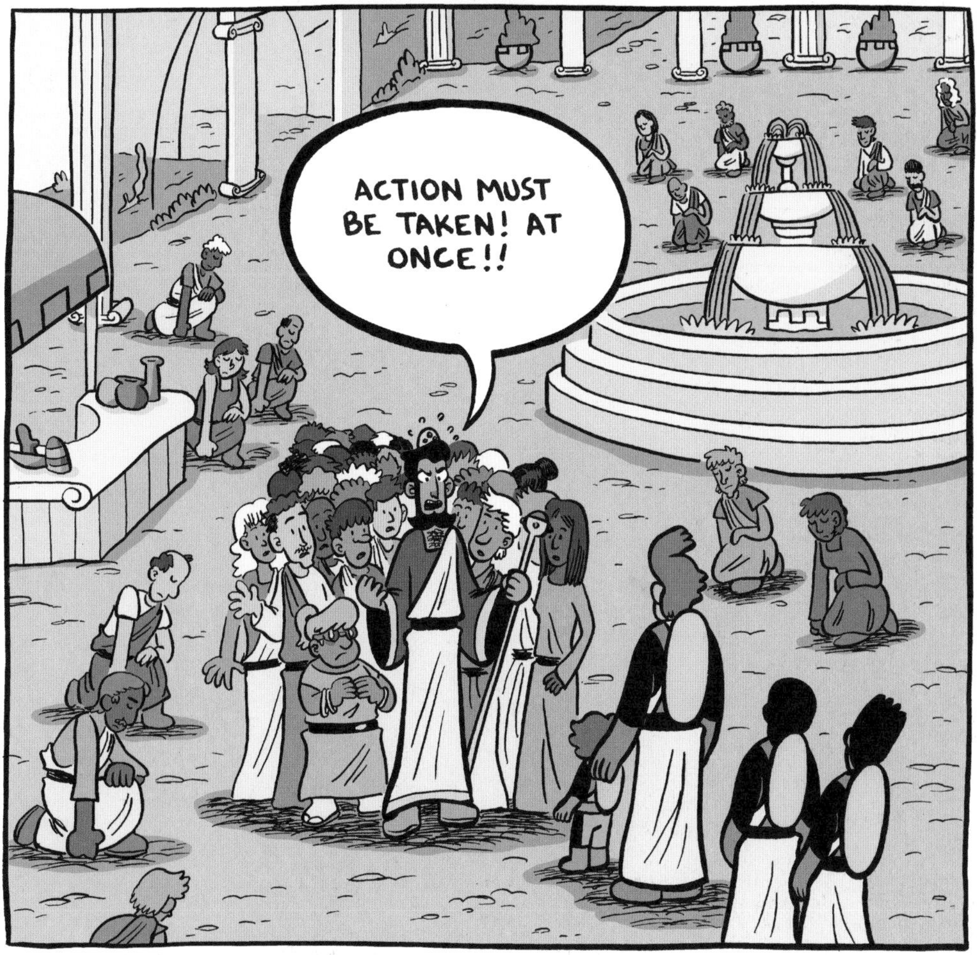
ACTION MUST BE TAKEN! AT ONCE!!

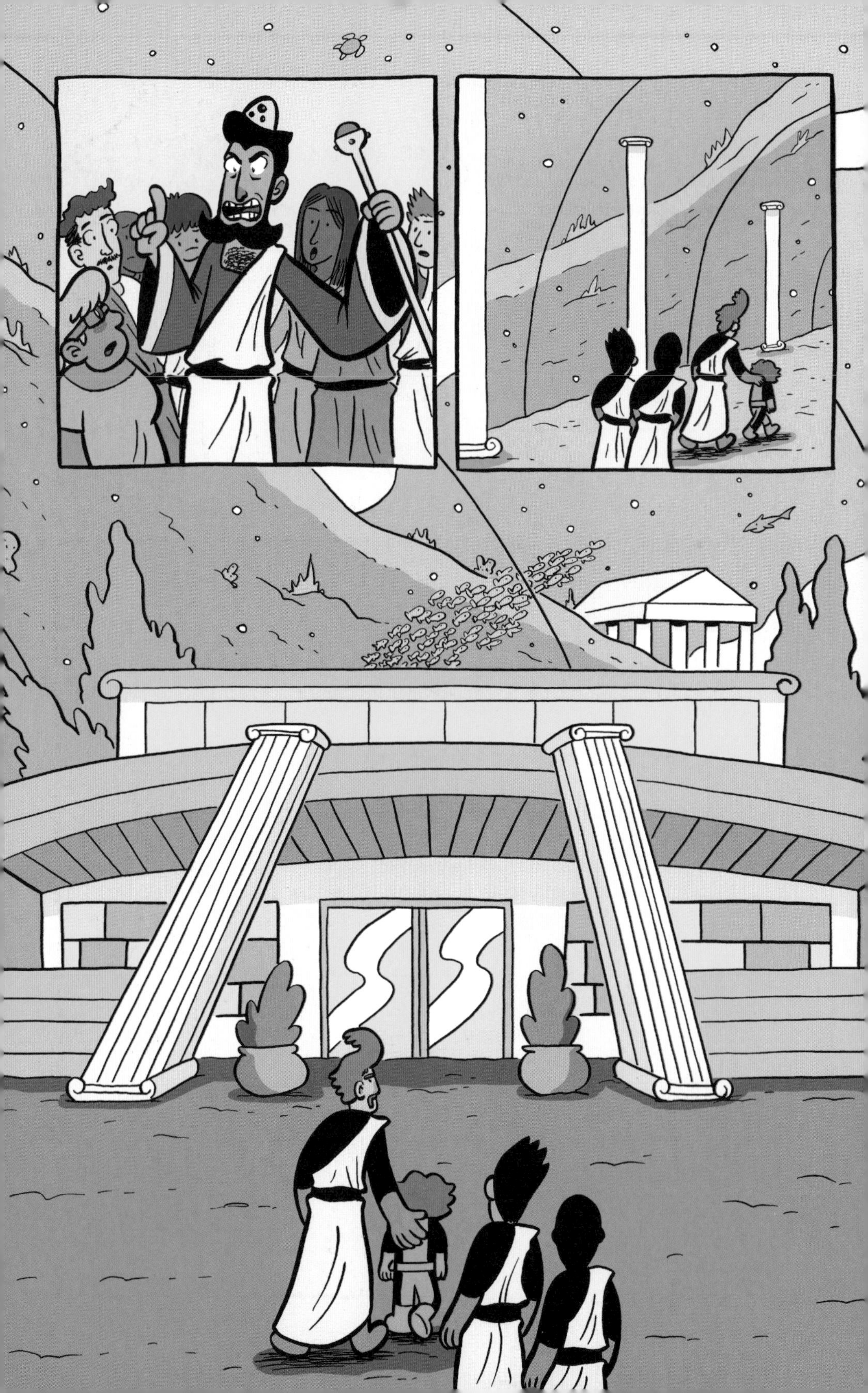

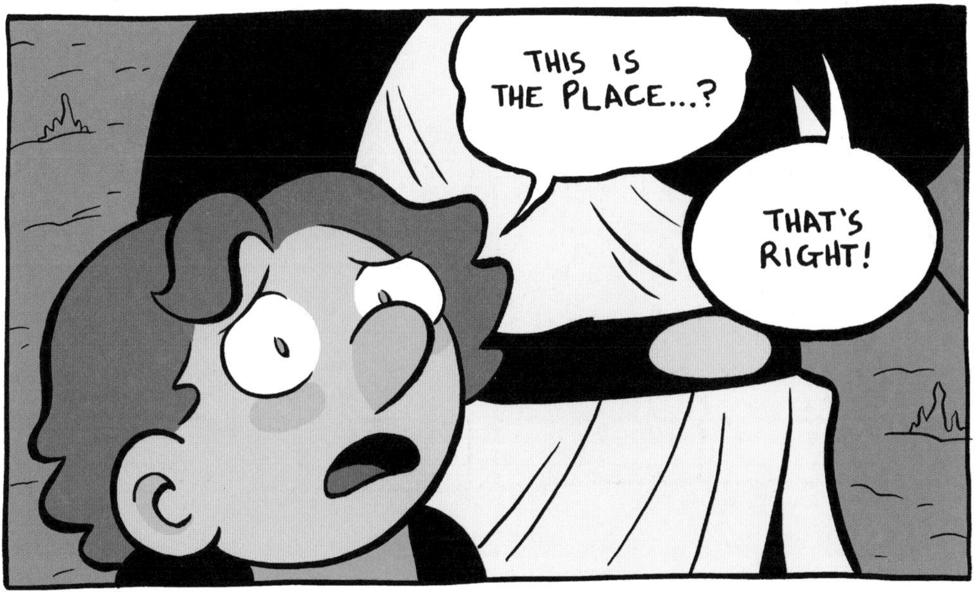
THIS IS THE PLACE...?
THAT'S RIGHT!

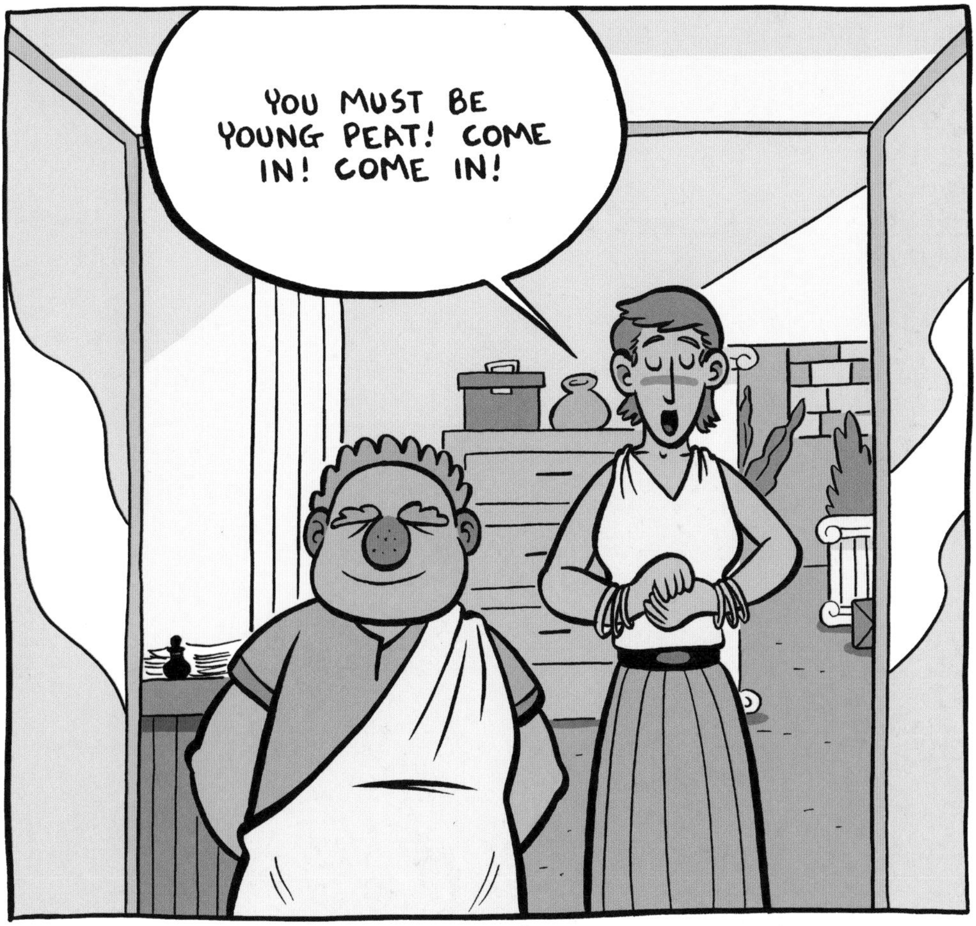
YOU MUST BE YOUNG PEAT! COME IN! COME IN!

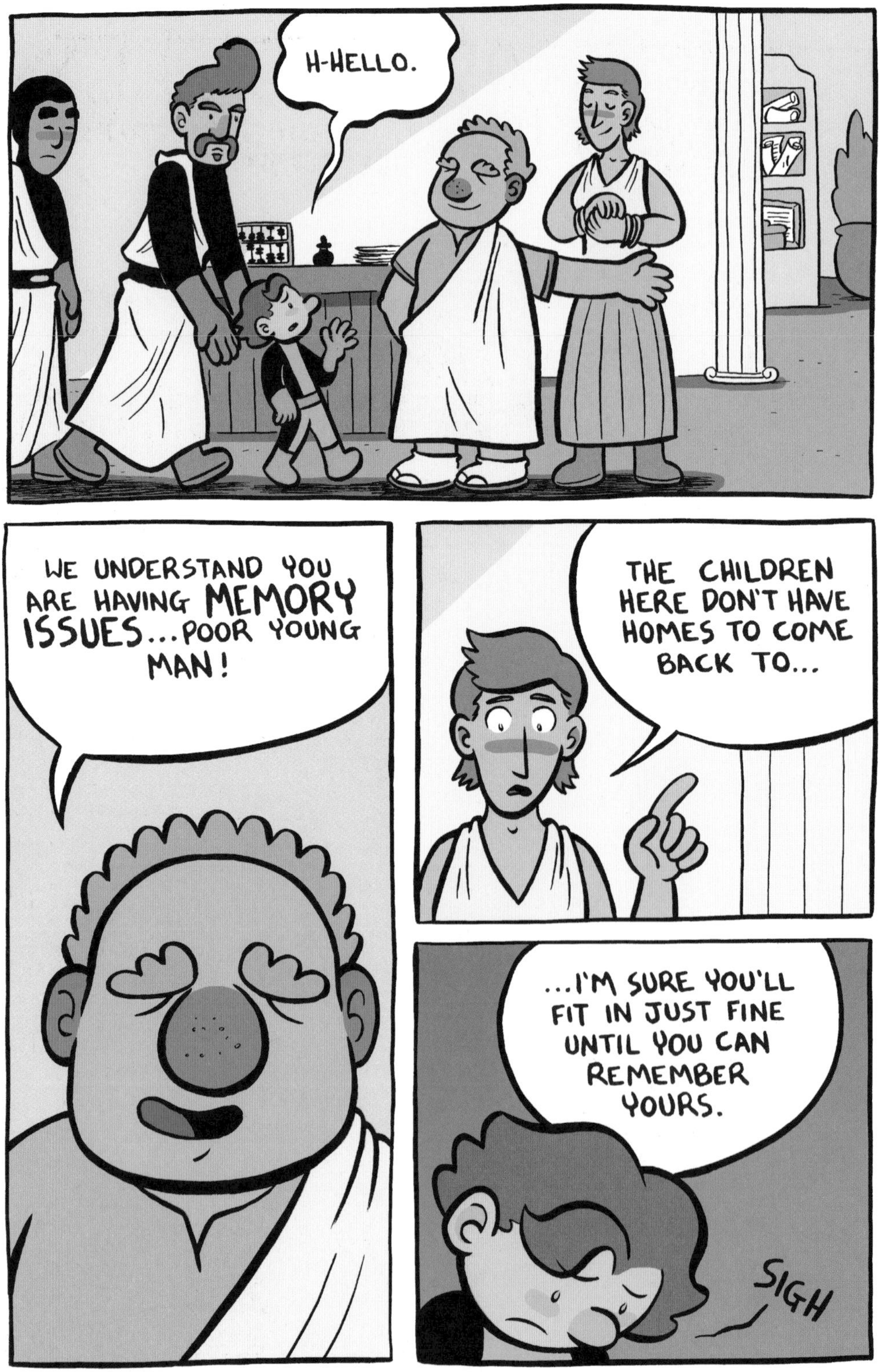
H-HELLO.
WE UNDERSTAND YOU ARE HAVING MEMORY ISSUES... POOR YOUNG MAN!
THE CHILDREN HERE DON'T HAVE HOMES TO COME BACK TO...
...I'M SURE YOU'LL FIT IN JUST FINE UNTIL YOU CAN REMEMBER YOURS.
SIGH

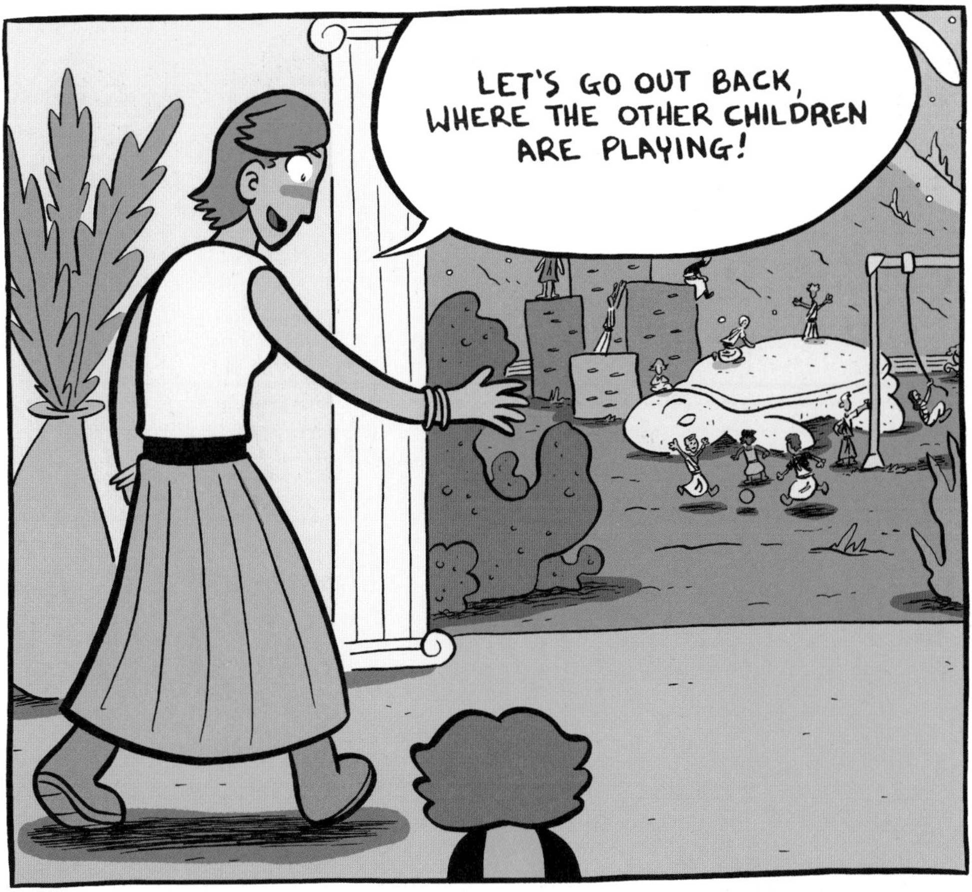
LET'S GO OUT BACK, WHERE THE OTHER CHILDREN ARE PLAYING!

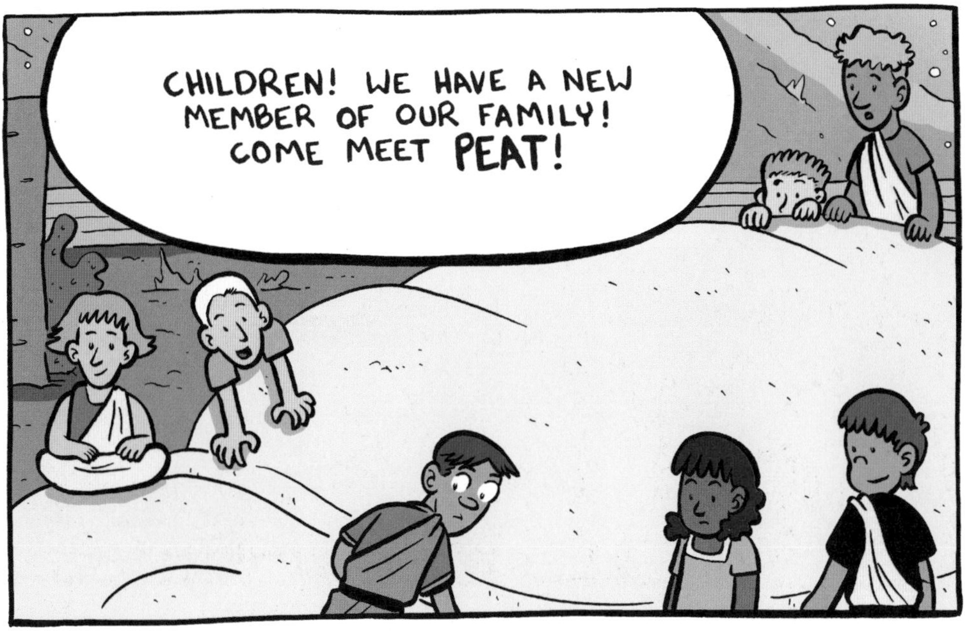
CHILDREN! WE HAVE A NEW MEMBER OF OUR FAMILY! COME MEET PEAT!

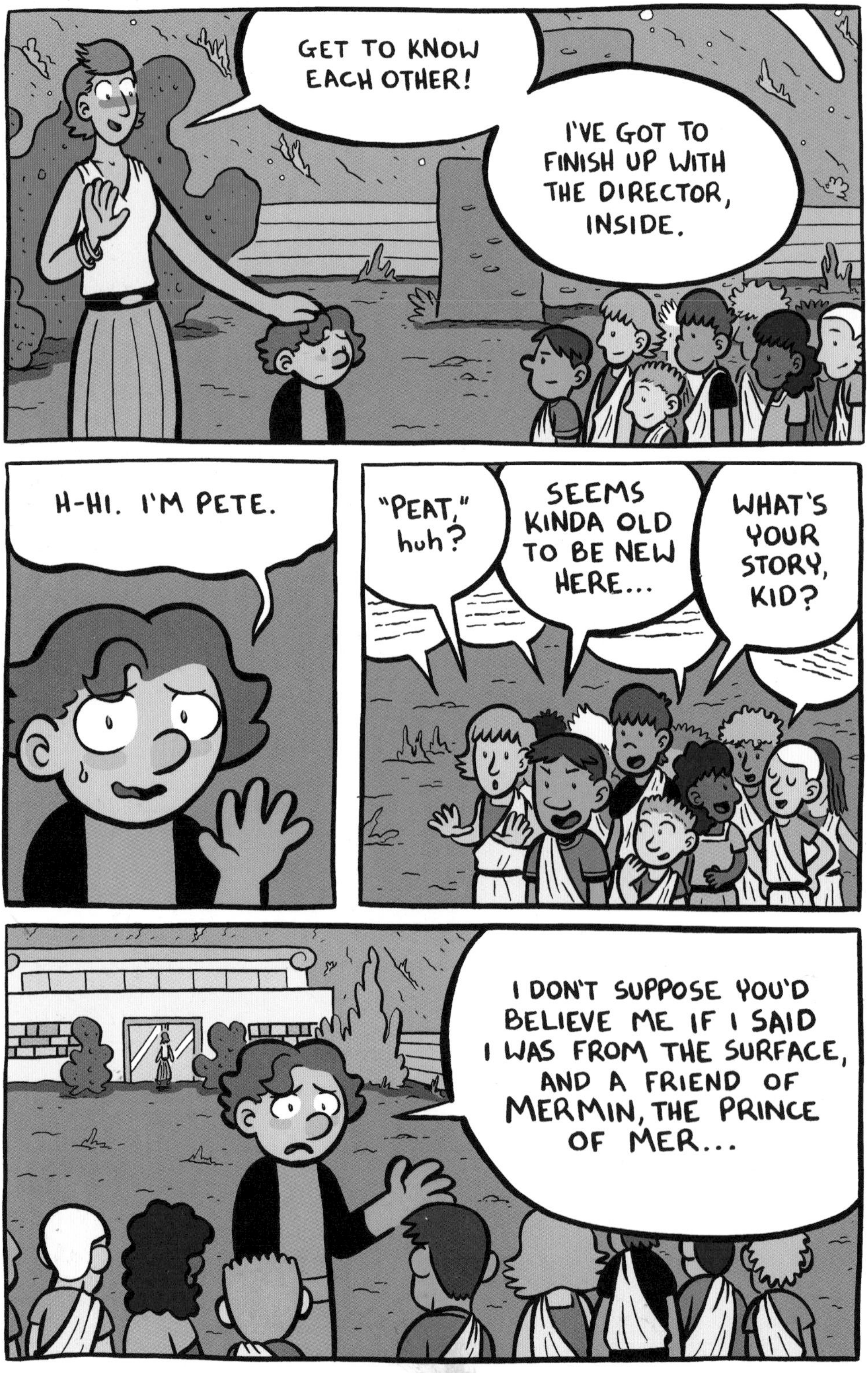
GET TO KNOW EACH OTHER!
I'VE GOT TO FINISH UP WITH THE DIRECTOR, INSIDE.
H-HI. I'M PETE.
"PEAT," huh?
SEEMS KINDA OLD TO BE NEW HERE...
WHAT'S YOUR STORY, KID?
I DON'T SUPPOSE YOU'D BELIEVE ME IF I SAID I WAS FROM THE SURFACE, AND A FRIEND OF MERMIN, THE PRINCE OF MER...

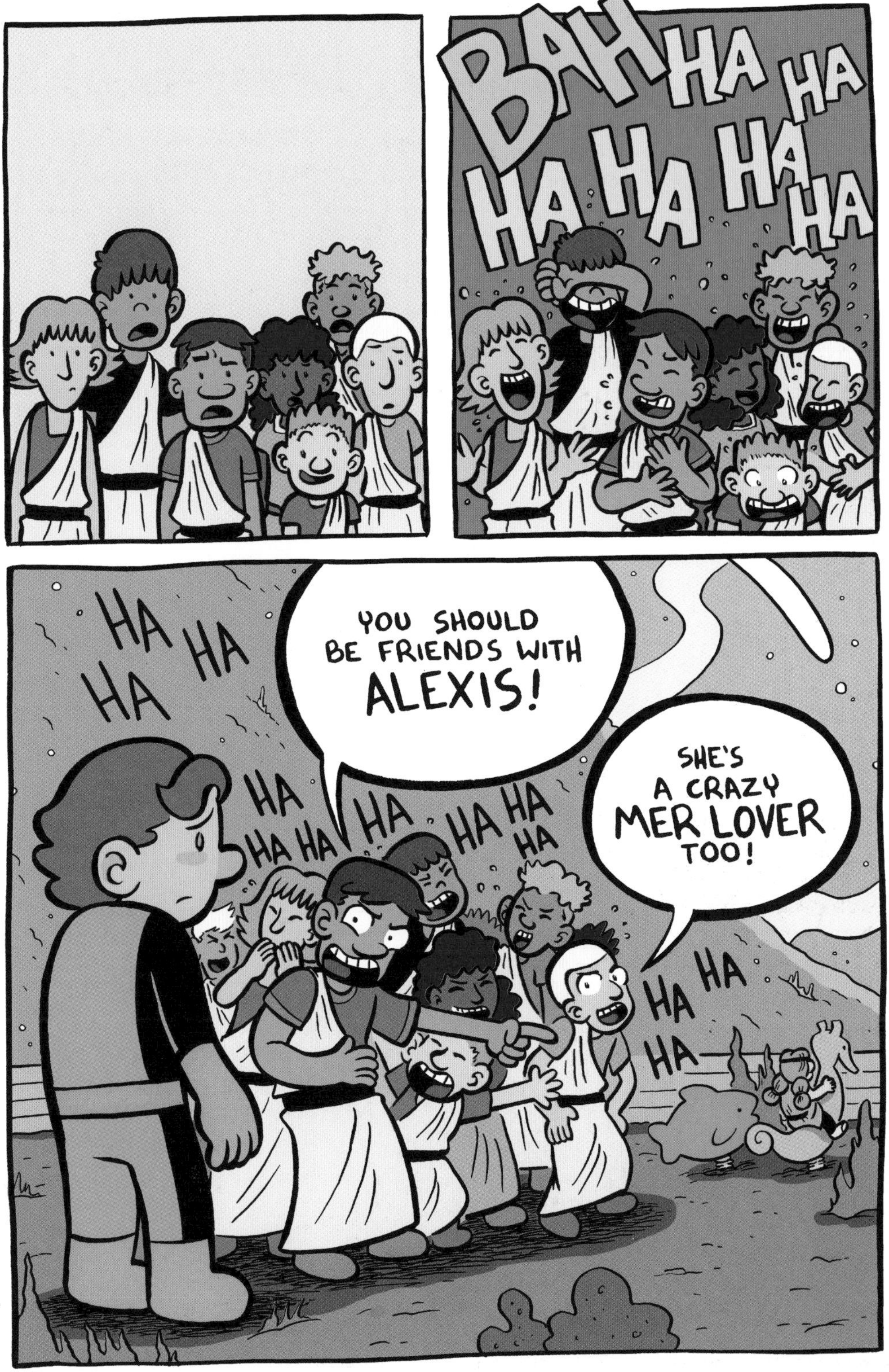
BAH HA HA HA HA HA HA HA HA
HA HA HA HA
YOU SHOULD BE FRIENDS WITH ALEXIS!
HA HA HA HA HA HA HA HA
SHE'S A CRAZY MER LOVER TOO!
HA HA HA

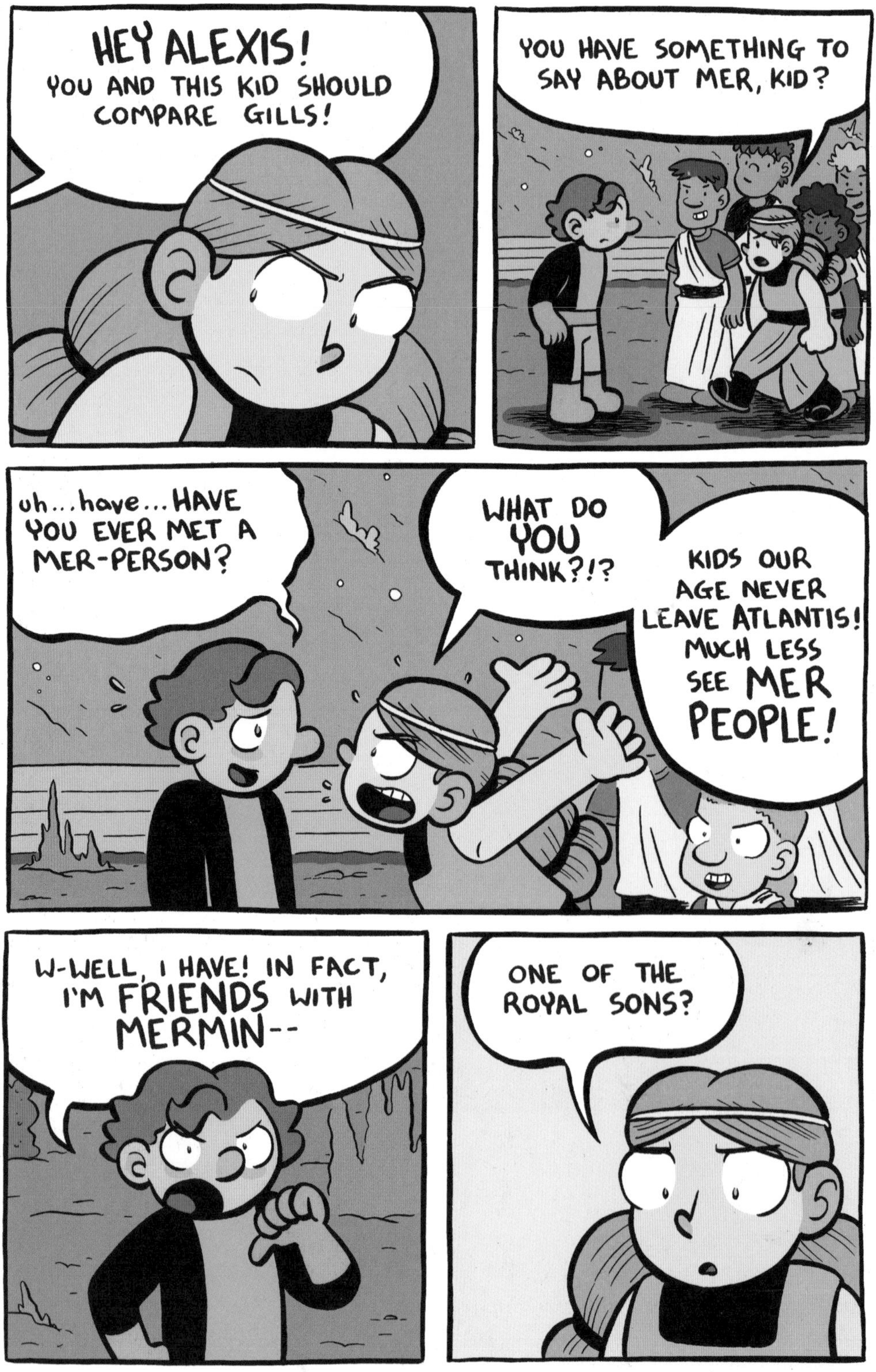
HEY ALEXIS! YOU AND THIS KID SHOULD COMPARE GILLS!
YOU HAVE SOMETHING TO SAY ABOUT MER, KID?
uh...have...HAVE YOU EVER MET A MER-PERSON?
WHAT DO YOU THINK?!?
KIDS OUR AGE NEVER LEAVE ATLANTIS! MUCH LESS SEE MER PEOPLE!
W-WELL, I HAVE! IN FACT, I'M FRIENDS WITH MERMIN--
ONE OF THE ROYAL SONS?

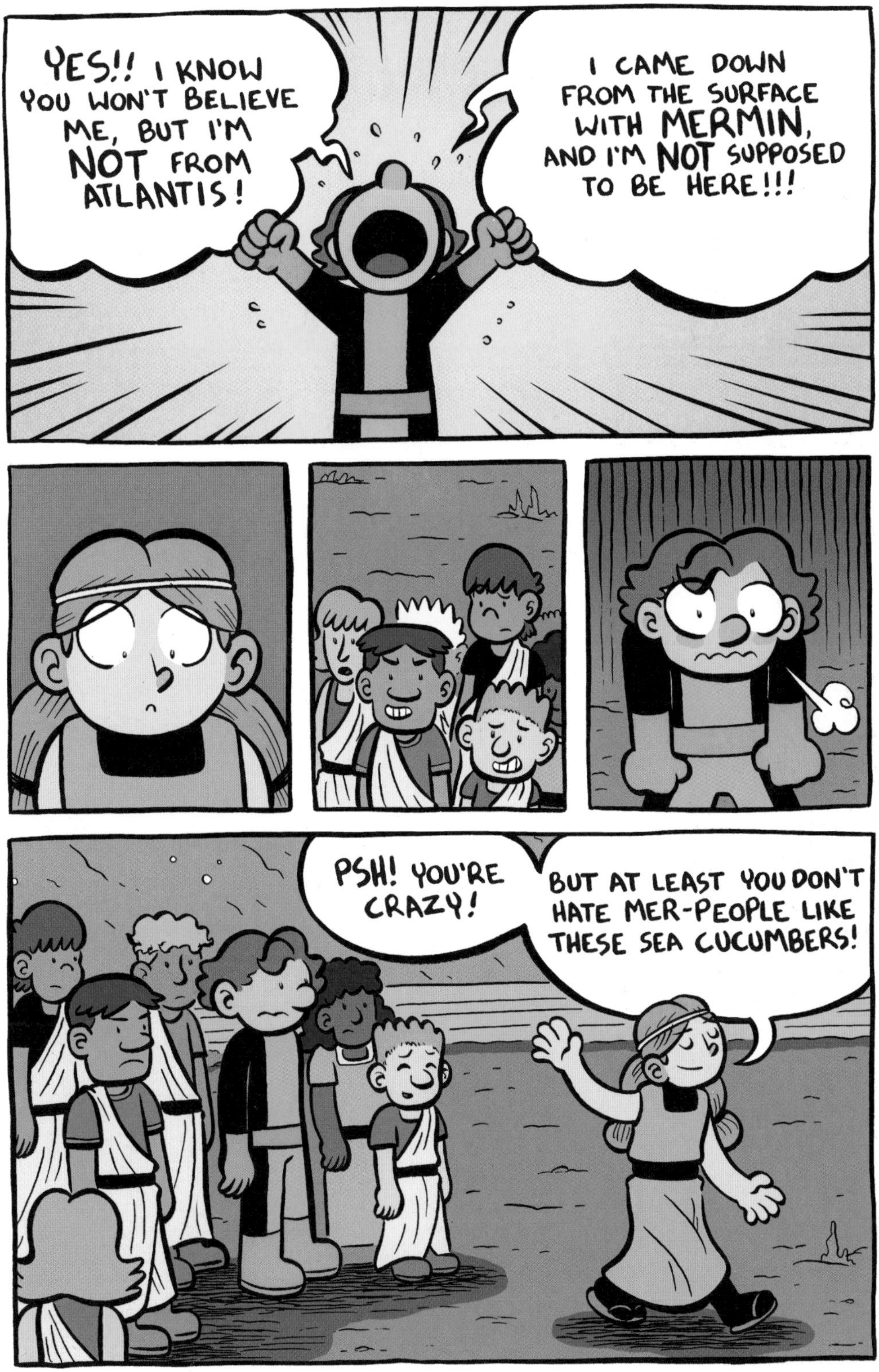
YES!! I KNOW YOU WON'T BELIEVE ME, BUT I'M NOT FROM ATLANTIS!
I CAME DOWN FROM THE SURFACE WITH MERMIN, AND I'M NOT SUPPOSED TO BE HERE!!!
PSH! YOU'RE CRAZY!
BUT AT LEAST YOU DON'T HATE MER-PEOPLE LIKE THESE SEA CUCUMBERS!

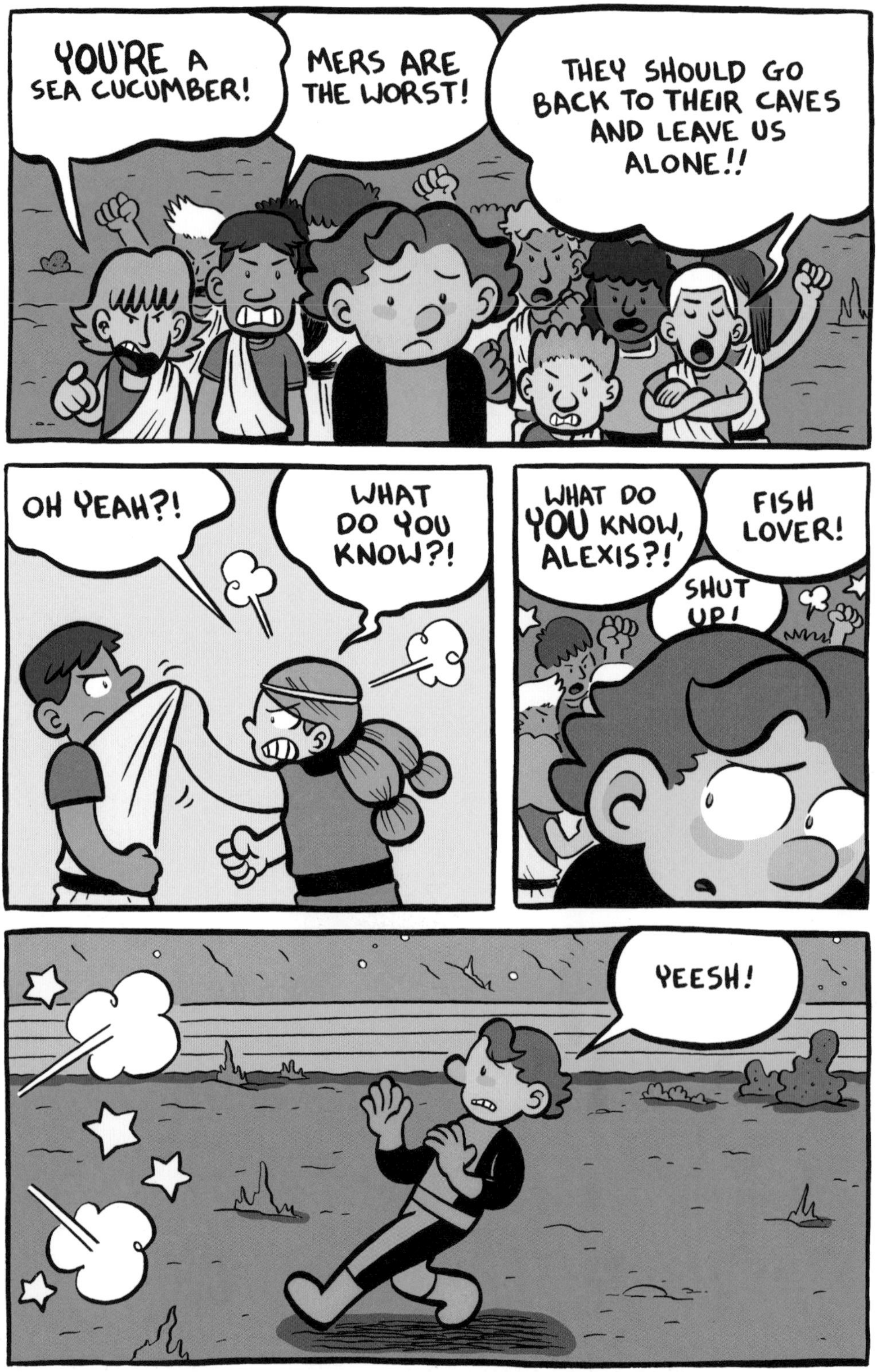
YOU'RE A SEA CUCUMBER!
MERS ARE THE WORST!
THEY SHOULD GO BACK TO THEIR CAVES AND LEAVE US ALONE!!
OH YEAH?!
WHAT DO YOU KNOW?!
WHAT DO YOU KNOW, ALEXIS?!
FISH LOVER!
SHUT UP!
YEESH!

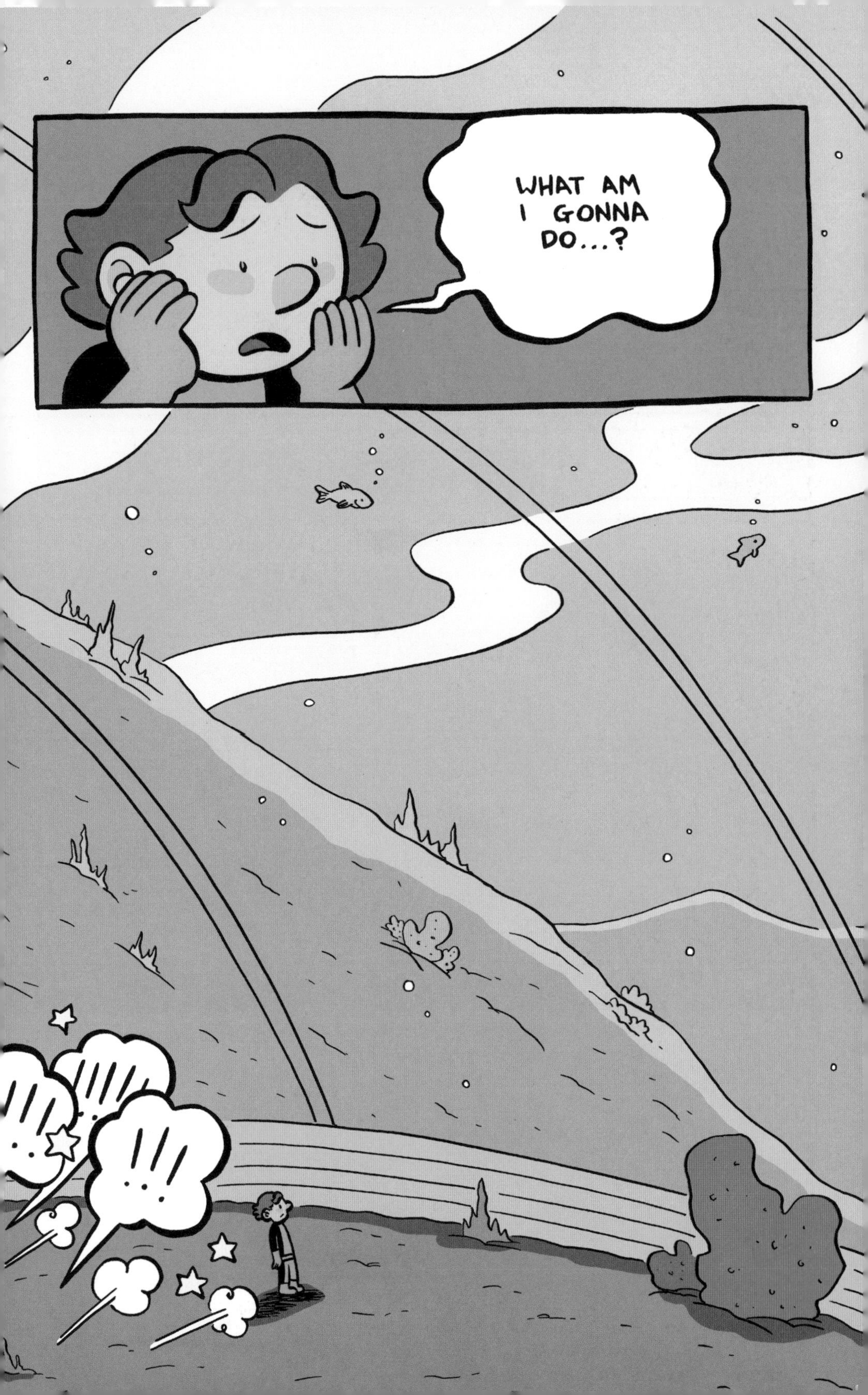
WHAT AM I GONNA DO...?
!!!...
!!!...
!!!...

CHAPTER THREE

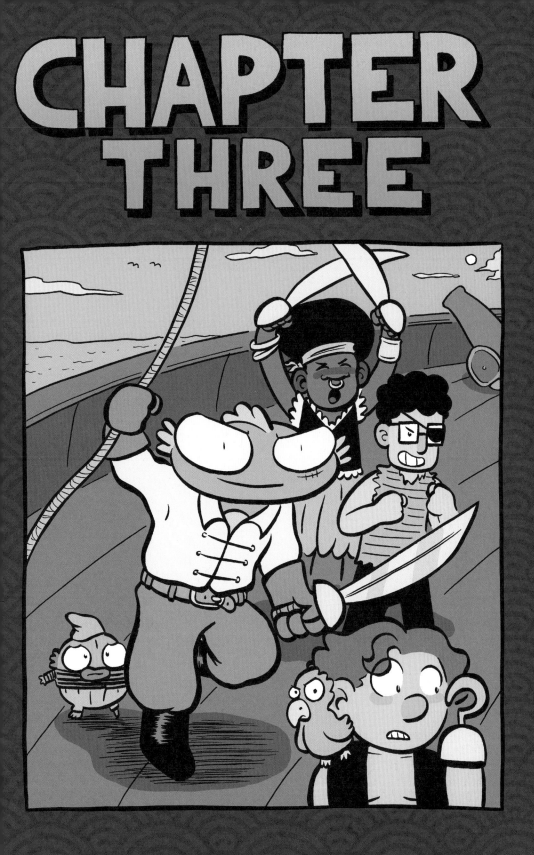

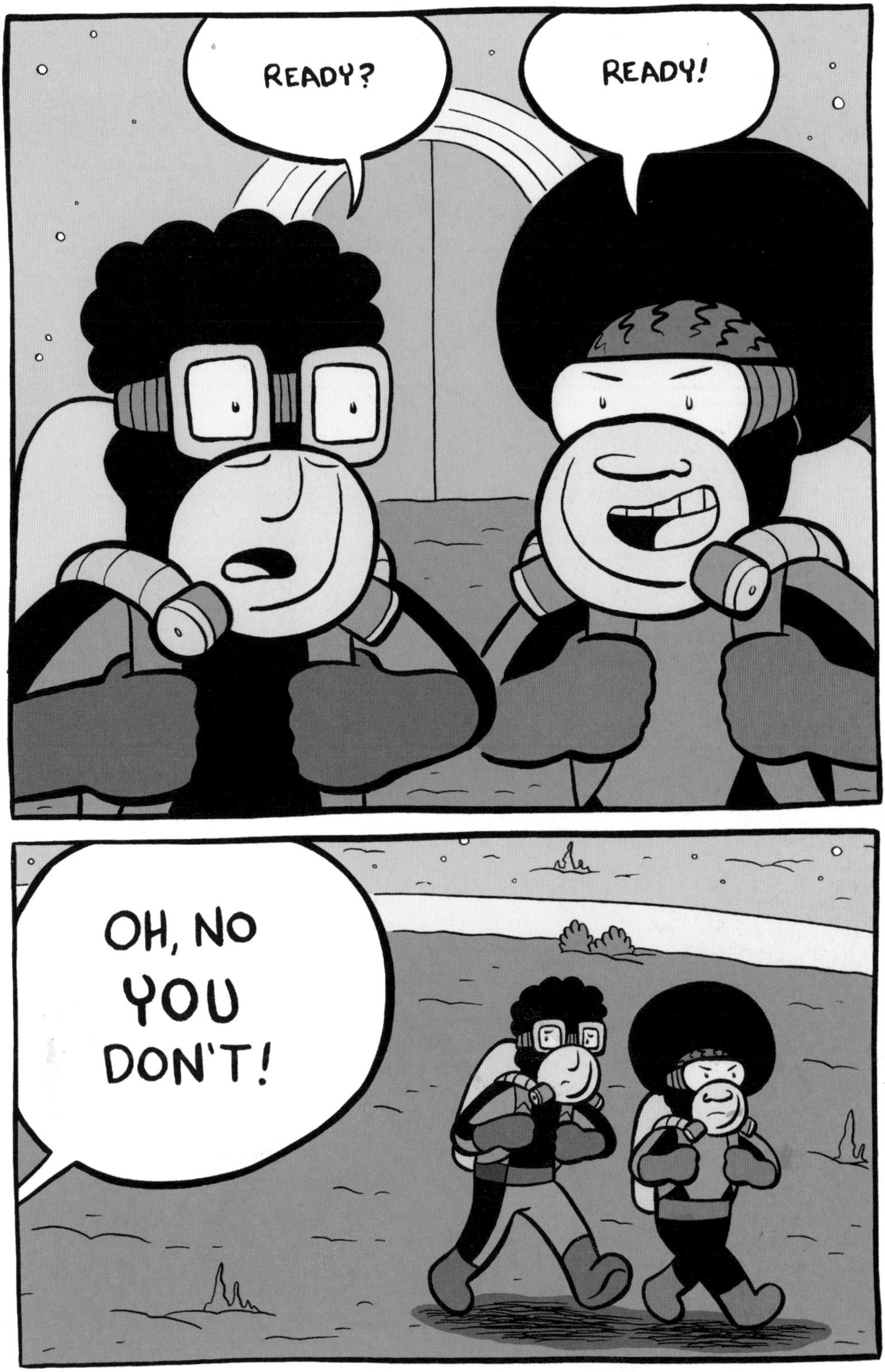
READY?
READY!
OH, NO YOU DON'T!

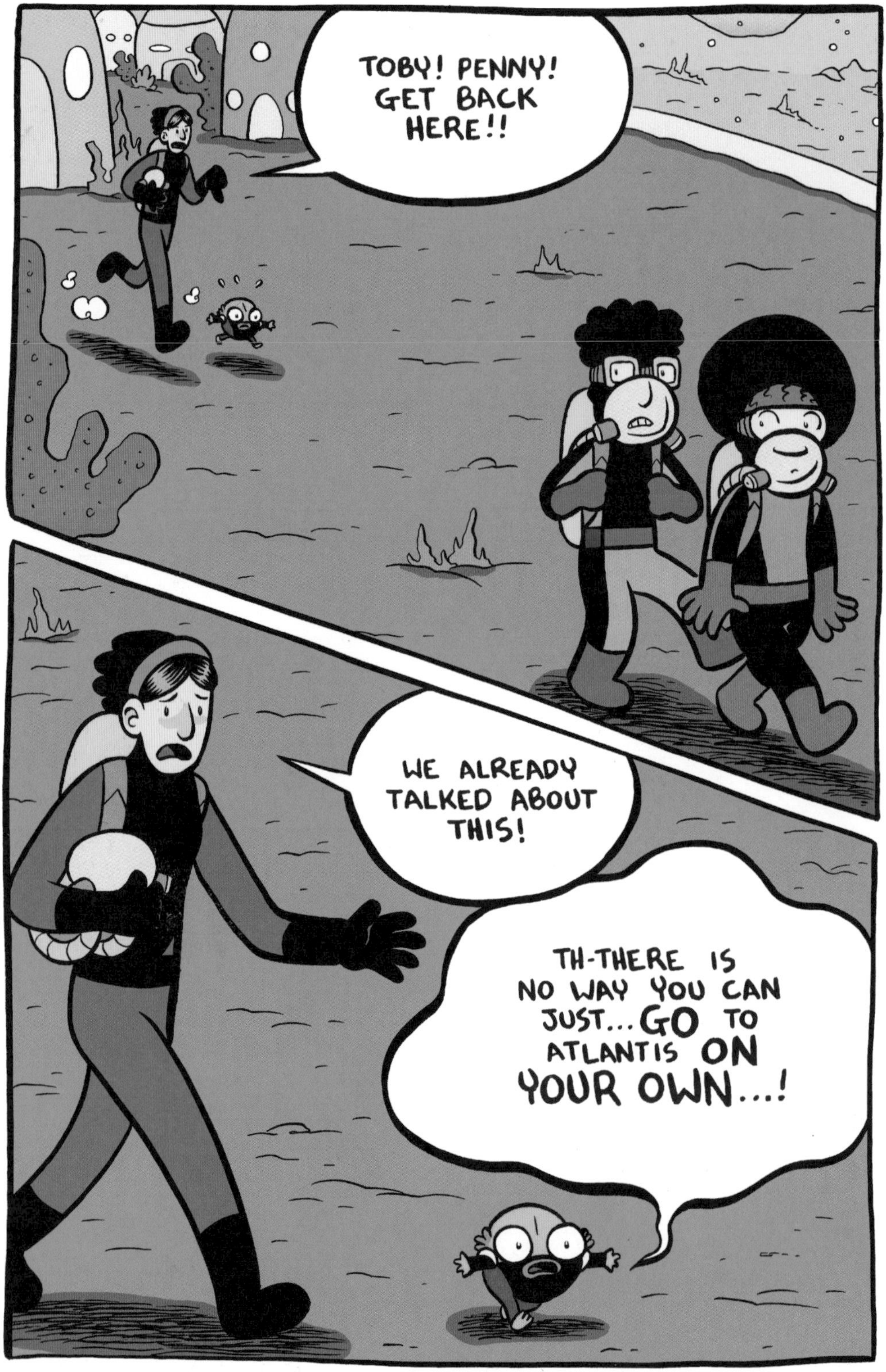
TOBY! PENNY! GET BACK HERE!!
WE ALREADY TALKED ABOUT THIS!
TH-THERE IS NO WAY YOU CAN JUST... GO TO ATLANTIS ON YOUR OWN...!

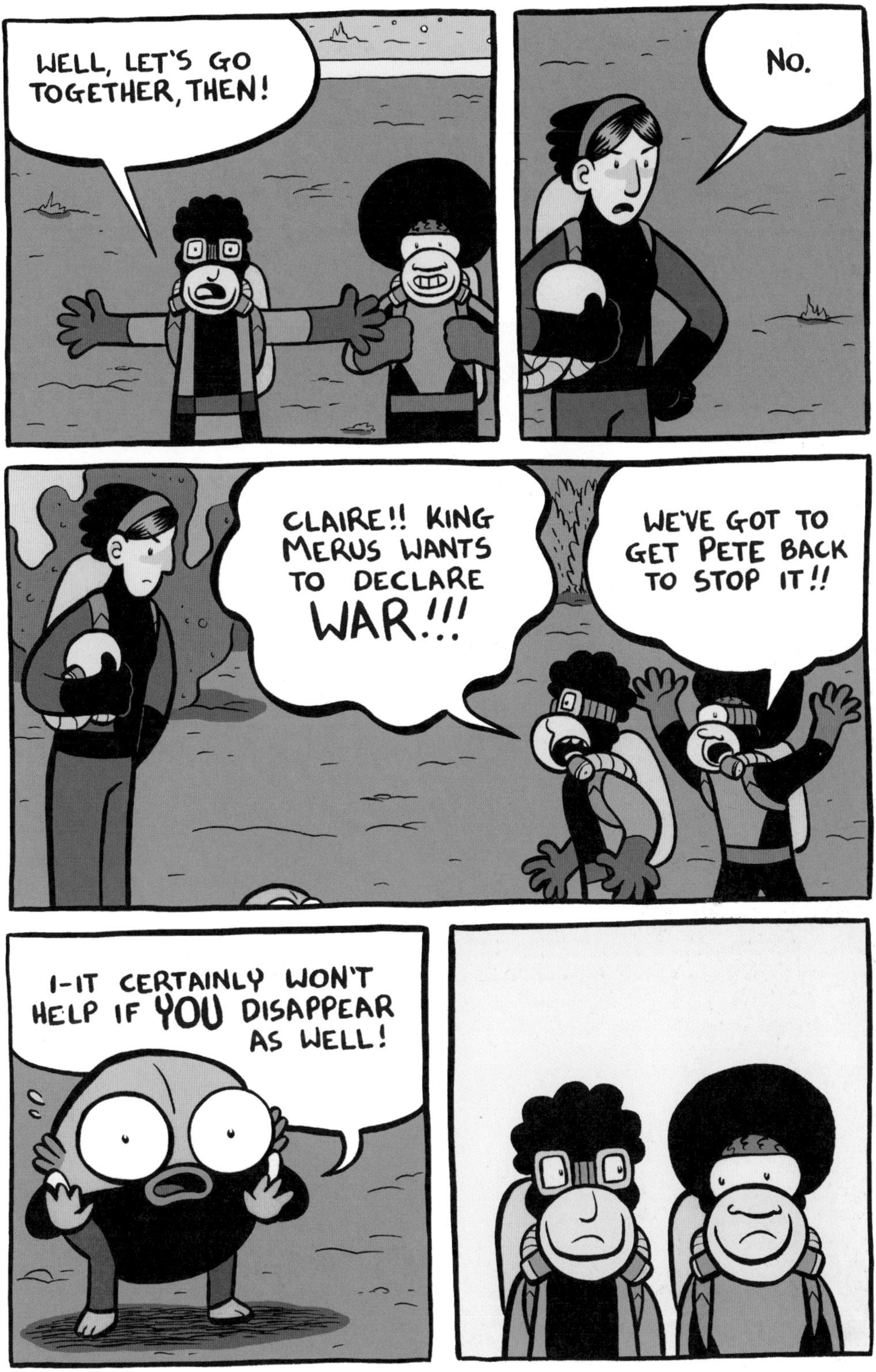
WELL, LET'S GO TOGETHER, THEN!
NO.
CLAIRE!! KING MERUS WANTS TO DECLARE WAR!!!
WE'VE GOT TO GET PETE BACK TO STOP IT!!
I-IT CERTAINLY WON'T HELP IF YOU DISAPPEAR AS WELL!

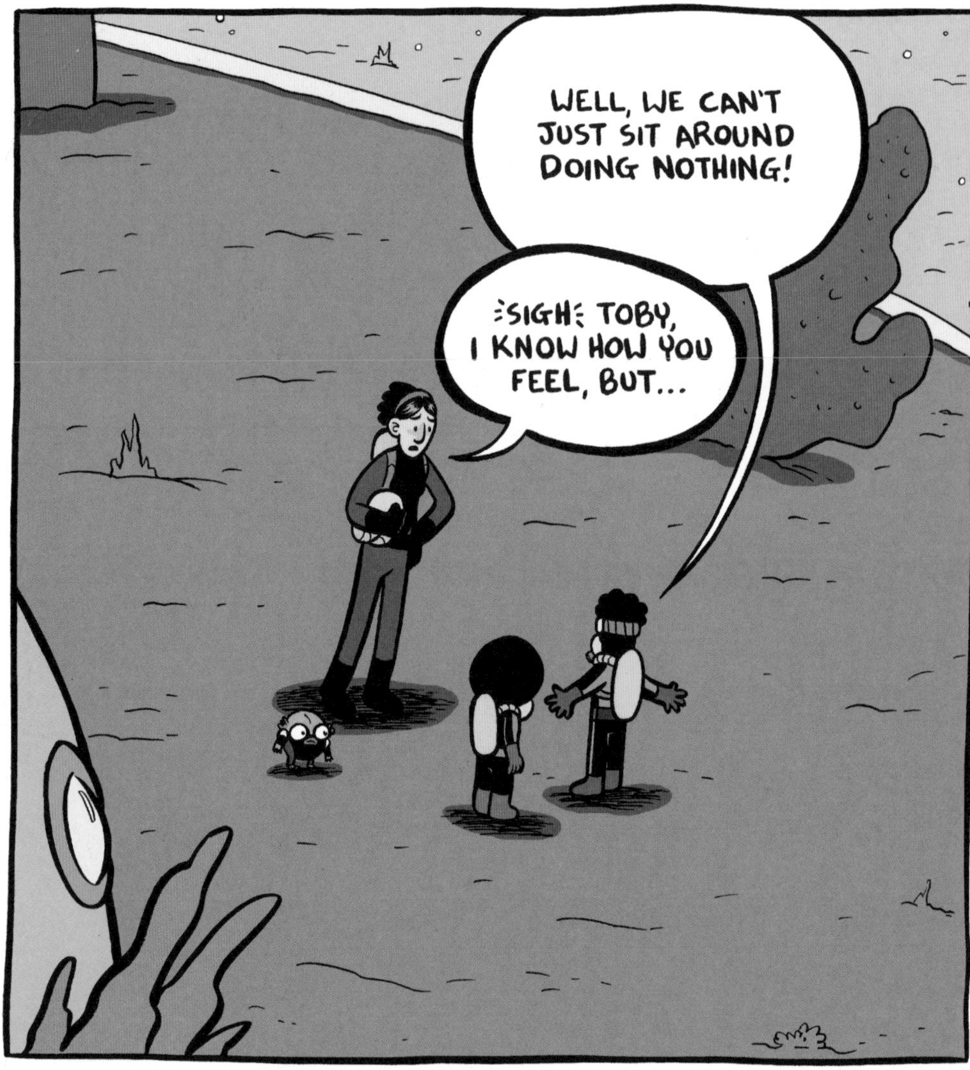
WELL, WE CAN'T JUST SIT AROUND DOING NOTHING!
SIGH TOBY, I KNOW HOW YOU FEEL, BUT...
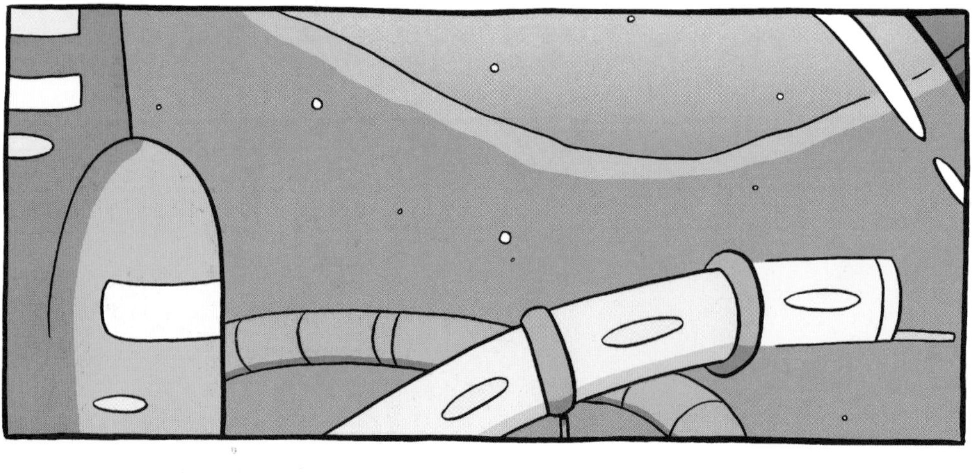

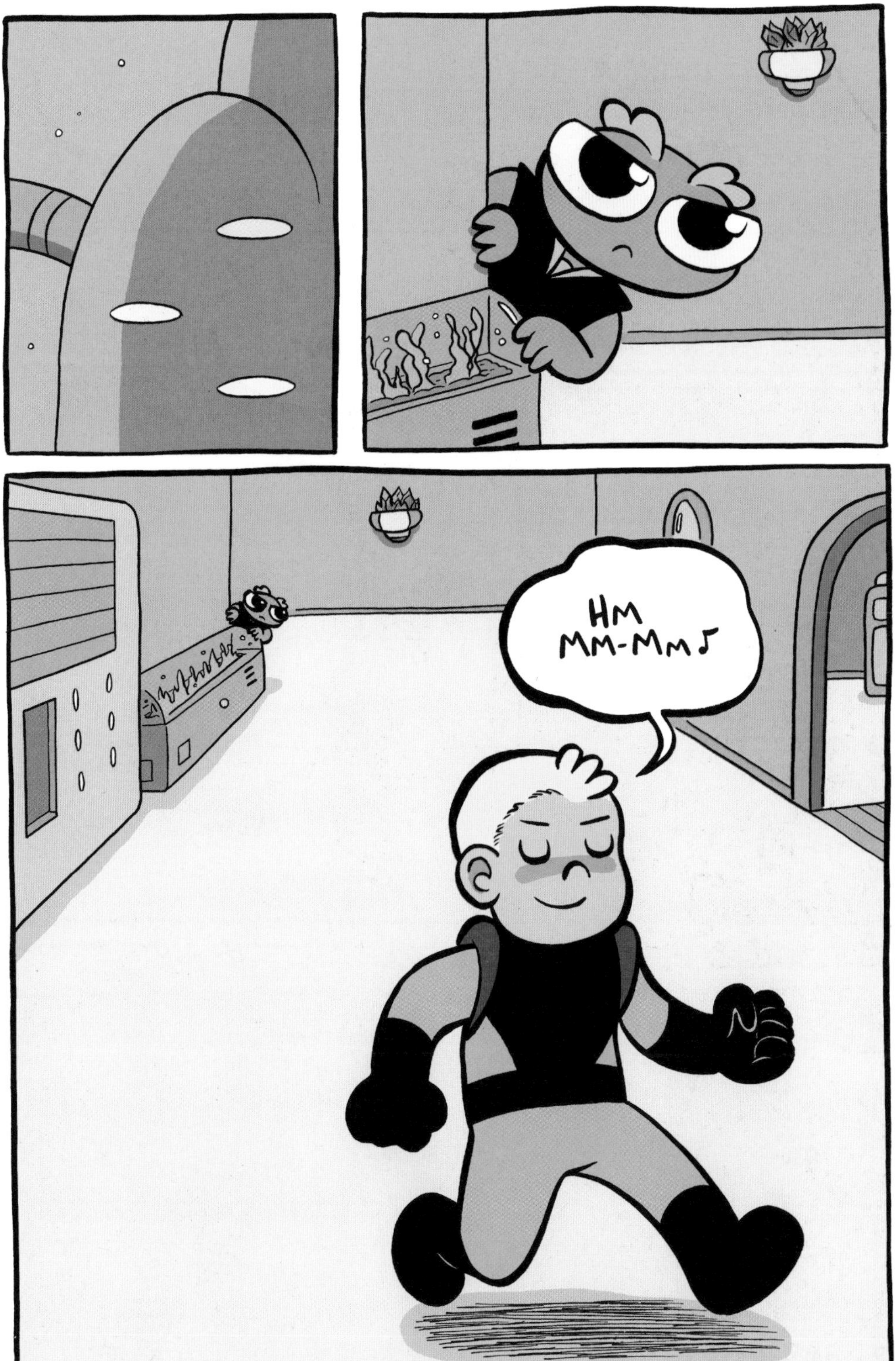
HM
MM-MM ♪

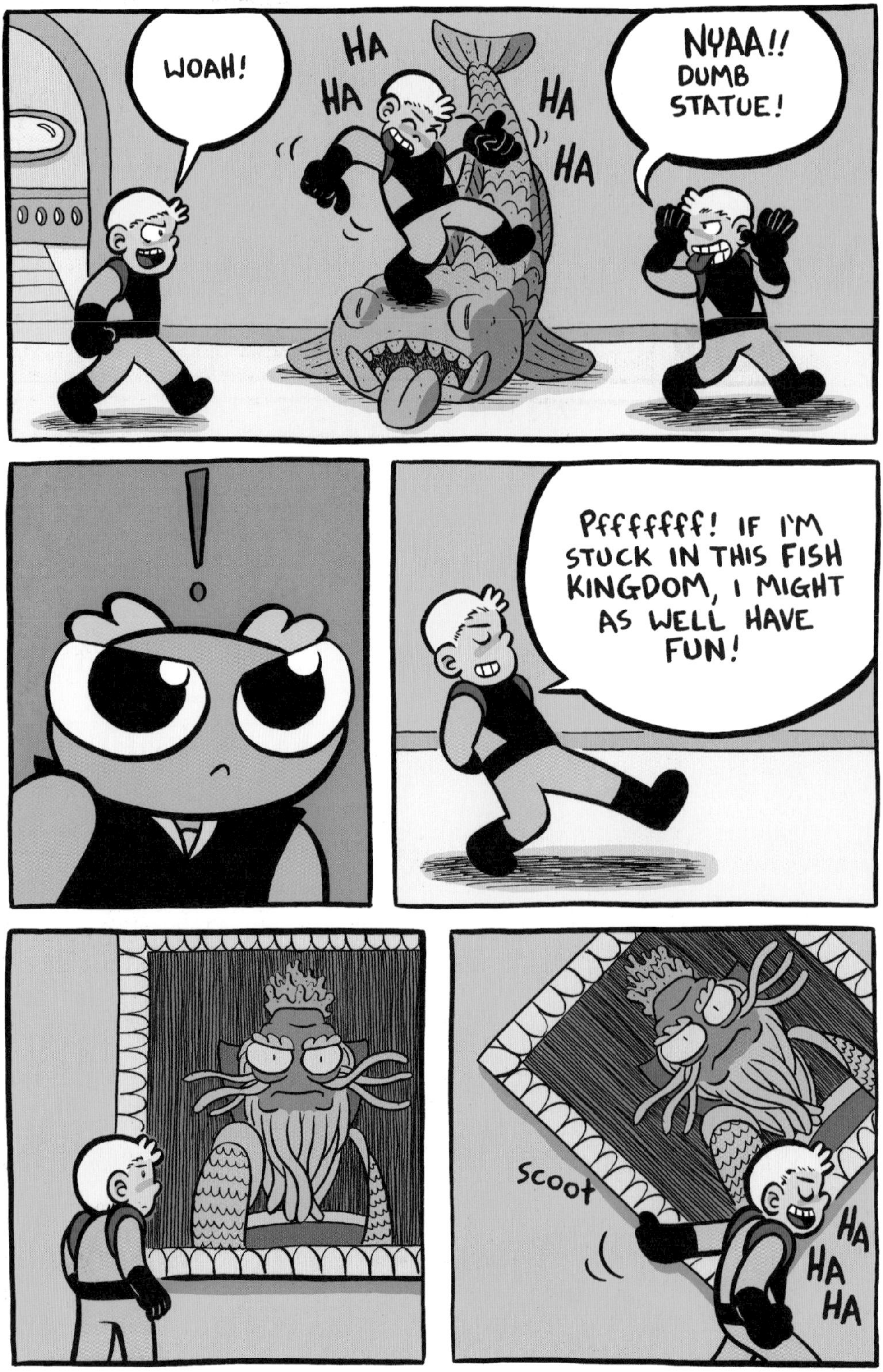
WOAH!
HA HA
HA HA
NYAA!! DUMB STATUE!
!
Pfffffff! IF I'M STUCK IN THIS FISH KINGDOM, I MIGHT AS WELL HAVE FUN!
scoot
HA HA HA

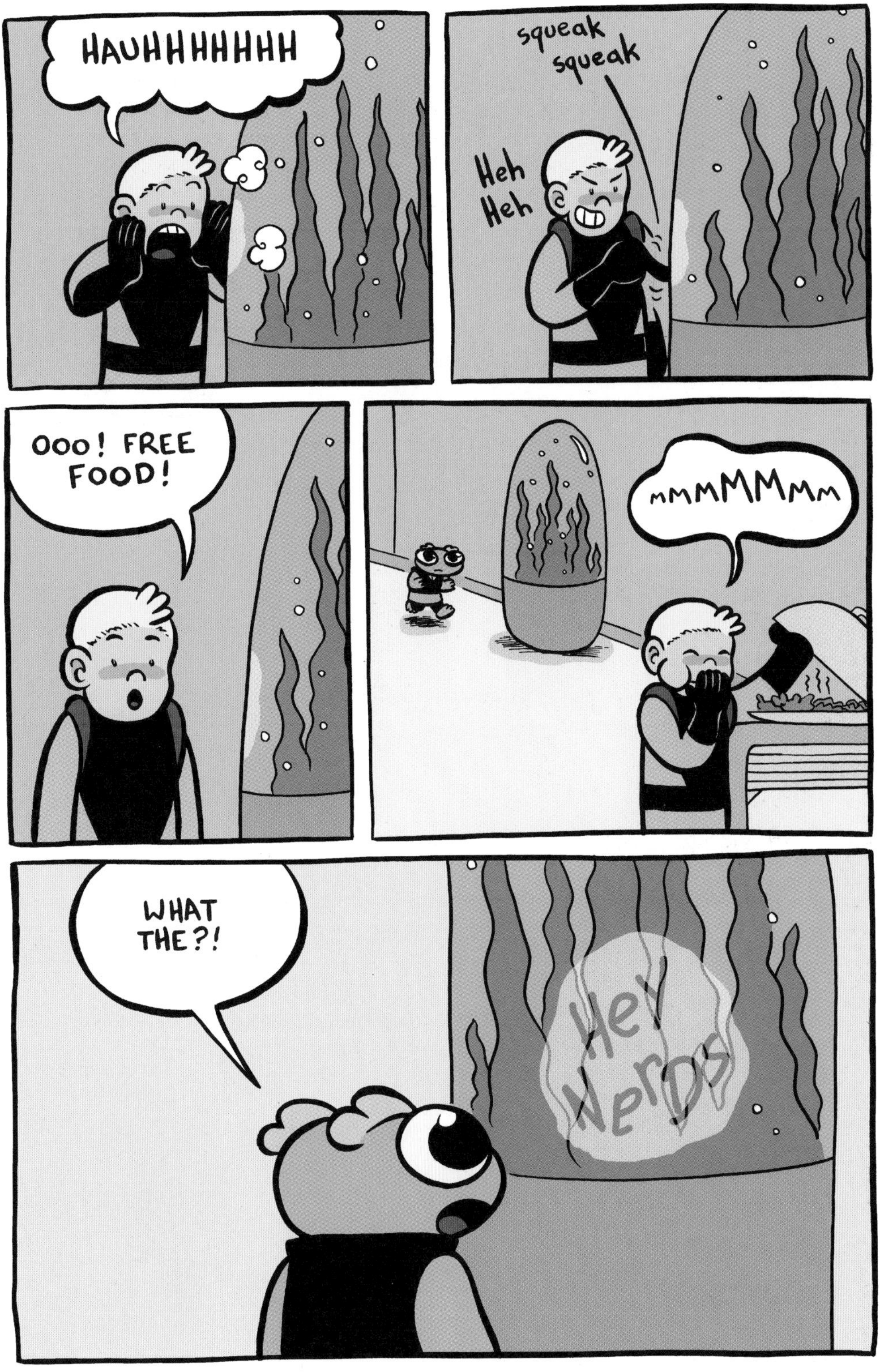
HAUHHHHHHH
squeak squeak
Heh Heh
OOO! FREE FOOD!
mMMMMMmm
WHAT THE?!
Hey Nerds

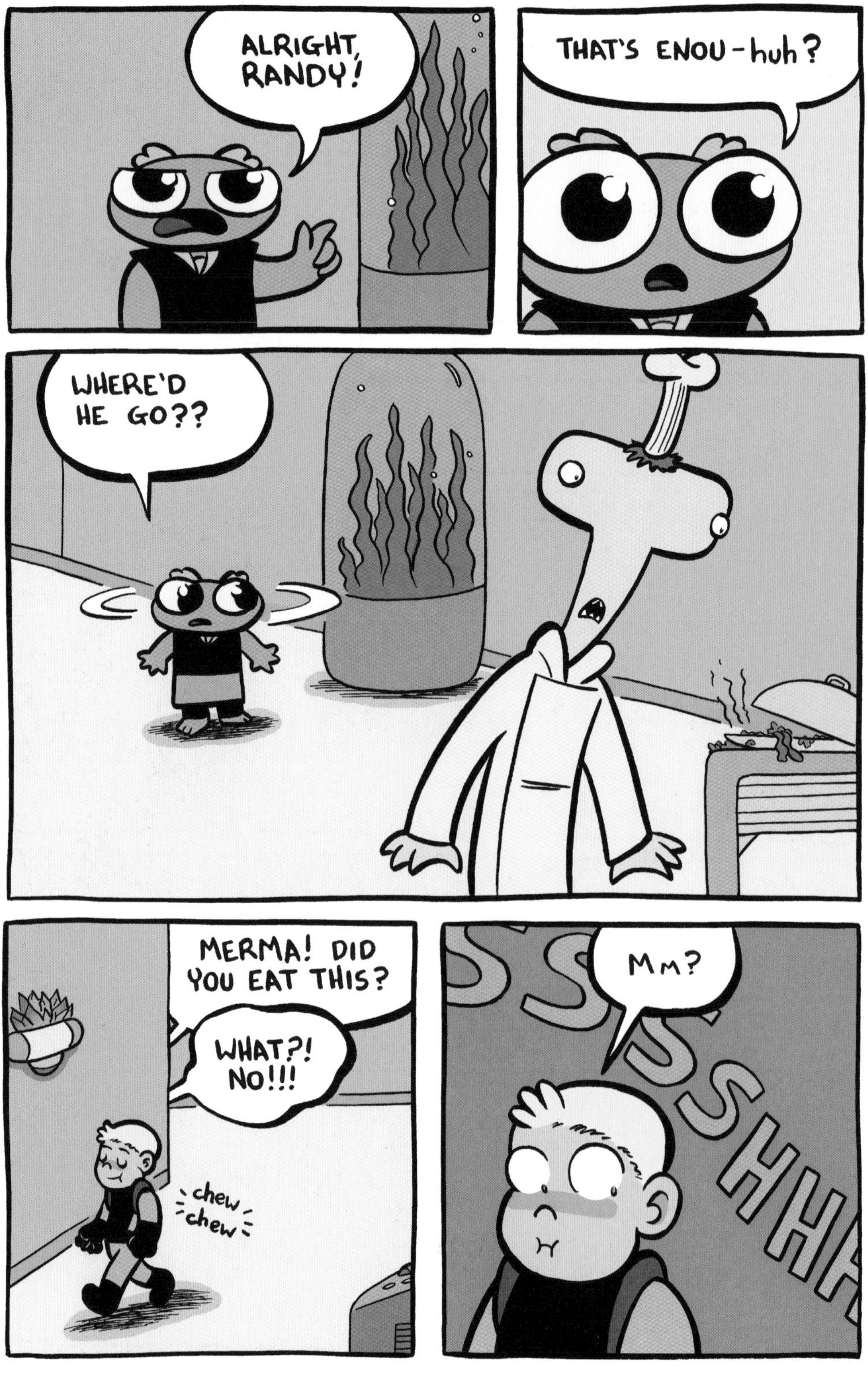
ALRIGHT, RANDY!
THAT'S ENOU-huh?
WHERE'D HE GO??
MERMA! DID YOU EAT THIS?
WHAT?! NO!!!
chew chew
Mm?
SSSSSHH

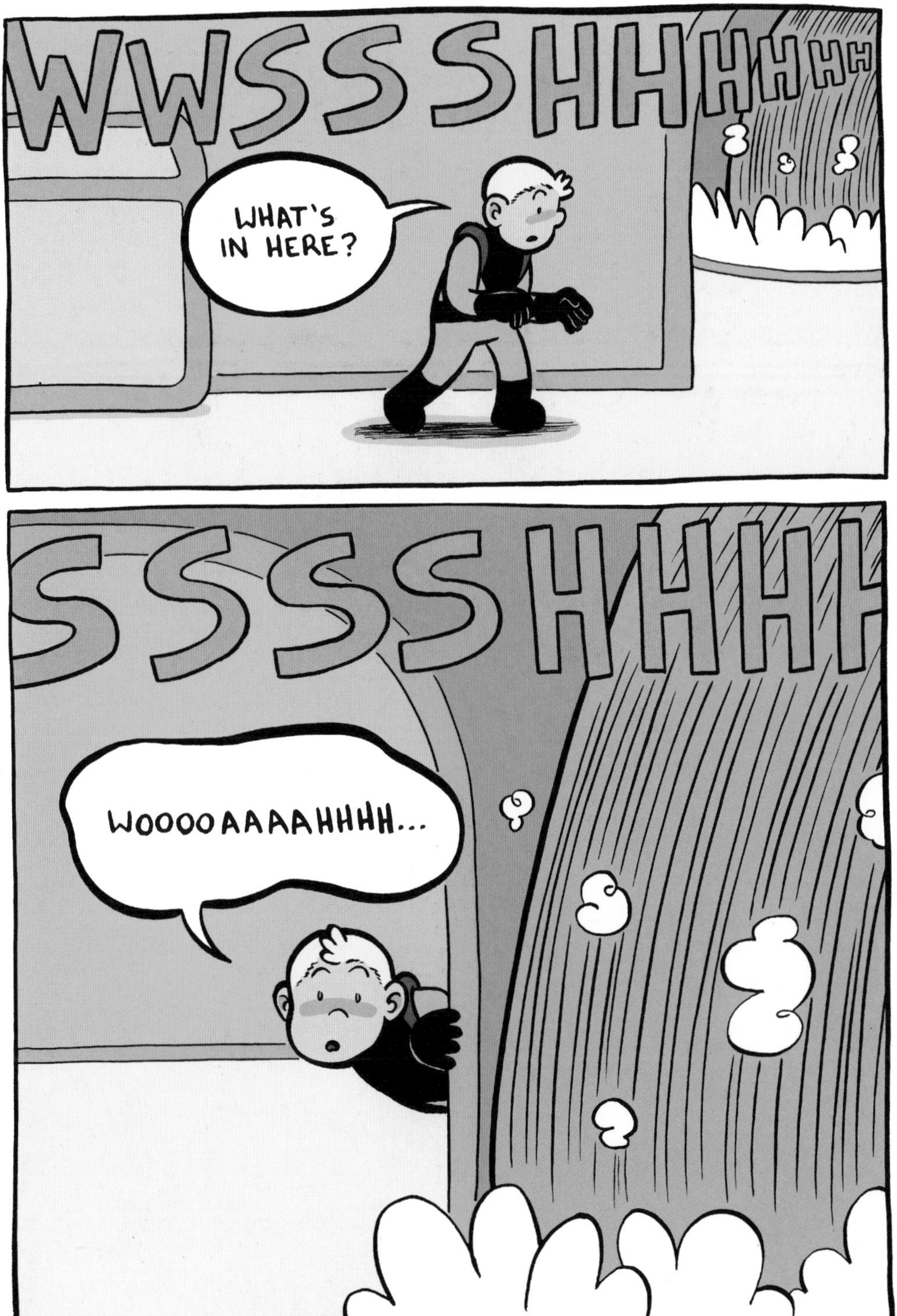
WWSSSSHHHHHH
WHAT'S IN HERE?
SSSSHHHH
WOOOOAAAAHHHH...

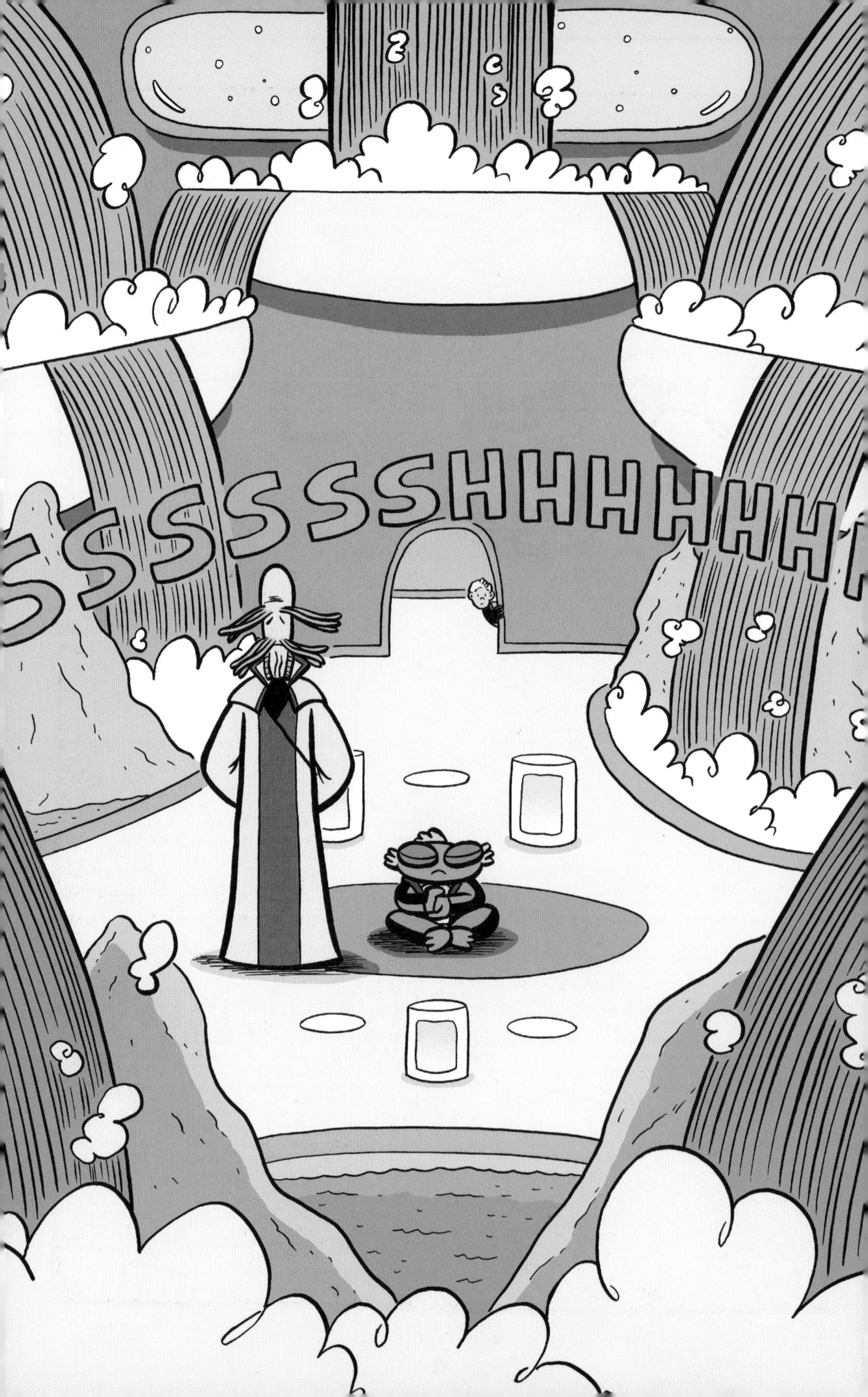
SSSSSSSHHHHHHHH

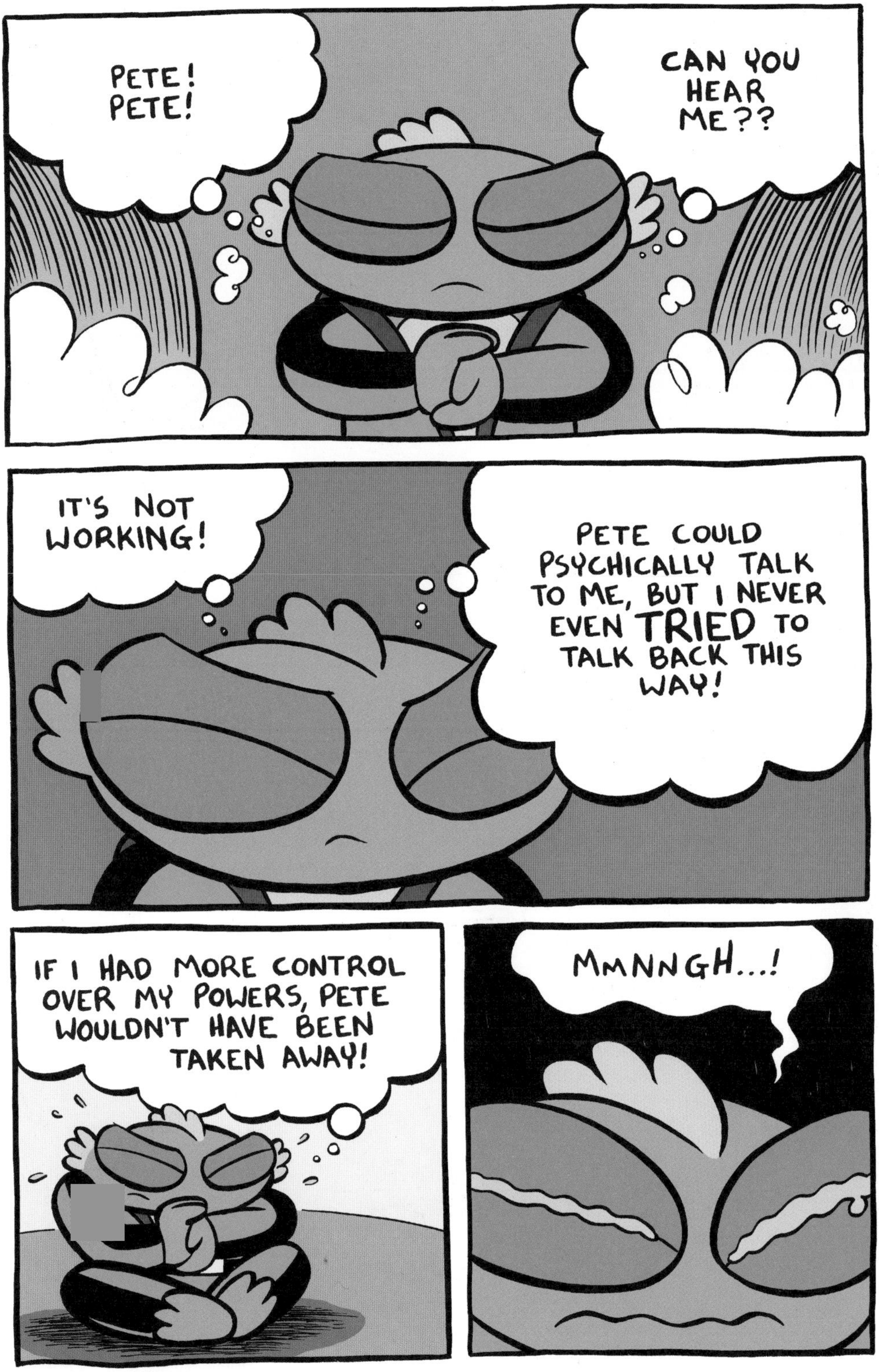
PETE! PETE!
CAN YOU HEAR ME??
IT'S NOT WORKING!
PETE COULD PSYCHICALLY TALK TO ME, BUT I NEVER EVEN TRIED TO TALK BACK THIS WAY!
IF I HAD MORE CONTROL OVER MY POWERS, PETE WOULDN'T HAVE BEEN TAKEN AWAY!
MMNNGH...!

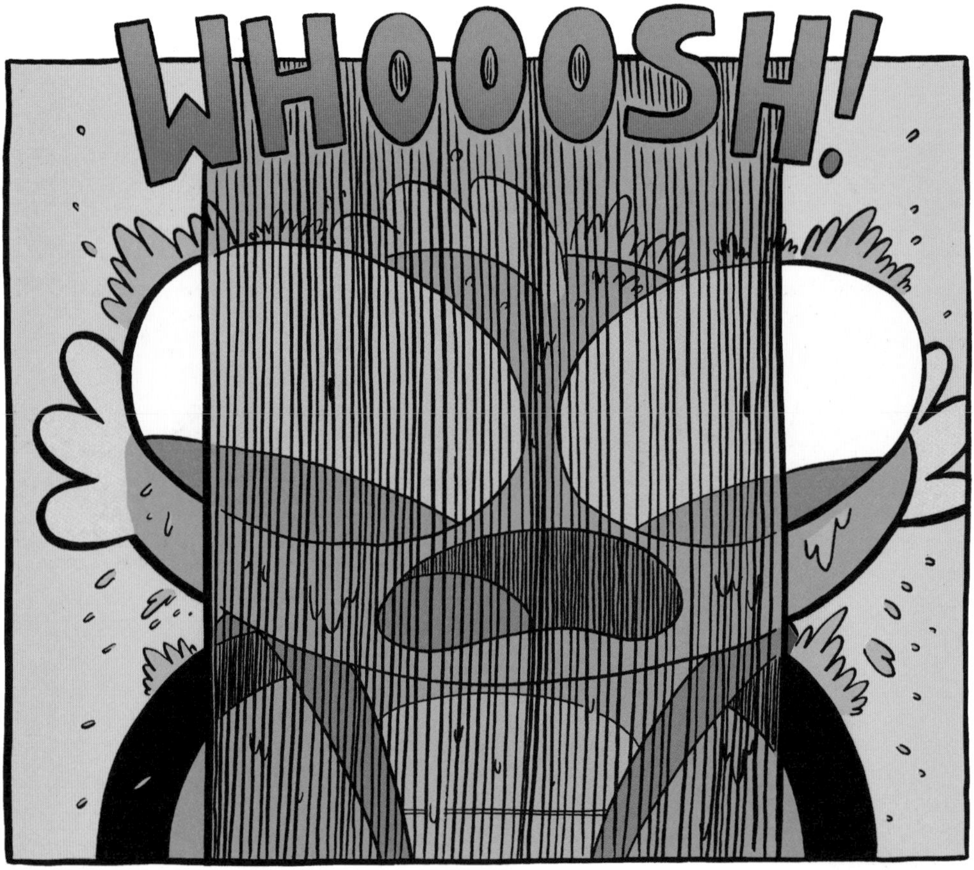
WHOOOSH!

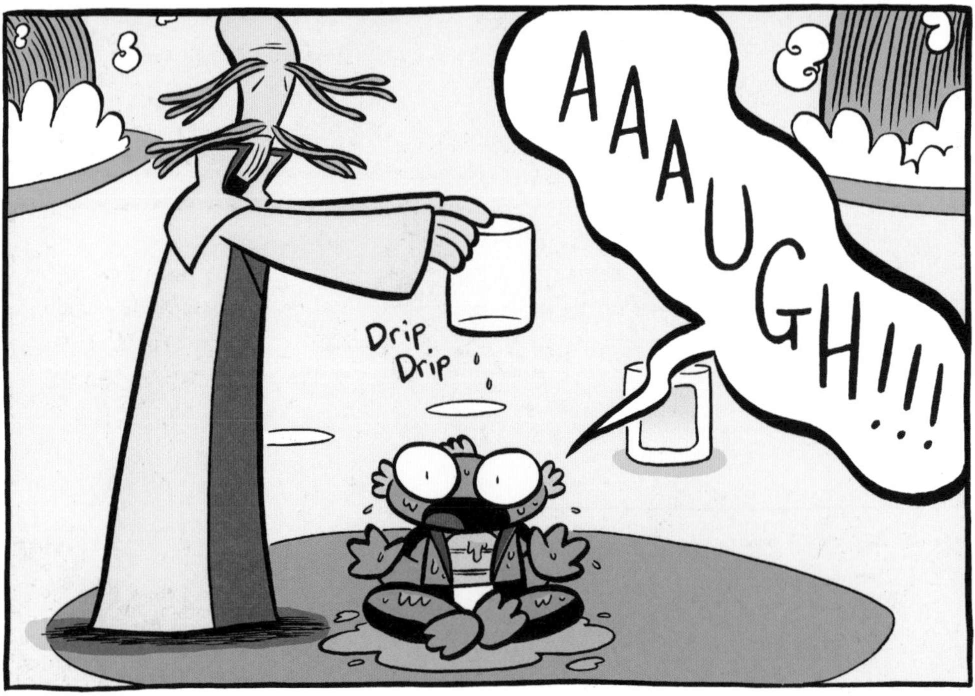
AAAAUGH!!!...
Drip Drip

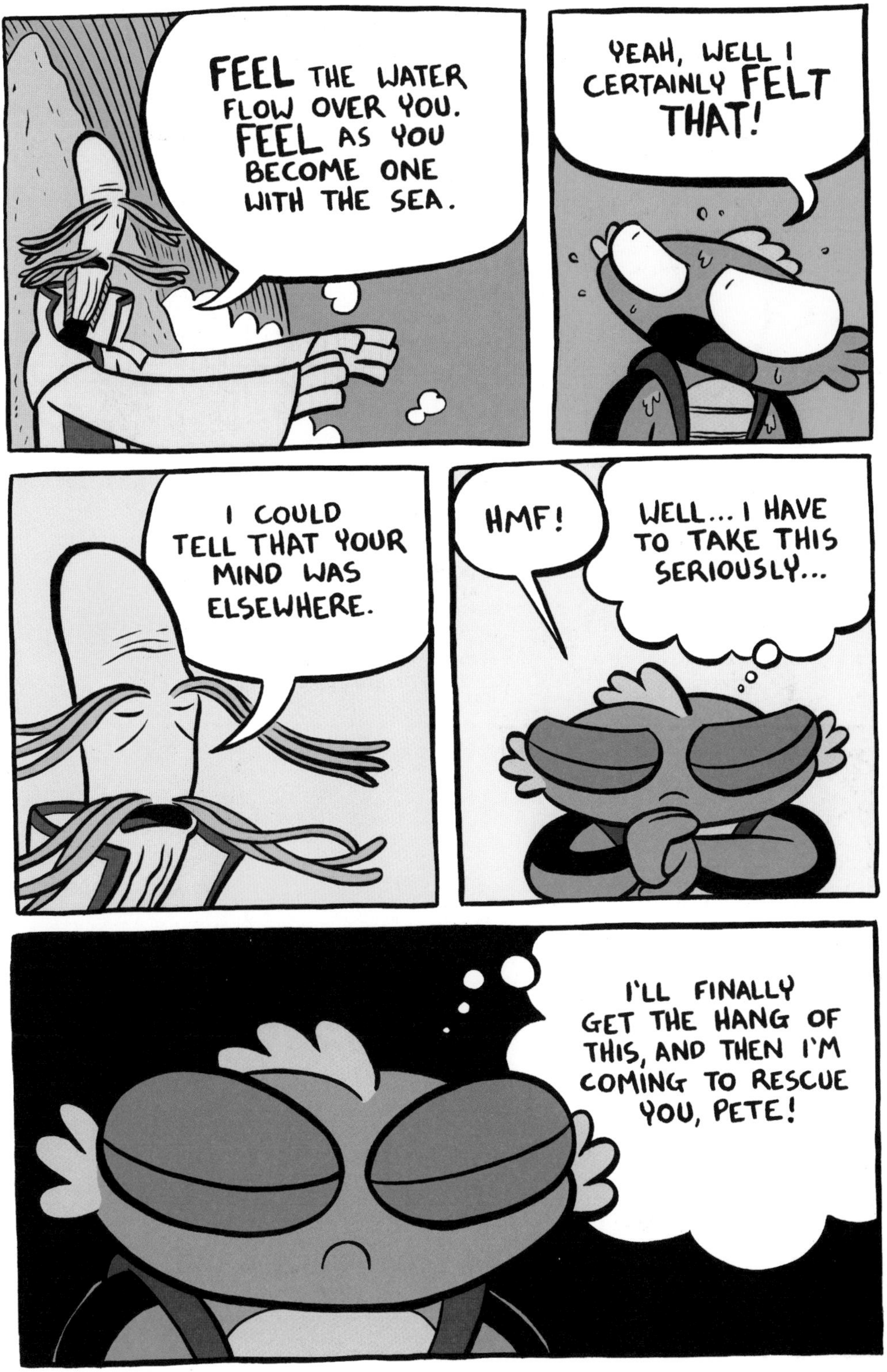
FEEL THE WATER FLOW OVER YOU. FEEL AS YOU BECOME ONE WITH THE SEA.
YEAH, WELL I CERTAINLY FELT THAT!
I COULD TELL THAT YOUR MIND WAS ELSEWHERE.
HMF!
WELL... I HAVE TO TAKE THIS SERIOUSLY...
I'LL FINALLY GET THE HANG OF THIS, AND THEN I'M COMING TO RESCUE YOU, PETE!

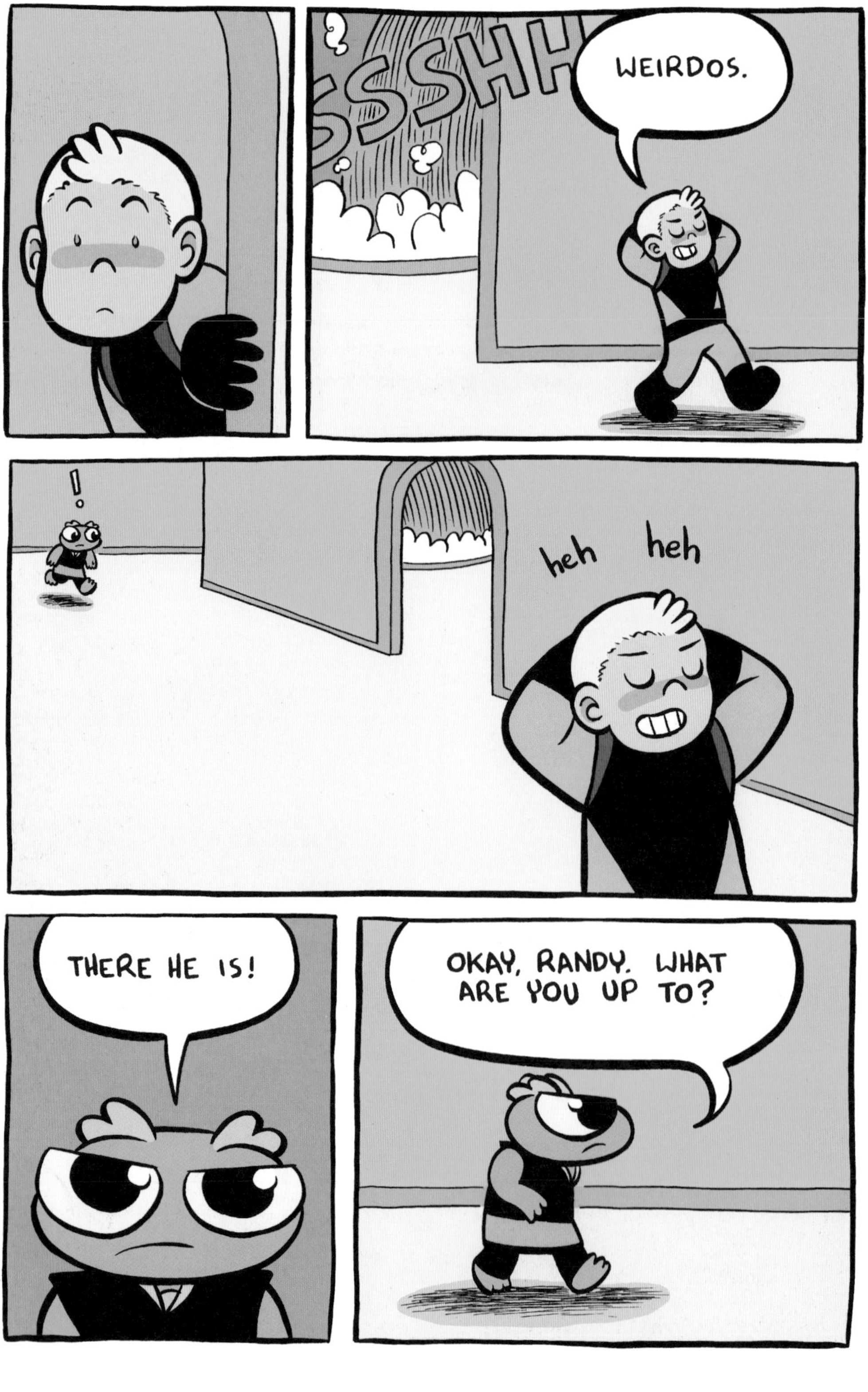
SSSHH
WEIRDOS.
!
heh heh
THERE HE IS!
OKAY, RANDY. WHAT ARE YOU UP TO?

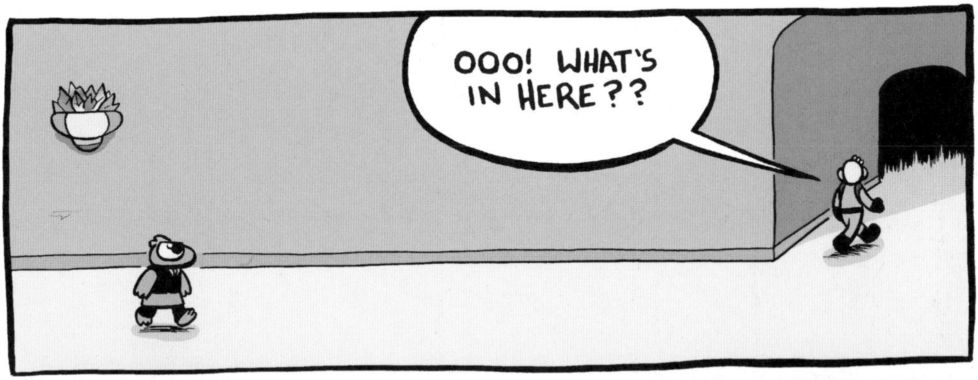
OOO! WHAT'S IN HERE??

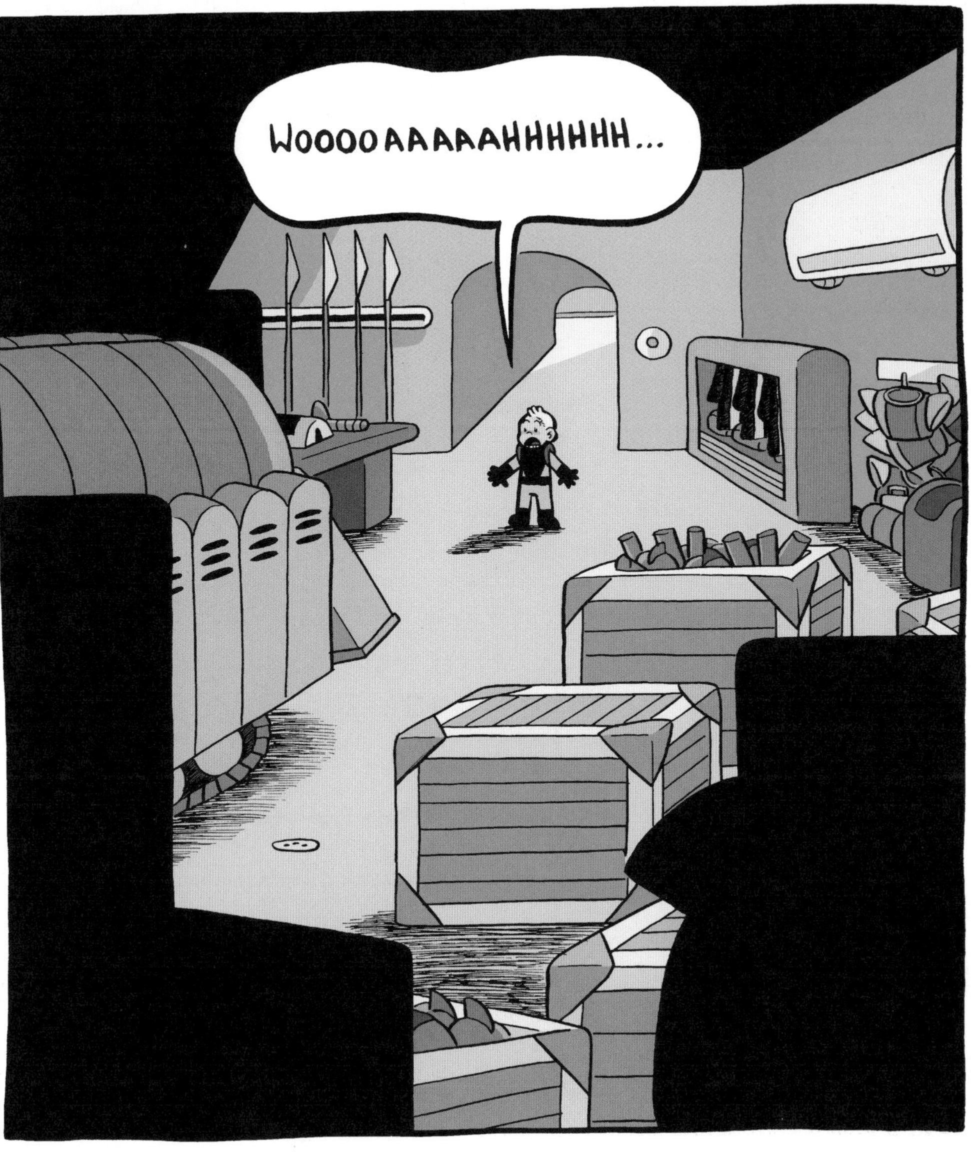
WOOOOAAAAAHHHHHH...

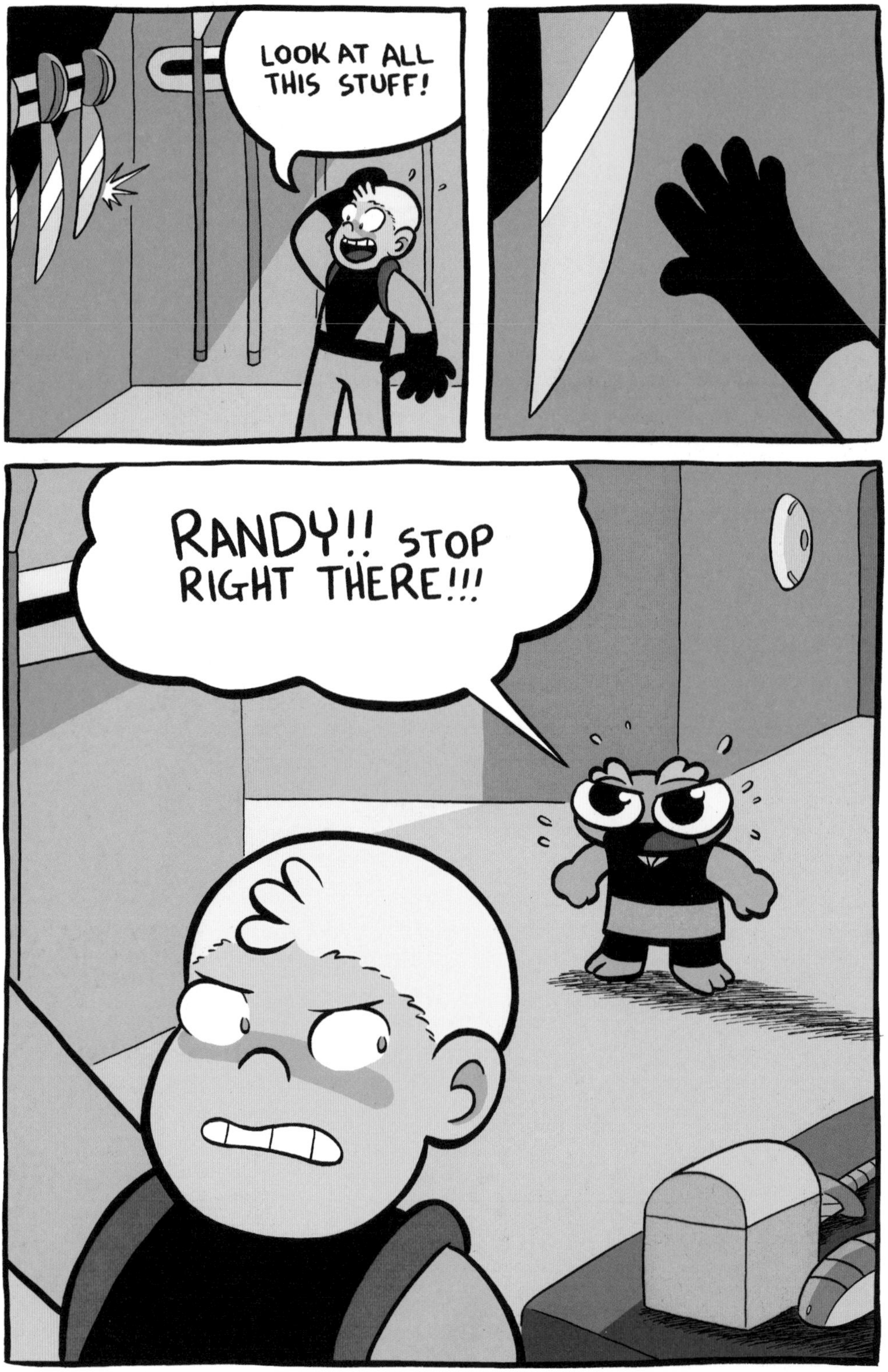
LOOK AT ALL THIS STUFF!
RANDY!! STOP RIGHT THERE!!!

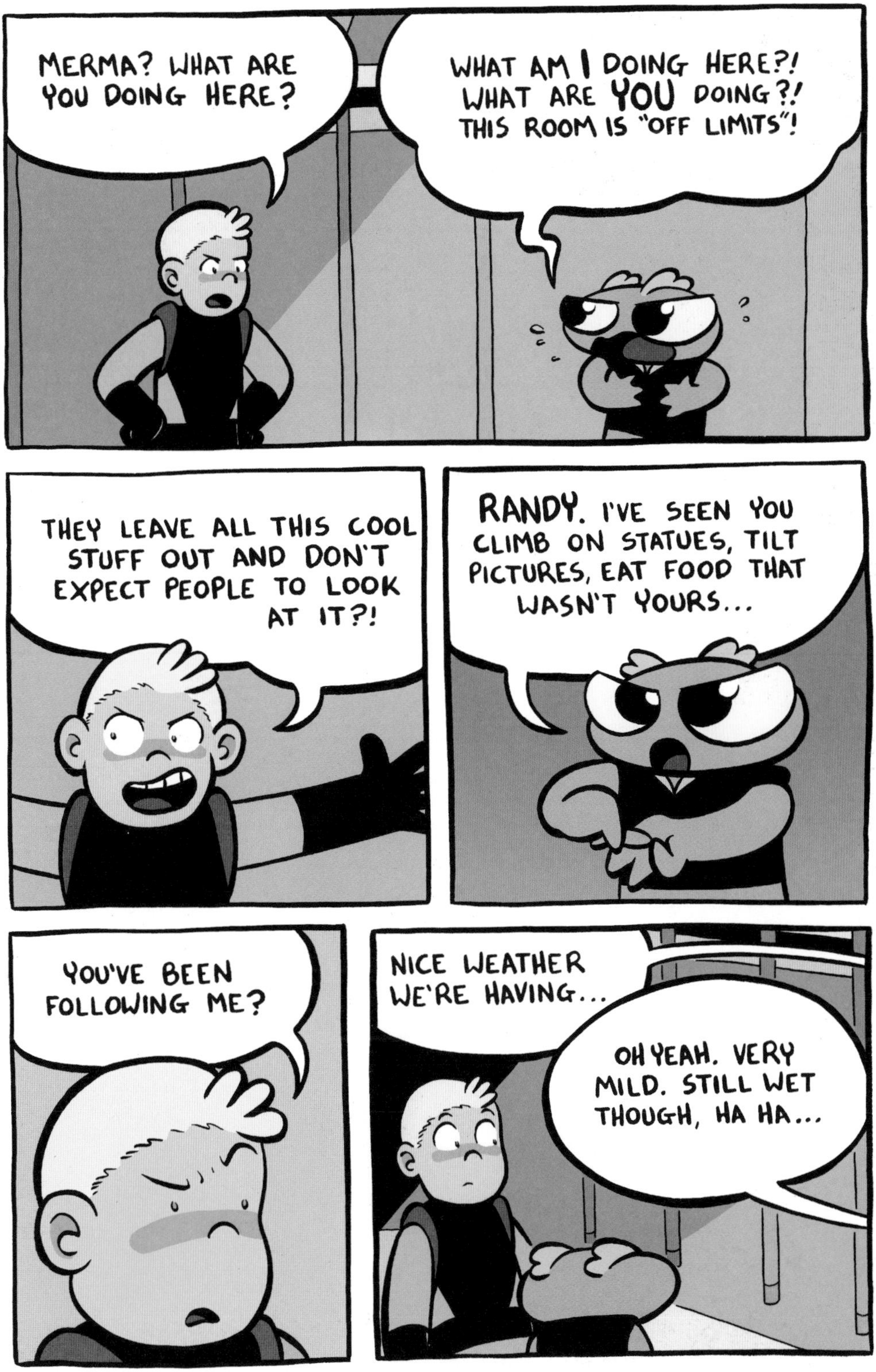
MERMA? WHAT ARE YOU DOING HERE?
WHAT AM I DOING HERE?! WHAT ARE YOU DOING?! THIS ROOM IS "OFF LIMITS"!
THEY LEAVE ALL THIS COOL STUFF OUT AND DON'T EXPECT PEOPLE TO LOOK AT IT?!
RANDY. I'VE SEEN YOU CLIMB ON STATUES, TILT PICTURES, EAT FOOD THAT WASN'T YOURS...
YOU'VE BEEN FOLLOWING ME?
NICE WEATHER WE'RE HAVING...
OH YEAH. VERY MILD. STILL WET THOUGH, HA HA...

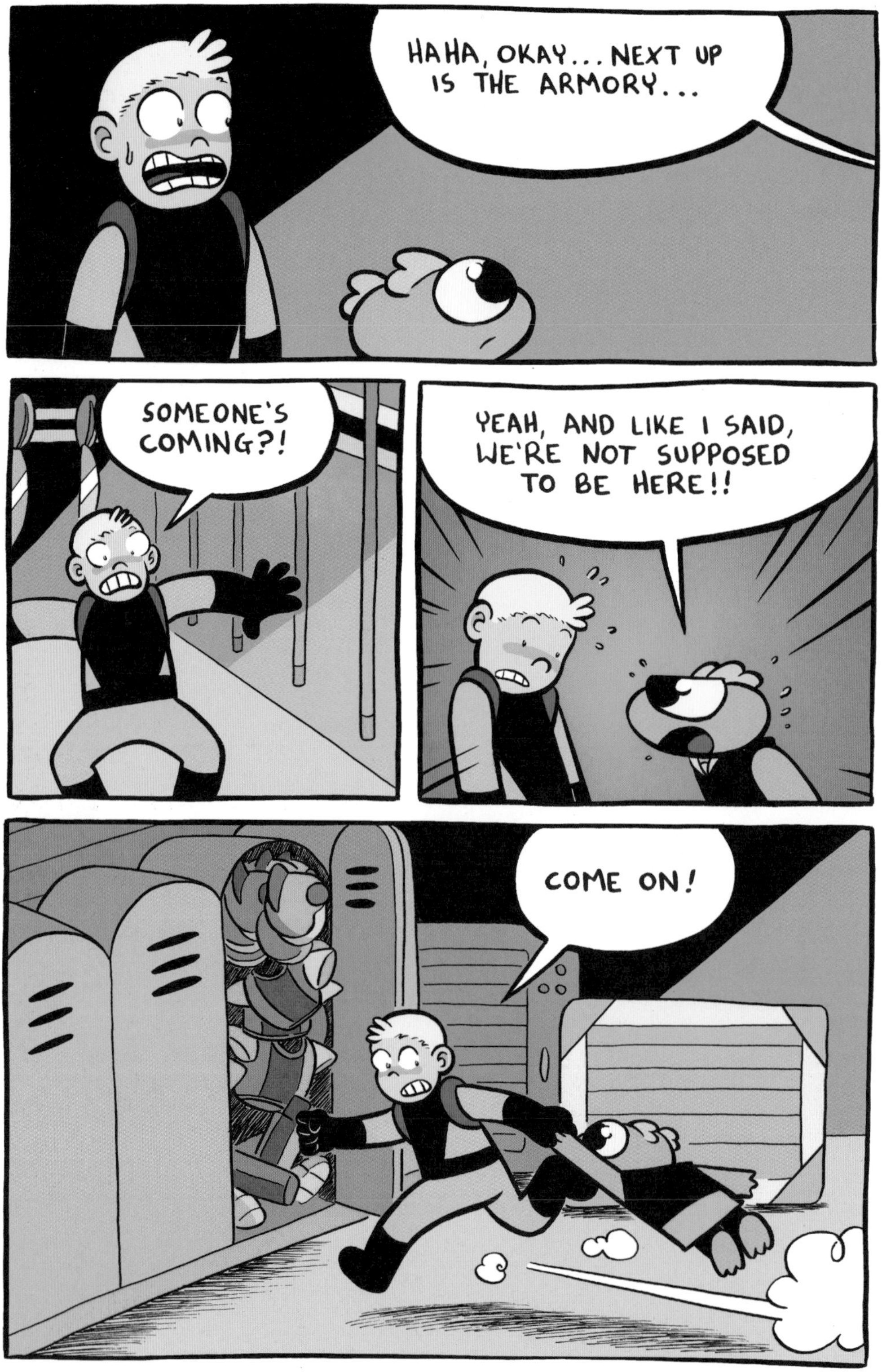
HAHA, OKAY... NEXT UP IS THE ARMORY...
SOMEONE'S COMING?!
YEAH, AND LIKE I SAID, WE'RE NOT SUPPOSED TO BE HERE!!
COME ON!

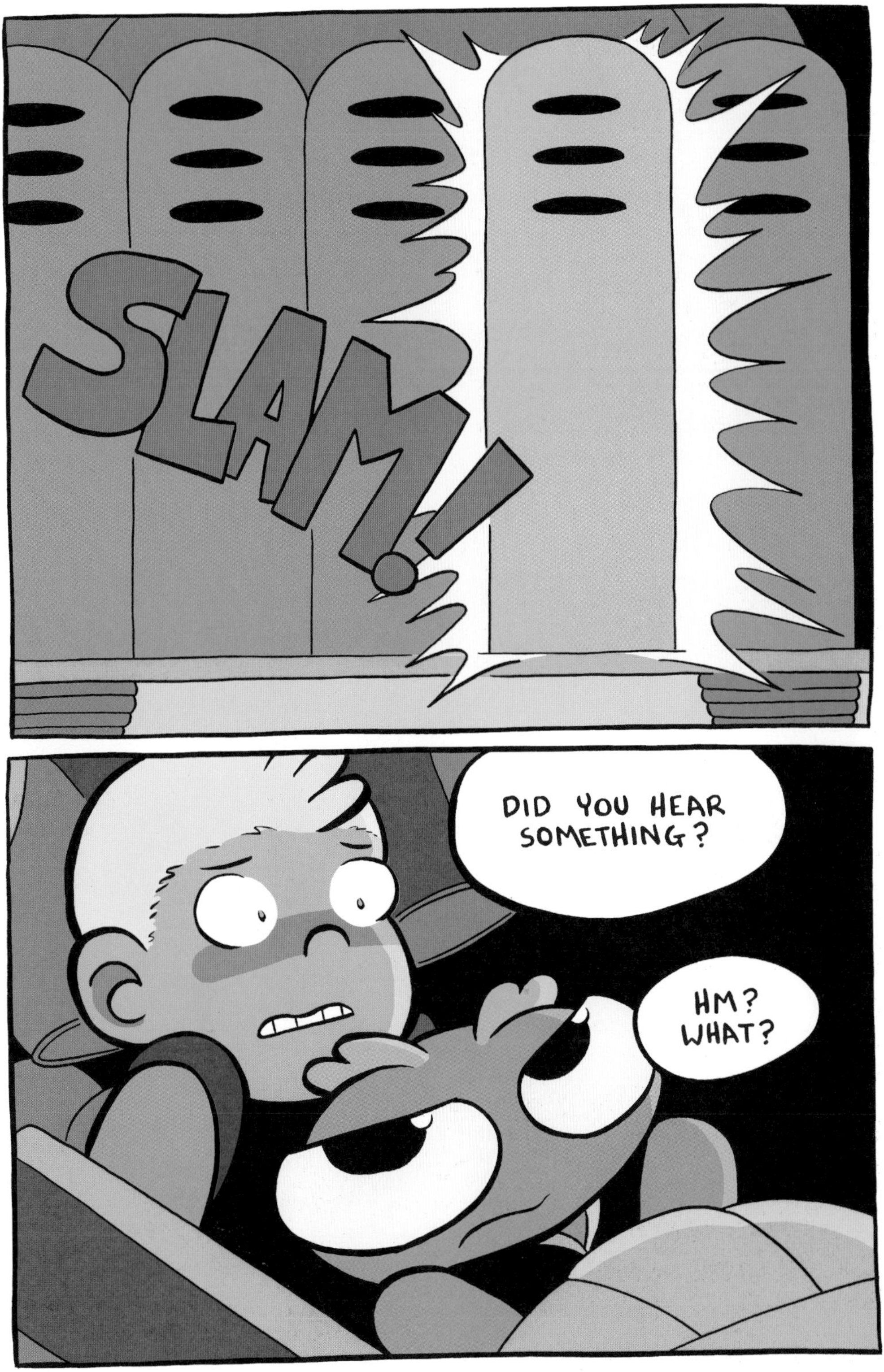
SLAM!!
DID YOU HEAR SOMETHING?
HM? WHAT?

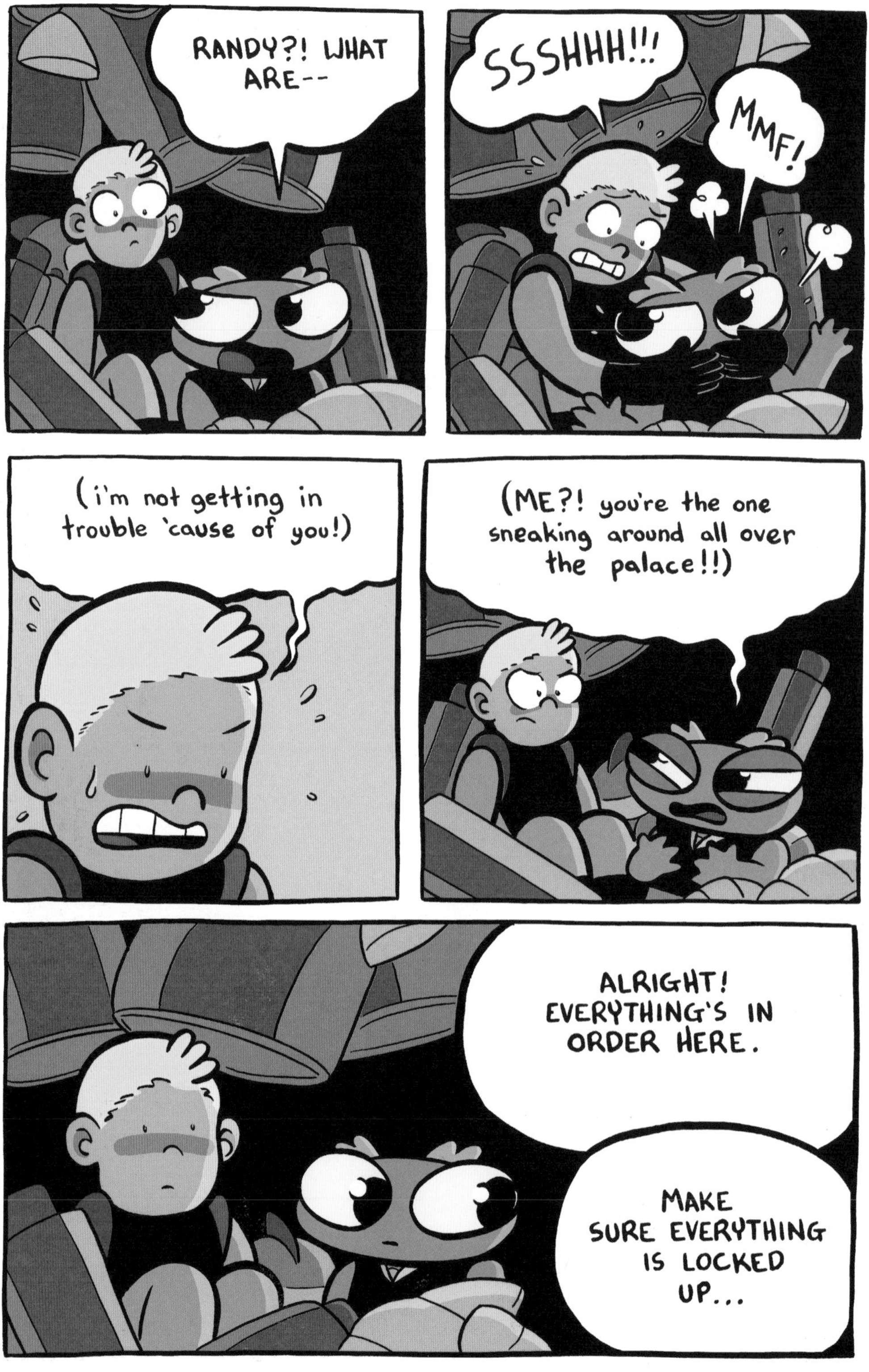
RANDY?! WHAT ARE--
SSSHHH!!!
MMF!
(i'm not getting in trouble 'cause of you!)
(ME?! you're the one sneaking around all over the palace!!)
ALRIGHT! EVERYTHING'S IN ORDER HERE.
MAKE SURE EVERYTHING IS LOCKED UP...

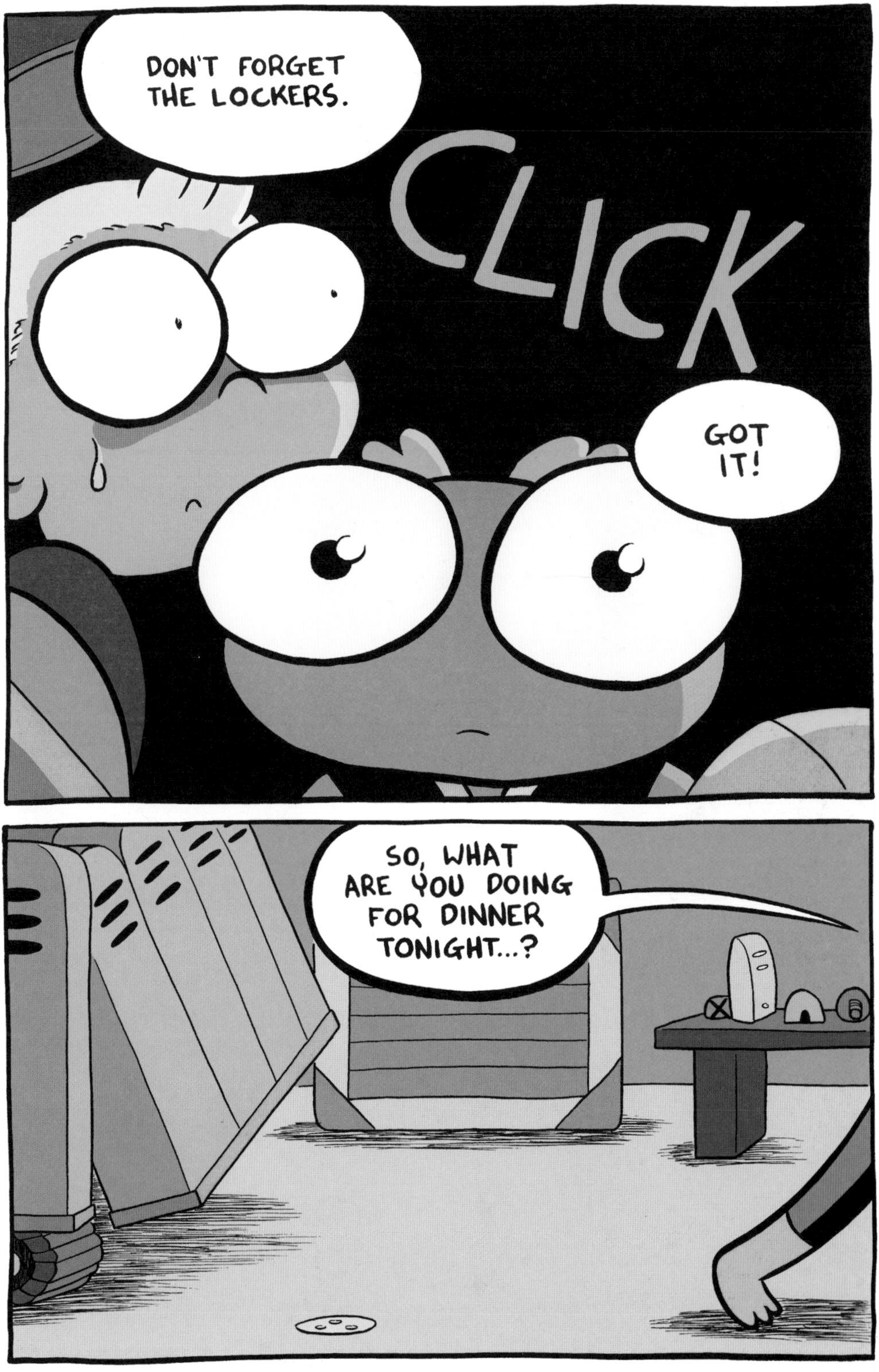
DON'T FORGET THE LOCKERS.
CLICK
GOT IT!
SO, WHAT ARE YOU DOING FOR DINNER TONIGHT...?

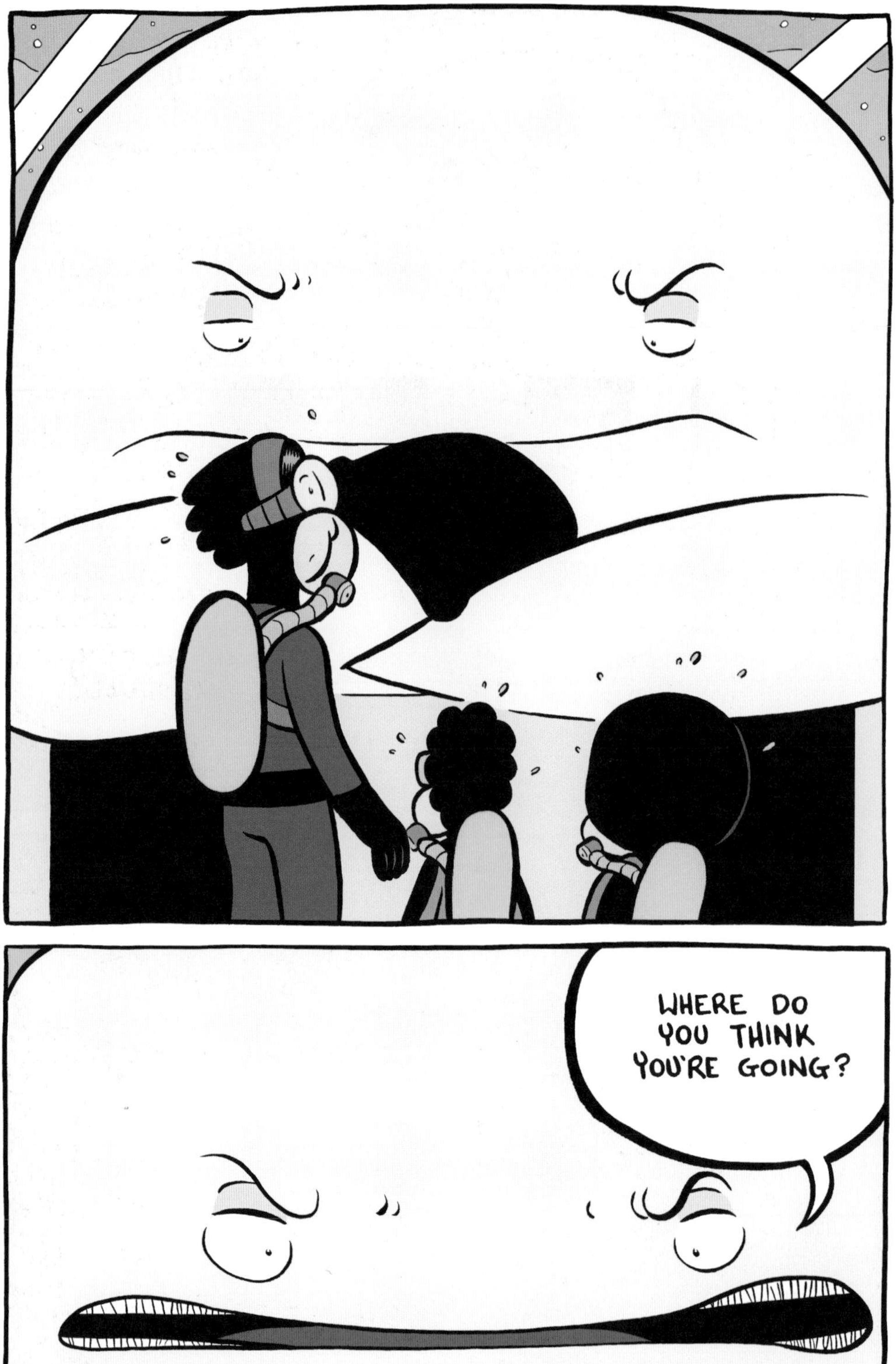
WHERE DO YOU THINK YOU'RE GOING?

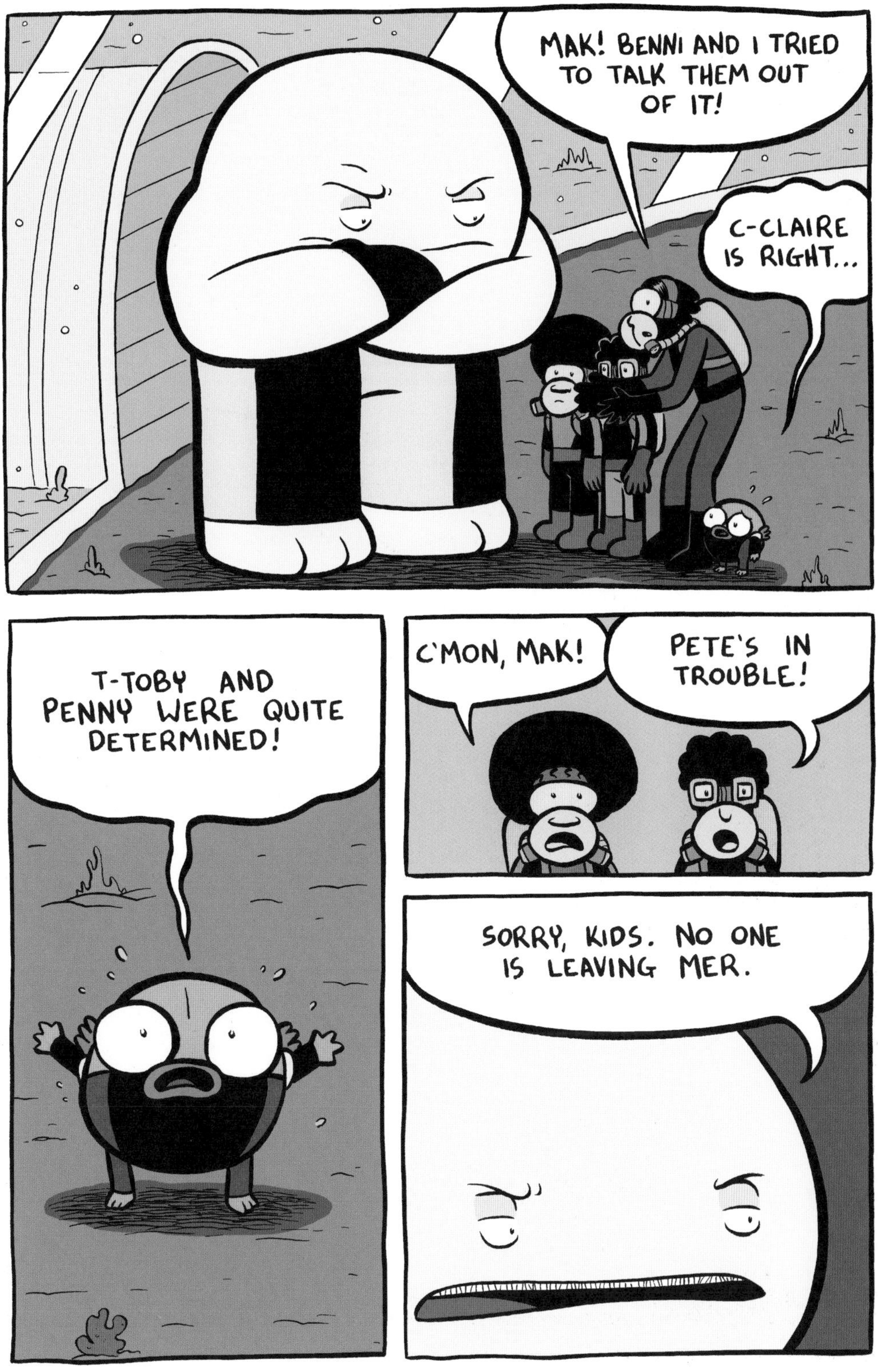
MAK! BENNI AND I TRIED TO TALK THEM OUT OF IT!
C-CLAIRE IS RIGHT...
T-TOBY AND PENNY WERE QUITE DETERMINED!
C'MON, MAK!
PETE'S IN TROUBLE!
SORRY, KIDS. NO ONE IS LEAVING MER.

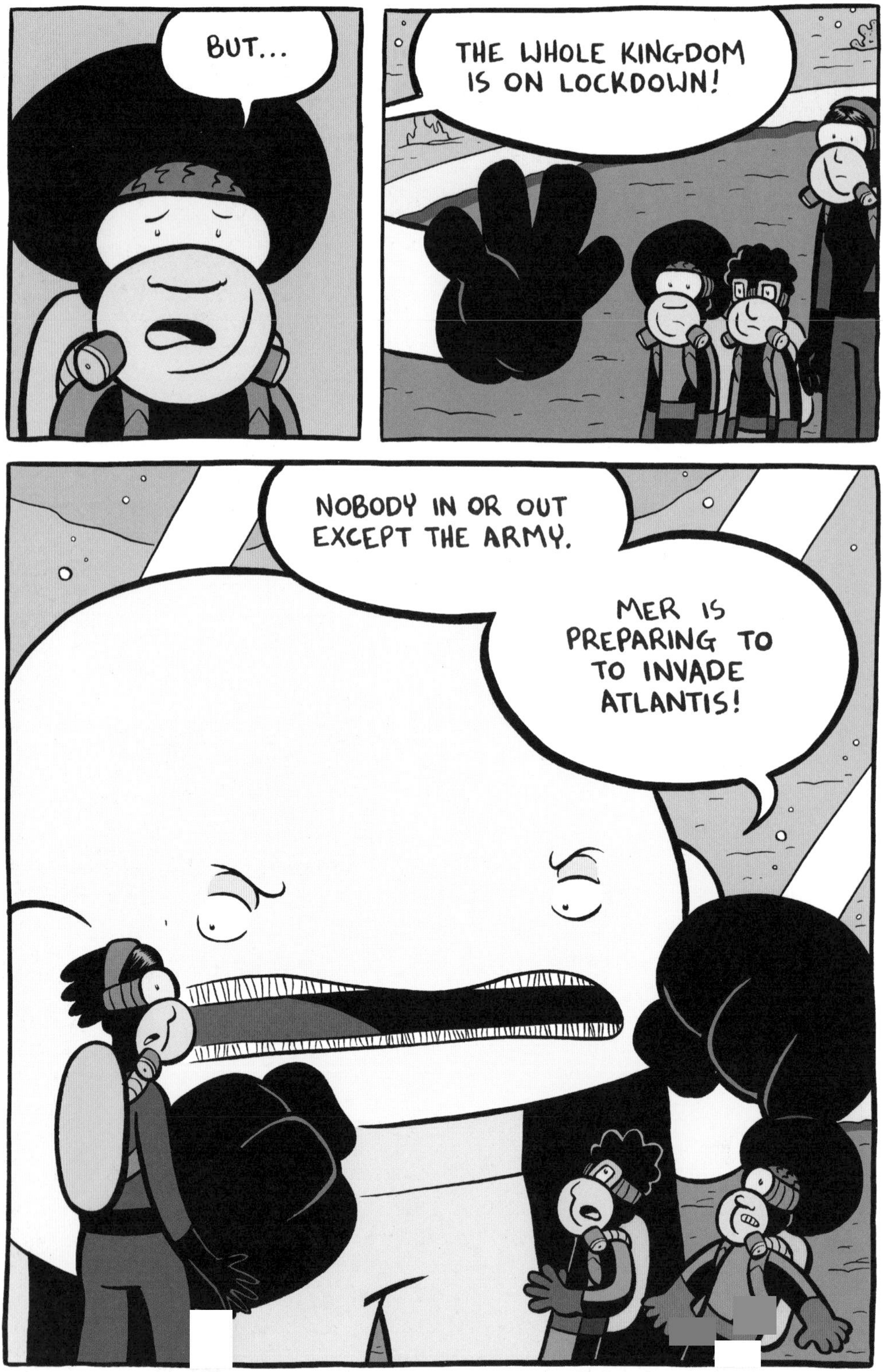
BUT...
THE WHOLE KINGDOM IS ON LOCKDOWN!
NOBODY IN OR OUT EXCEPT THE ARMY.
MER IS PREPARING TO TO INVADE ATLANTIS!

CHAPTER FOUR

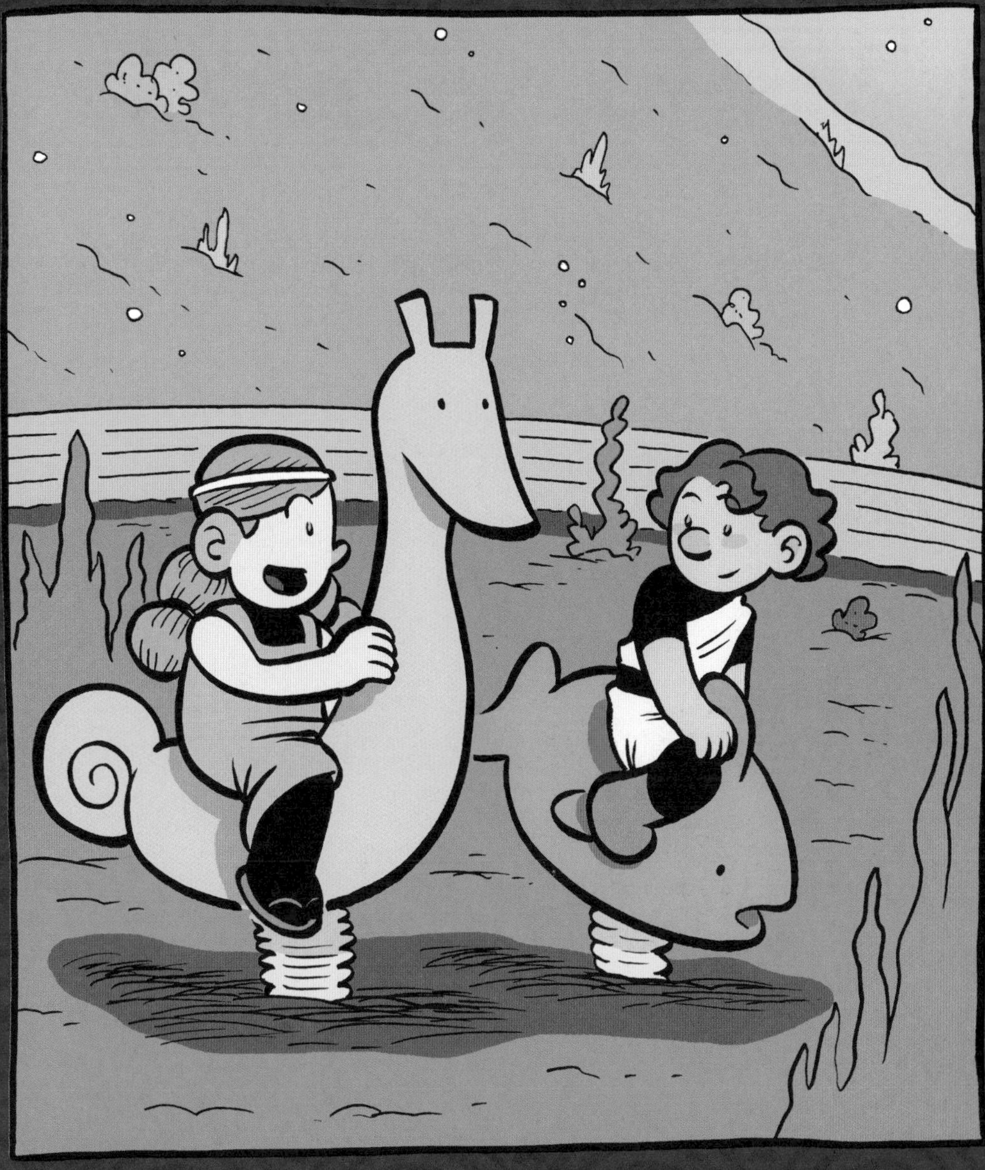

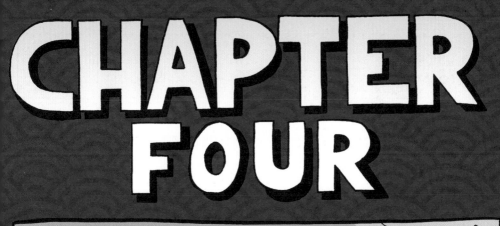

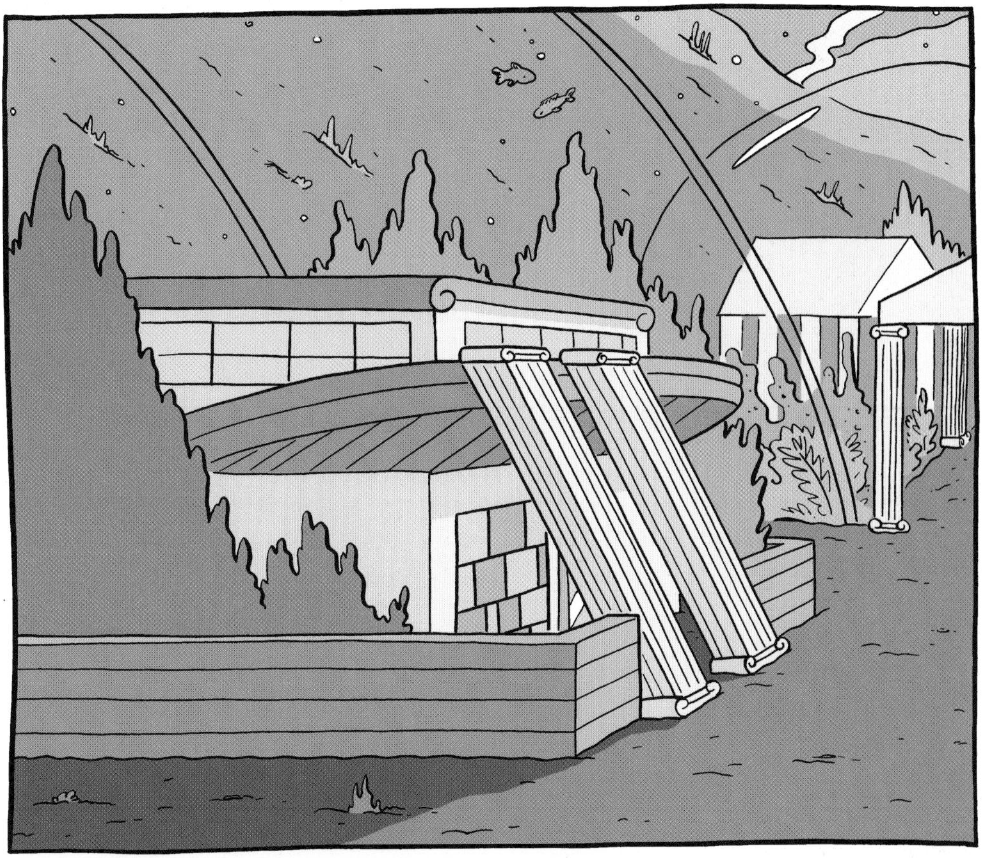

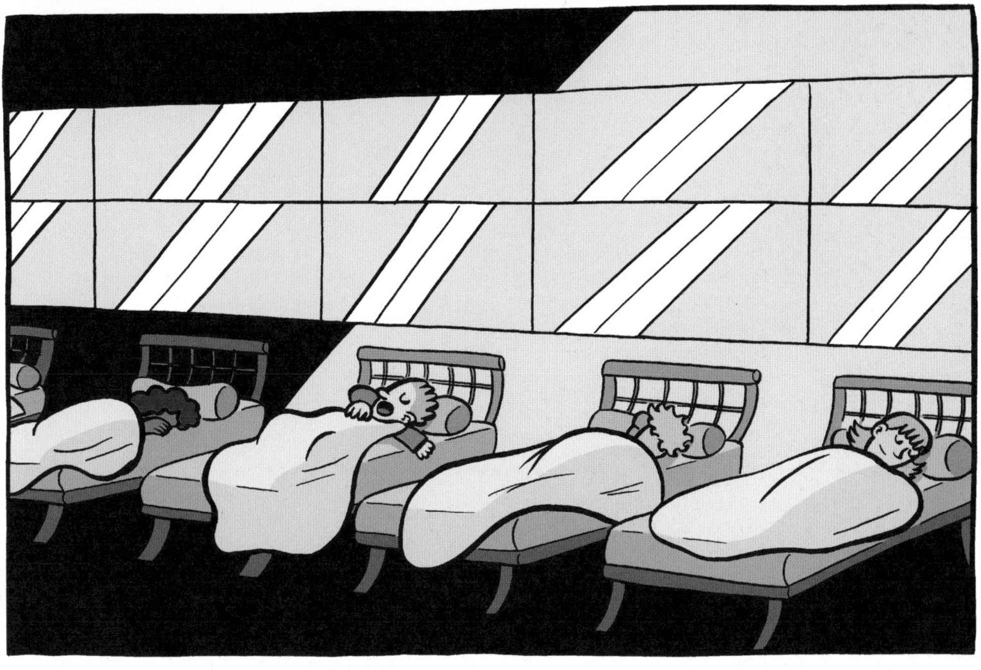

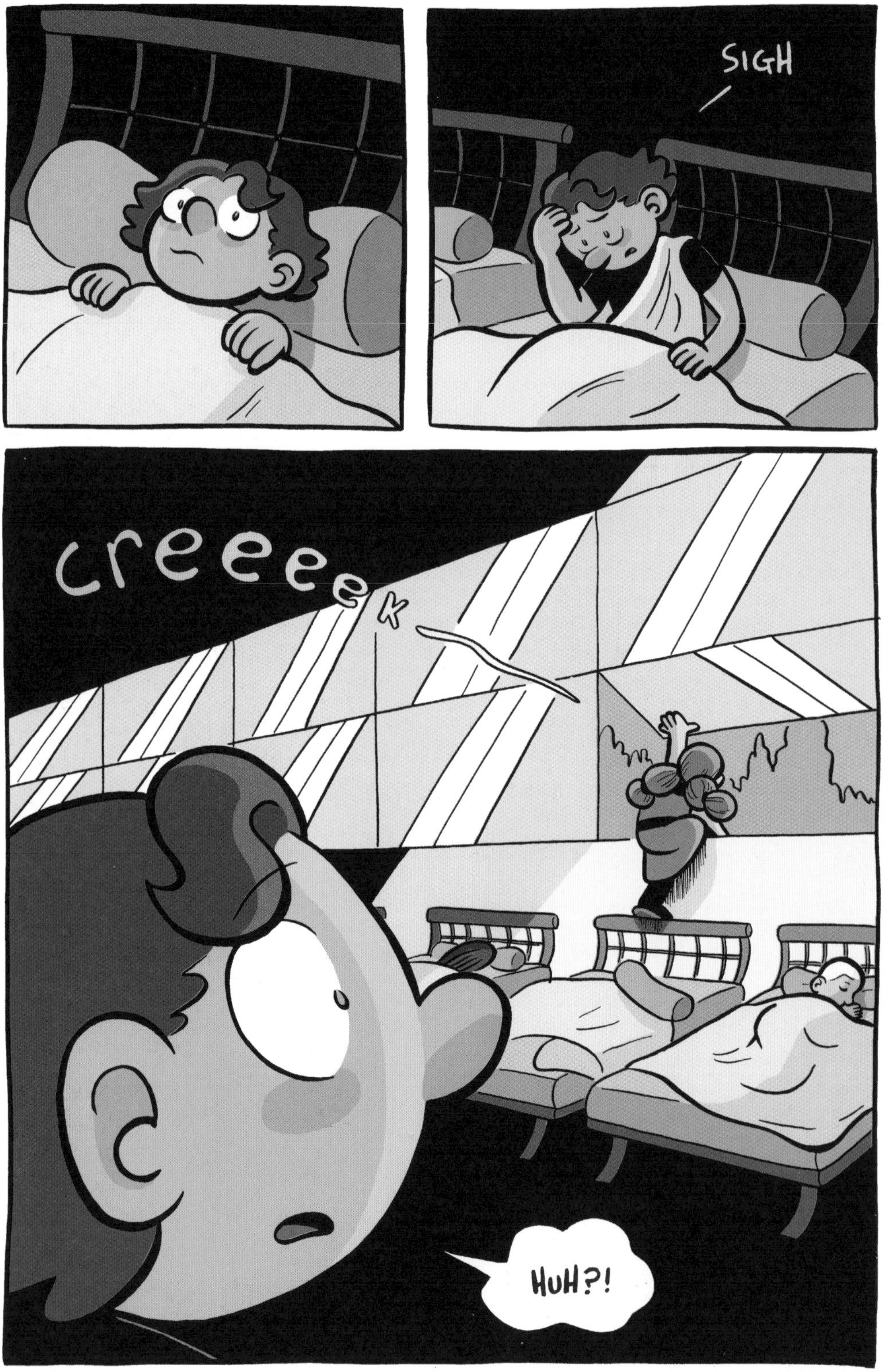
SIGH
creeeek
HUH?!

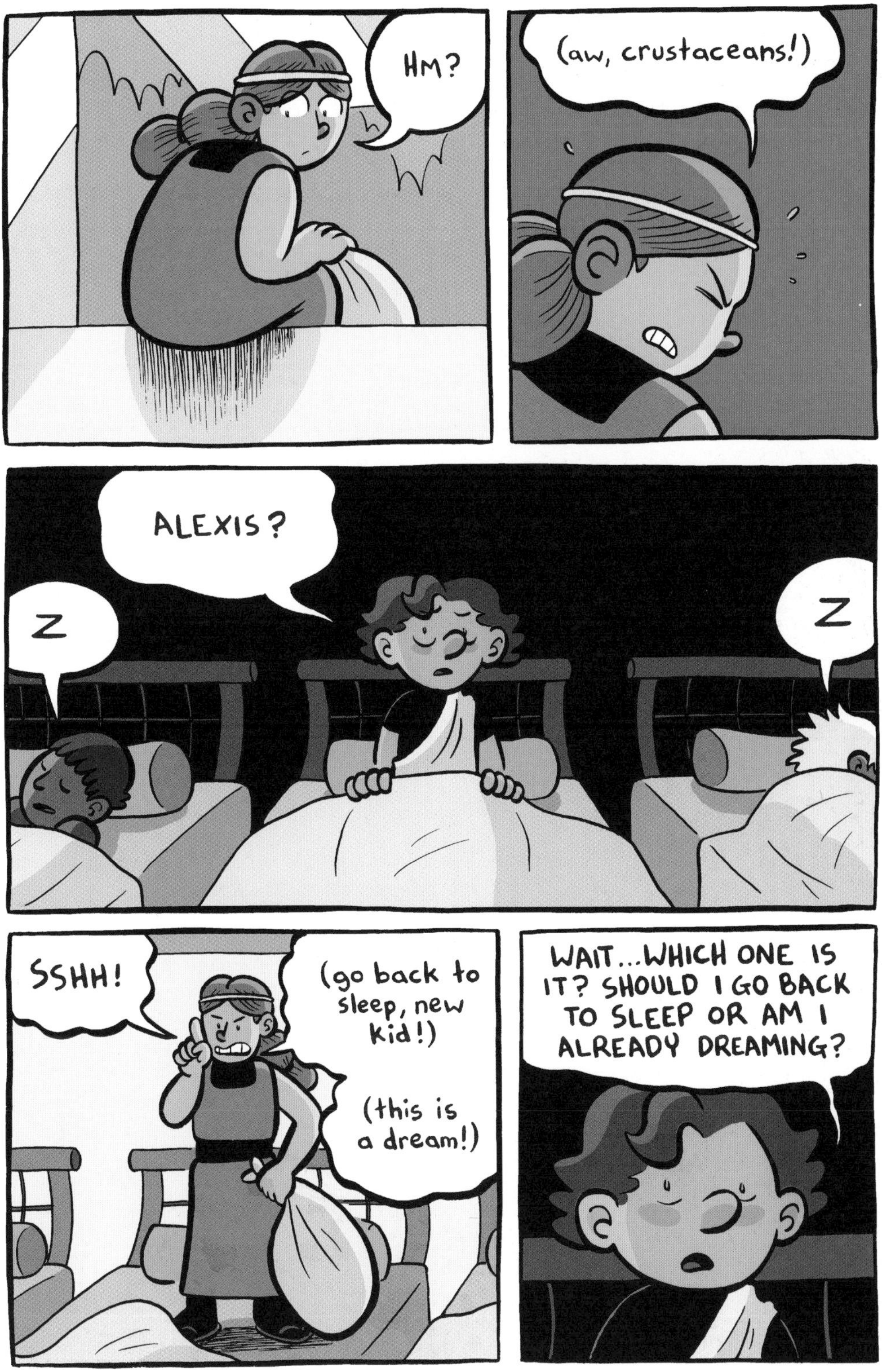
HM?
(aw, crustaceans!)
ALEXIS?
Z
Z
SSHH!
(go back to sleep, new kid!)
(this is a dream!)
WAIT...WHICH ONE IS IT? SHOULD I GO BACK TO SLEEP OR AM I ALREADY DREAMING?

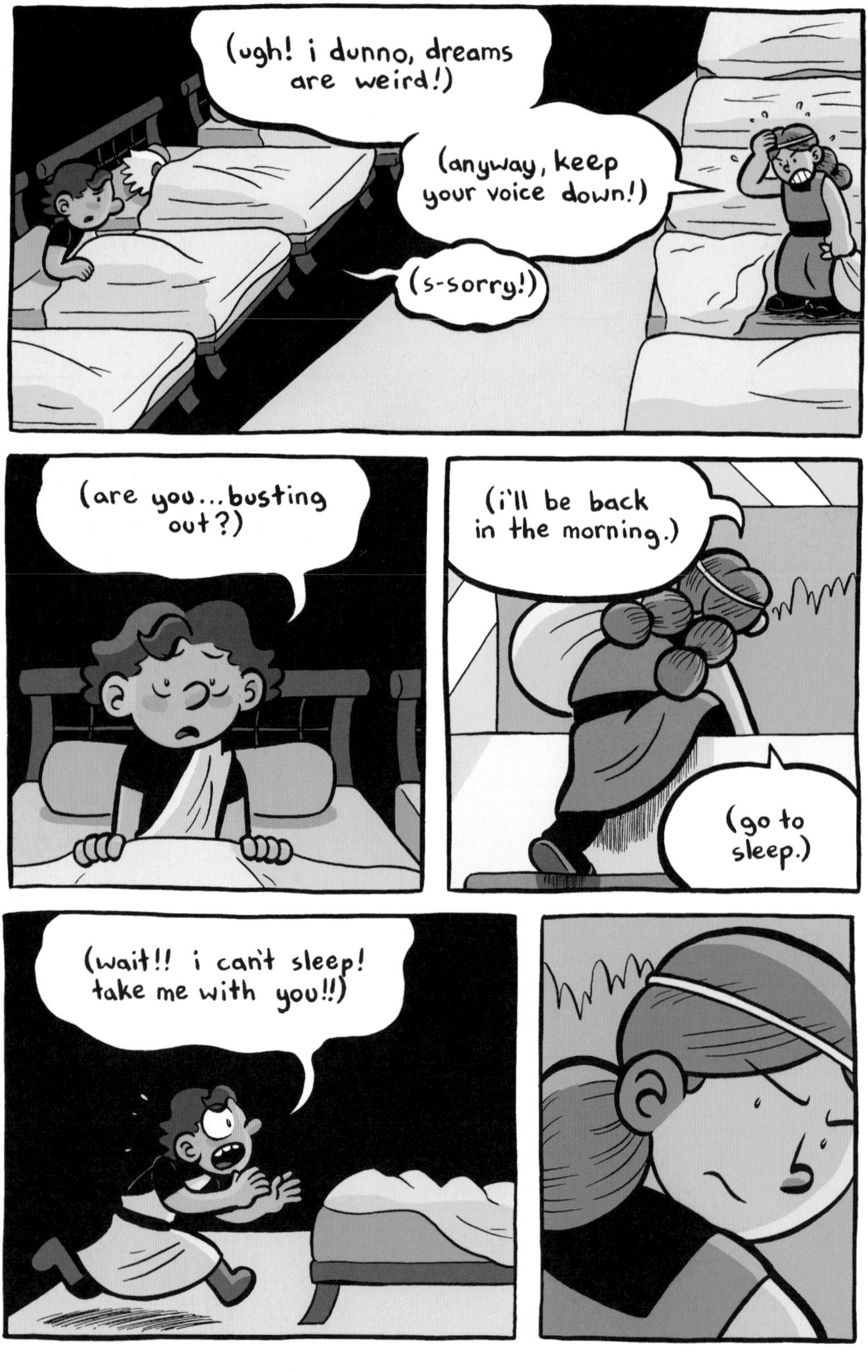

(ugh! i dunno, dreams are weird!)
(anyway, keep your voice down!)
(s-sorry!)
(are you...busting out?)
(i'll be back in the morning.)
(go to sleep.)
(wait!! i can't sleep! take me with you!!)

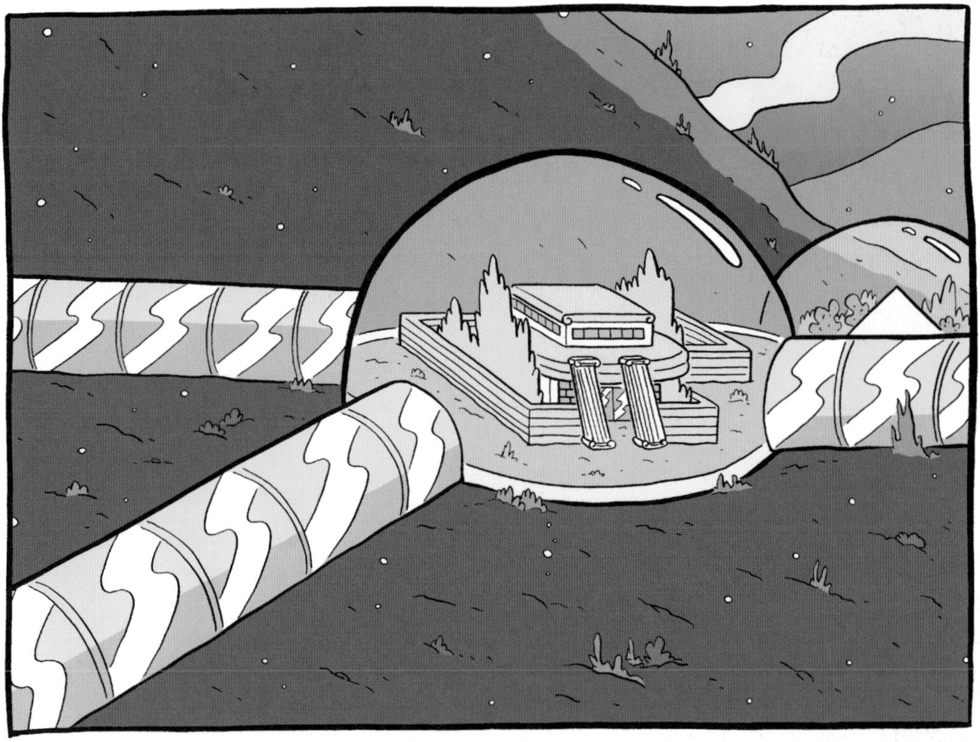

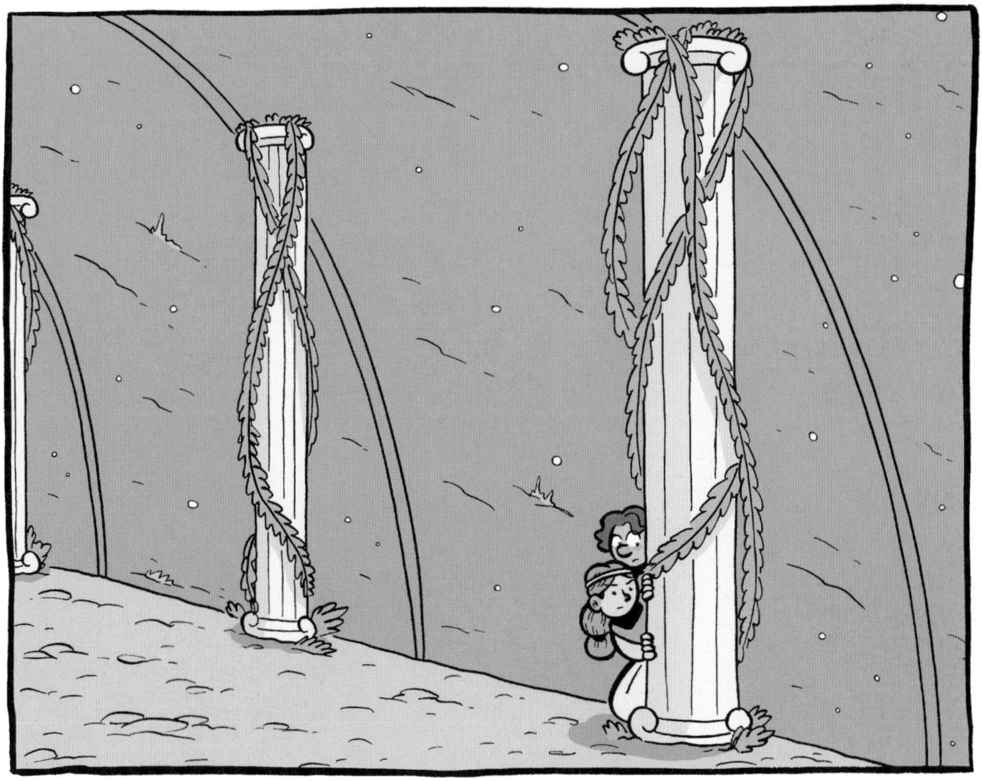

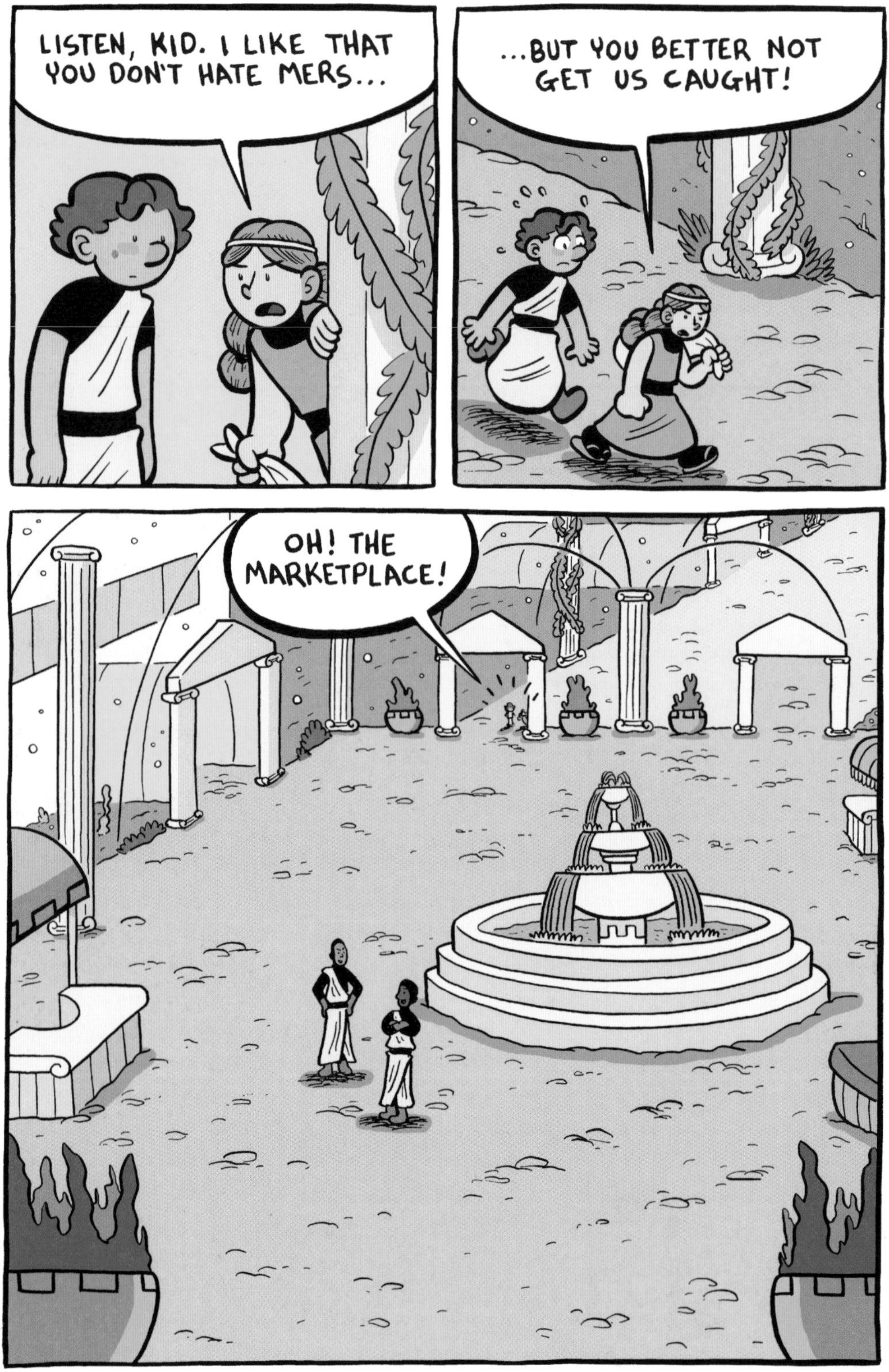
LISTEN, KID. I LIKE THAT YOU DON'T HATE MERS...
...BUT YOU BETTER NOT GET US CAUGHT!
OH! THE MARKETPLACE!

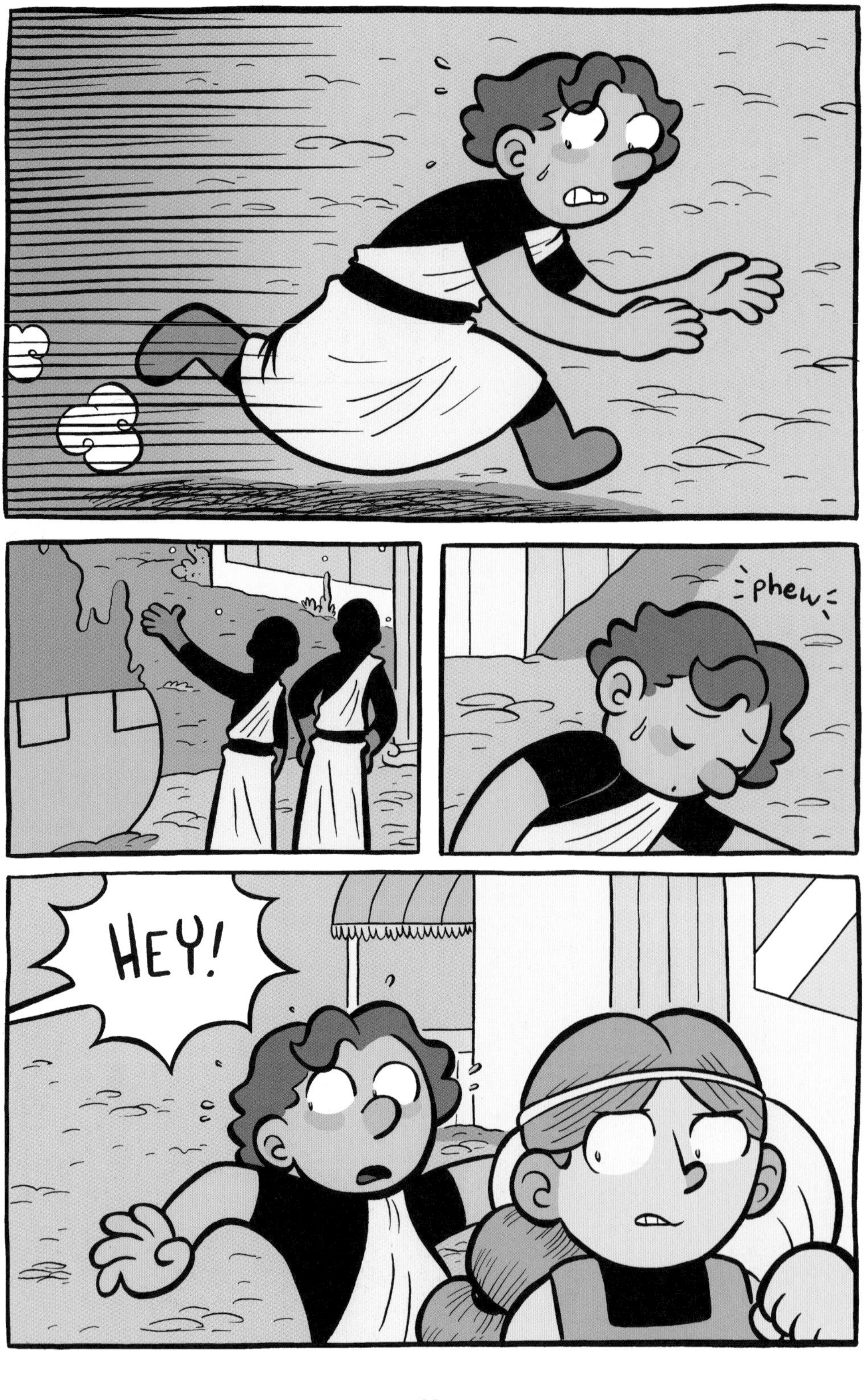
phew
HEY!

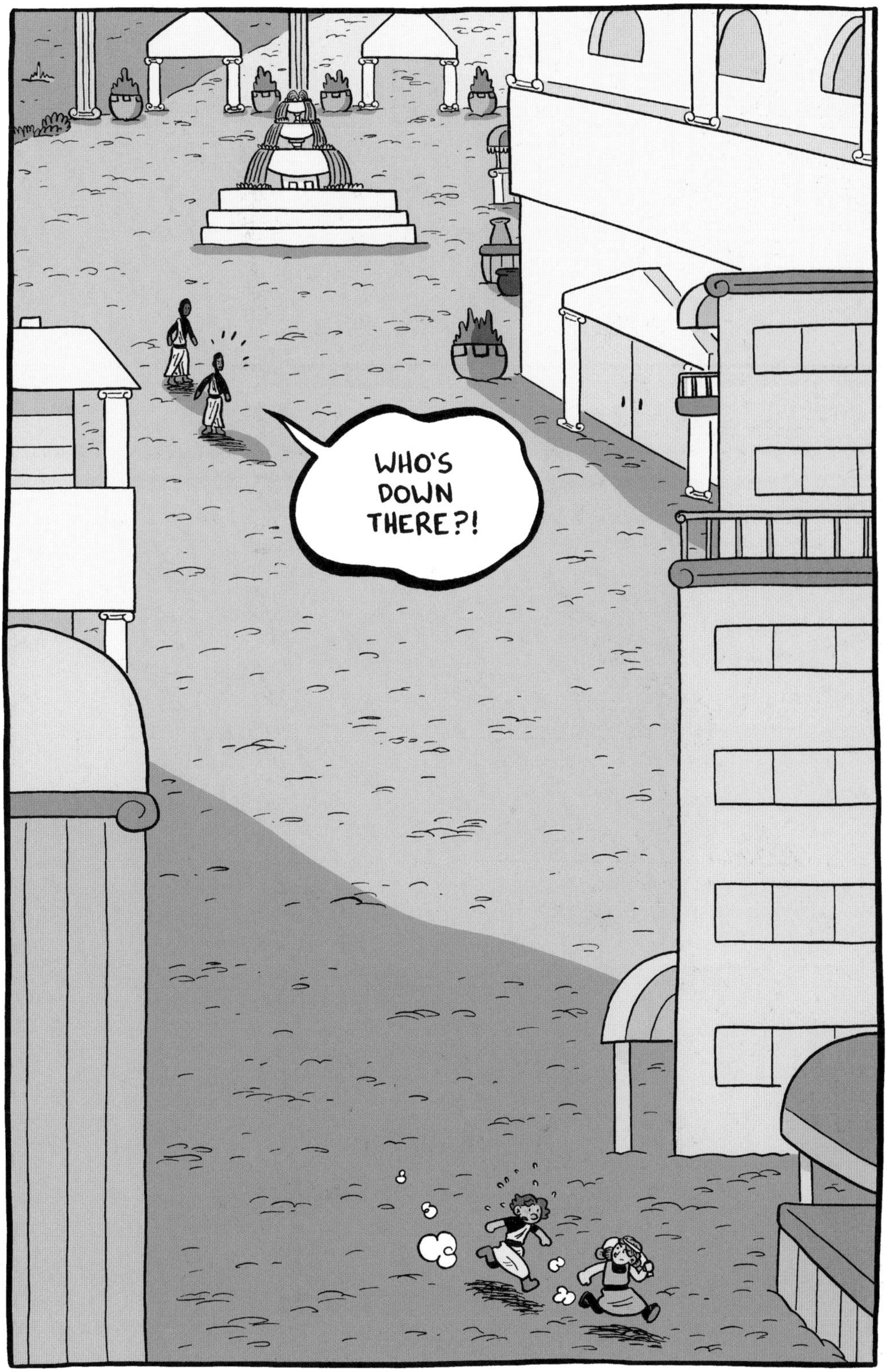
WHO'S DOWN THERE?!

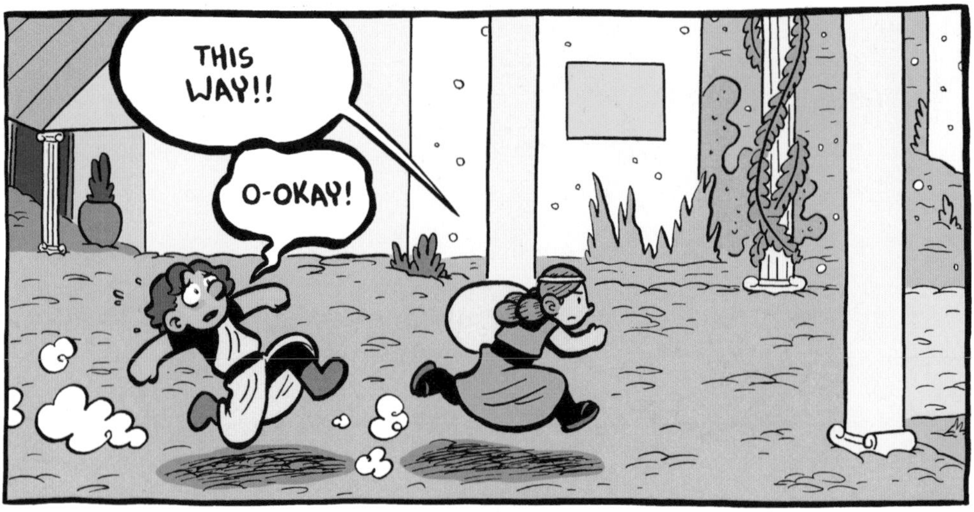
THIS WAY!!
O-OKAY!

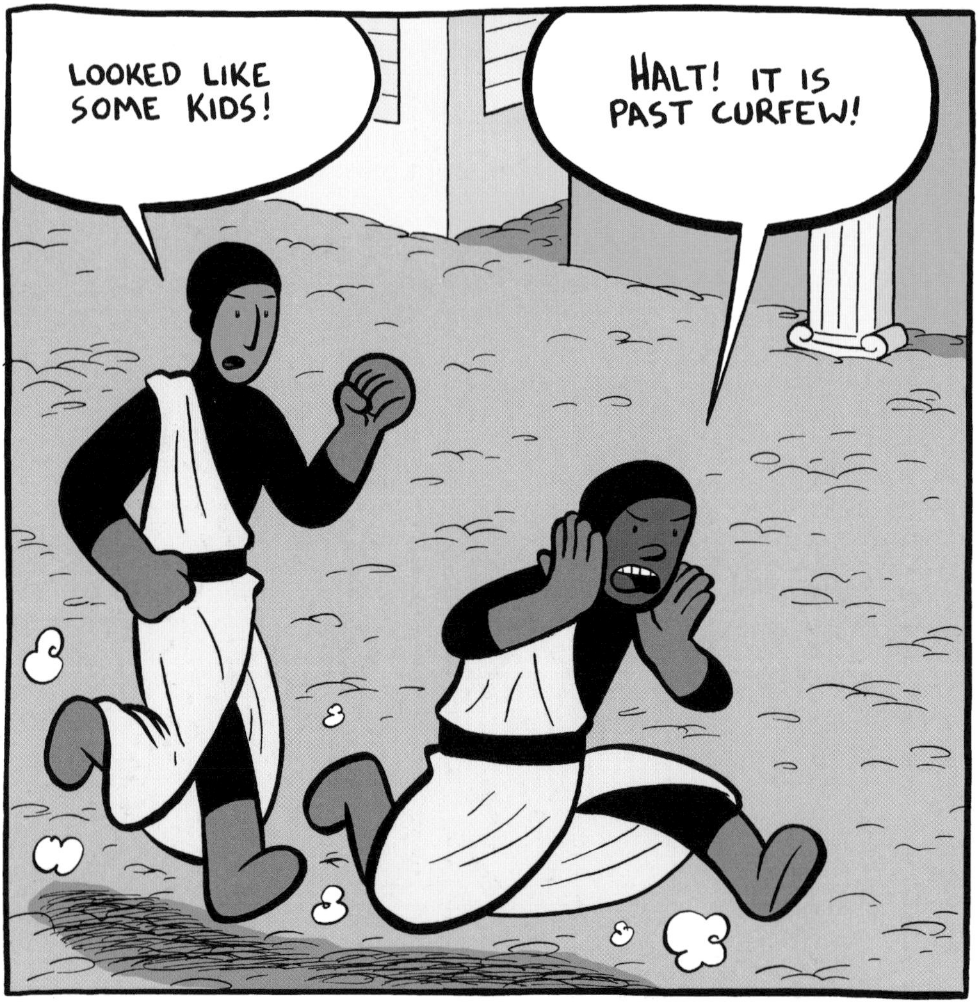
LOOKED LIKE SOME KIDS!
HALT! IT IS PAST CURFEW!

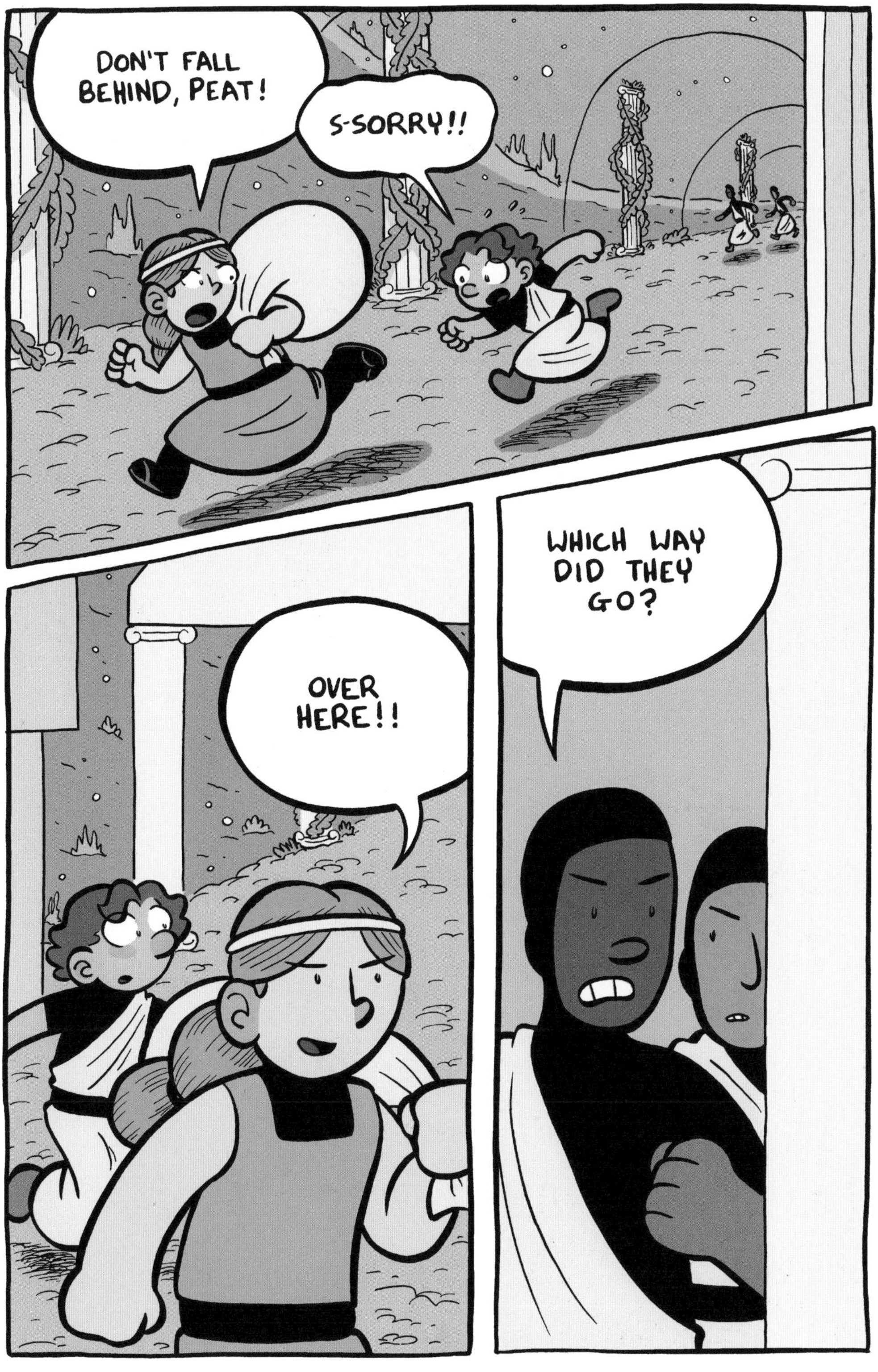
DON'T FALL BEHIND, PEAT!
S-SORRY!!
OVER HERE!!
WHICH WAY DID THEY GO?

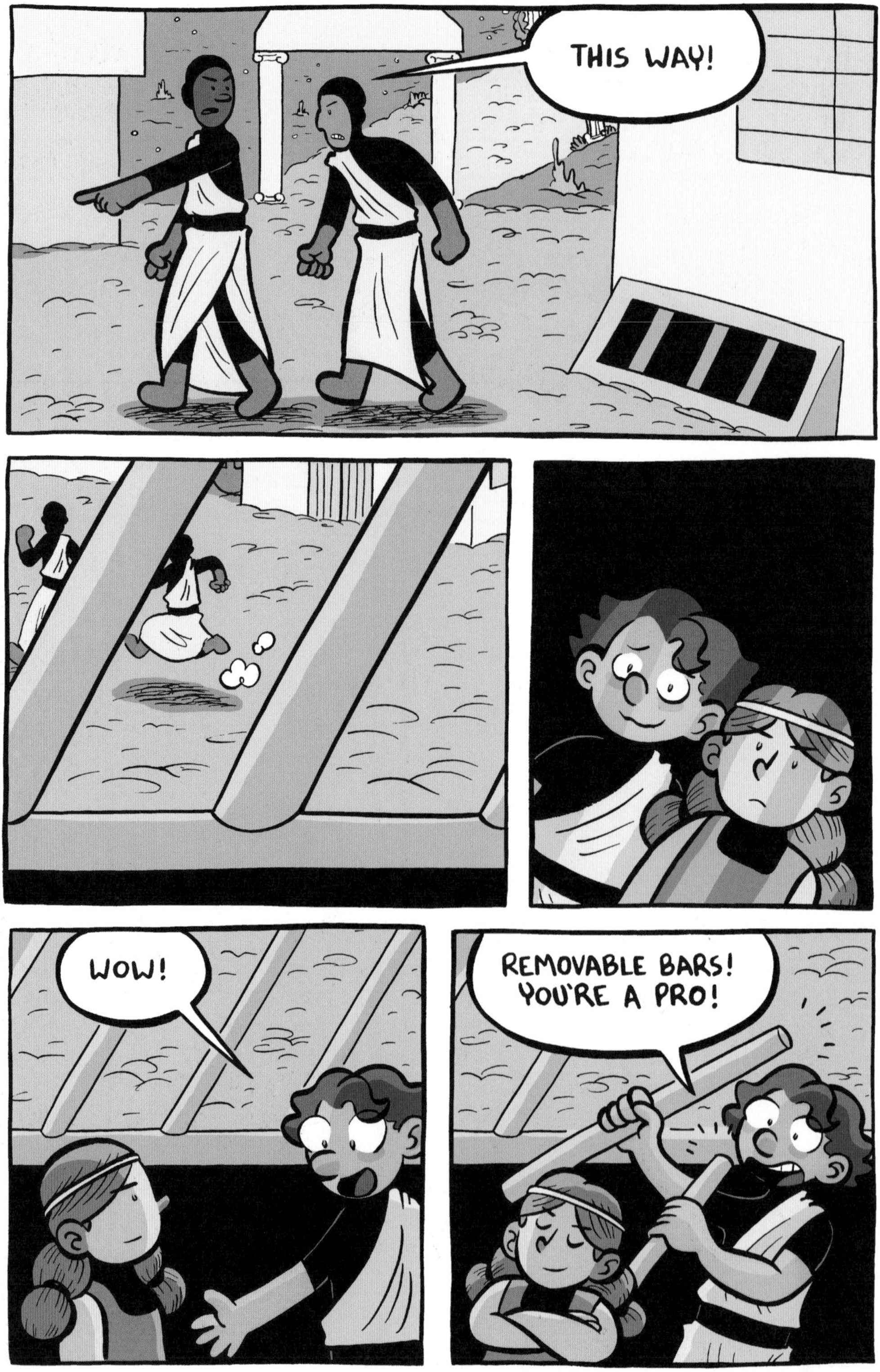
THIS WAY!
WOW!
REMOVABLE BARS! YOU'RE A PRO!

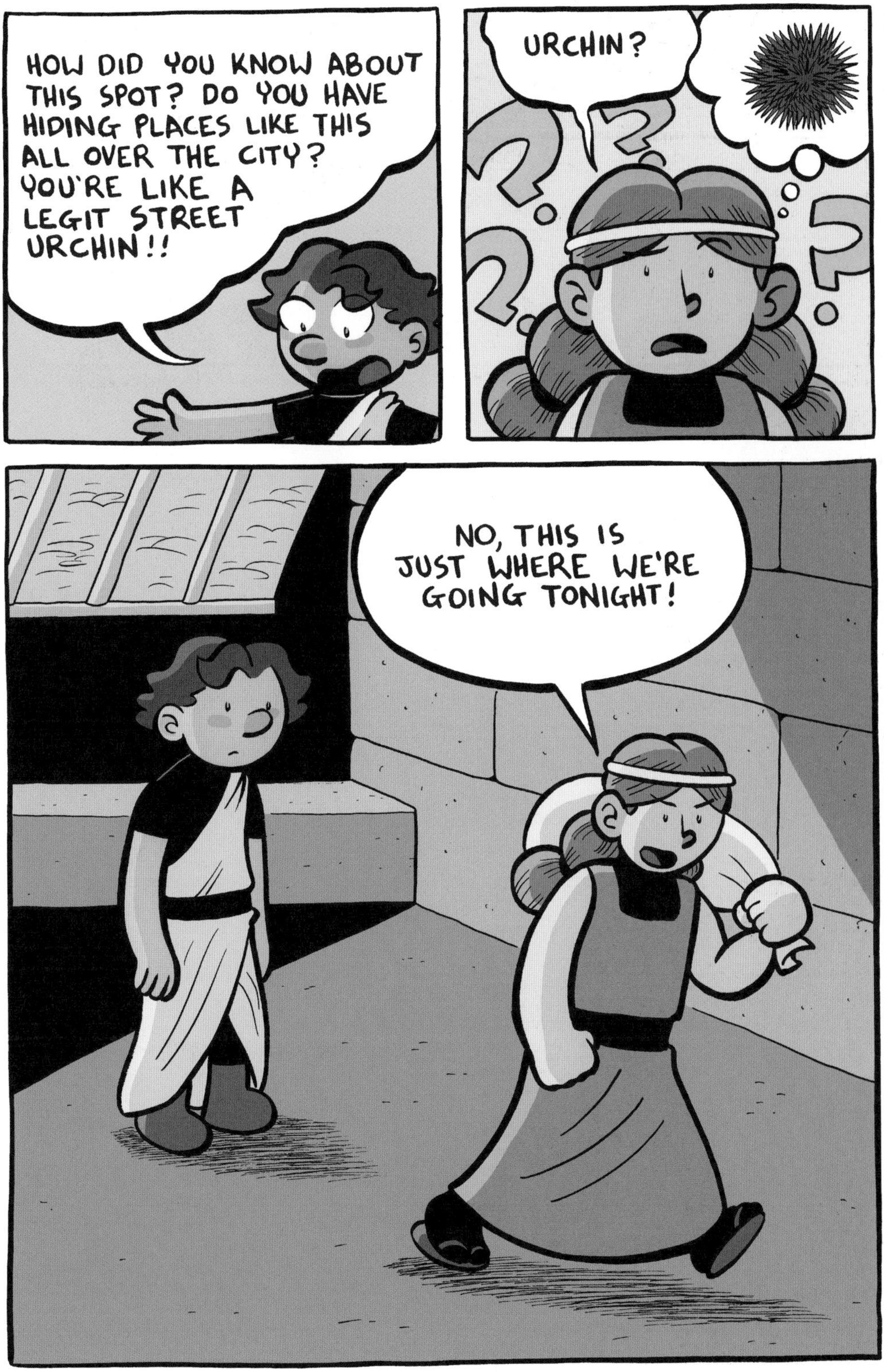
HOW DID YOU KNOW ABOUT THIS SPOT? DO YOU HAVE HIDING PLACES LIKE THIS ALL OVER THE CITY? YOU'RE LIKE A LEGIT STREET URCHIN!!
URCHIN?
NO, THIS IS JUST WHERE WE'RE GOING TONIGHT!

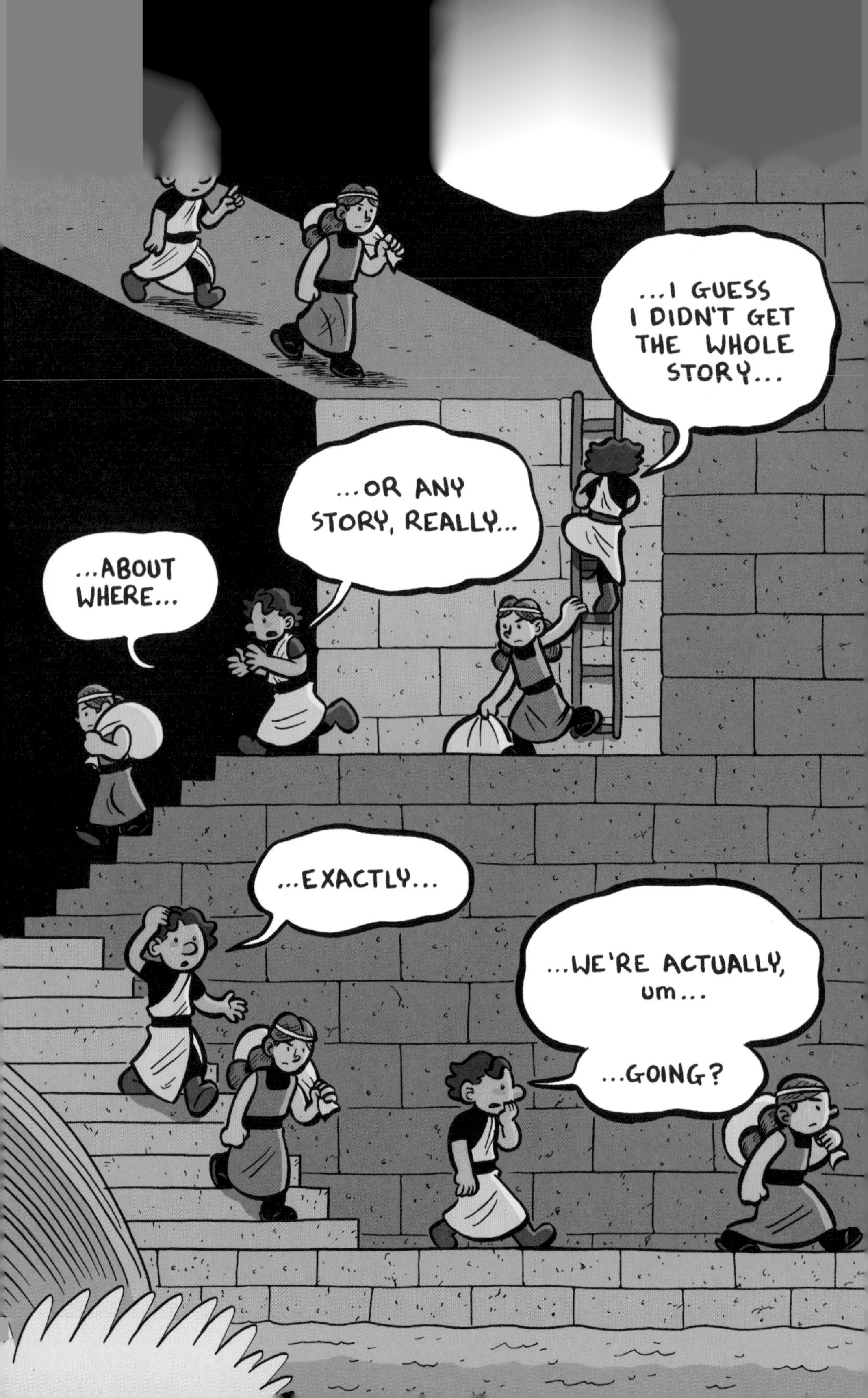
...I GUESS I DIDN'T GET THE WHOLE STORY...
...OR ANY STORY, REALLY...
...ABOUT WHERE...
...EXACTLY...
...WE'RE ACTUALLY, um...
...GOING?

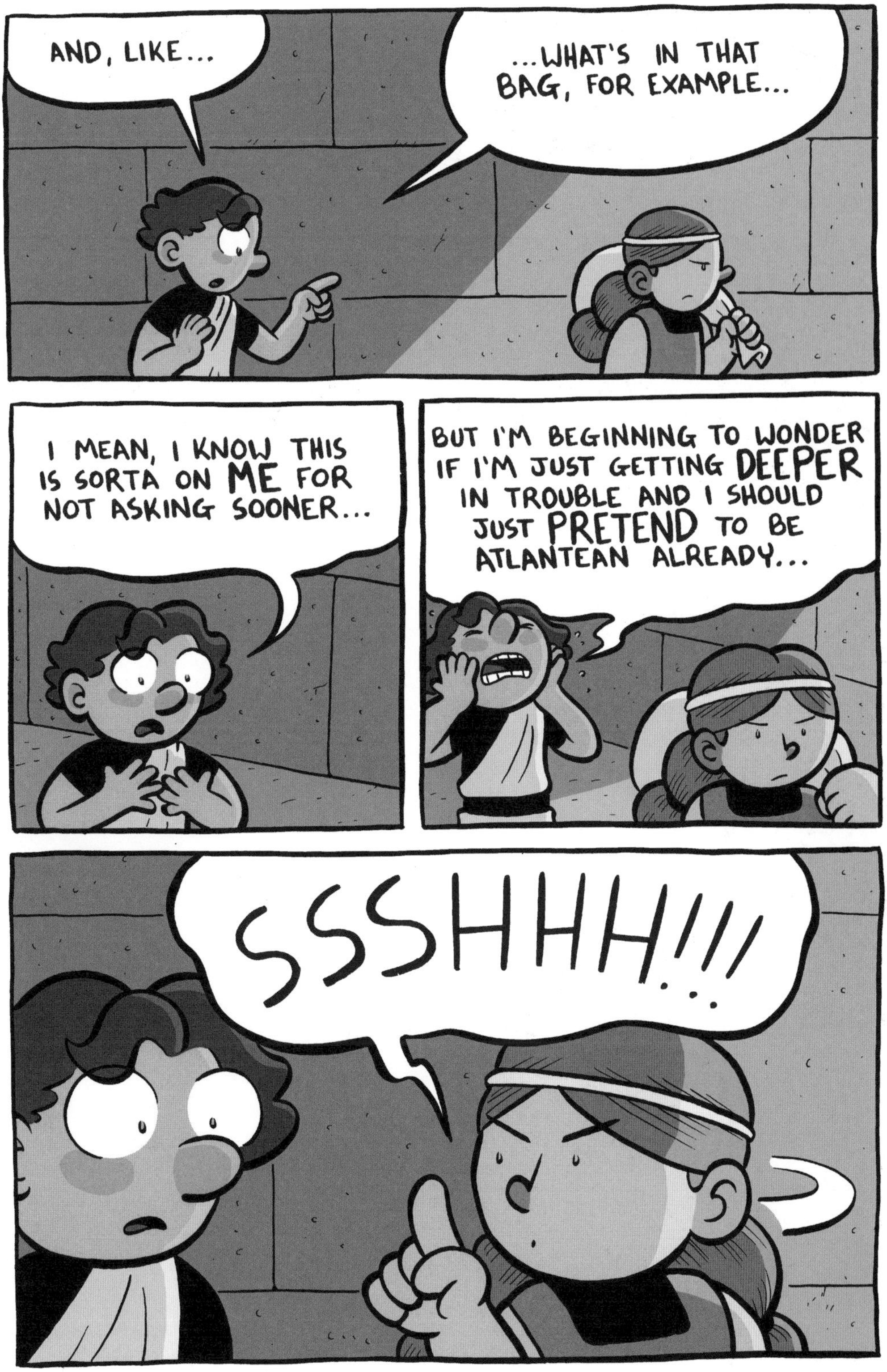
AND, LIKE...
...WHAT'S IN THAT BAG, FOR EXAMPLE...
I MEAN, I KNOW THIS IS SORTA ON ME FOR NOT ASKING SOONER...
BUT I'M BEGINNING TO WONDER IF I'M JUST GETTING DEEPER IN TROUBLE AND I SHOULD JUST PRETEND TO BE ATLANTEAN ALREADY...
SSSHHH!!!

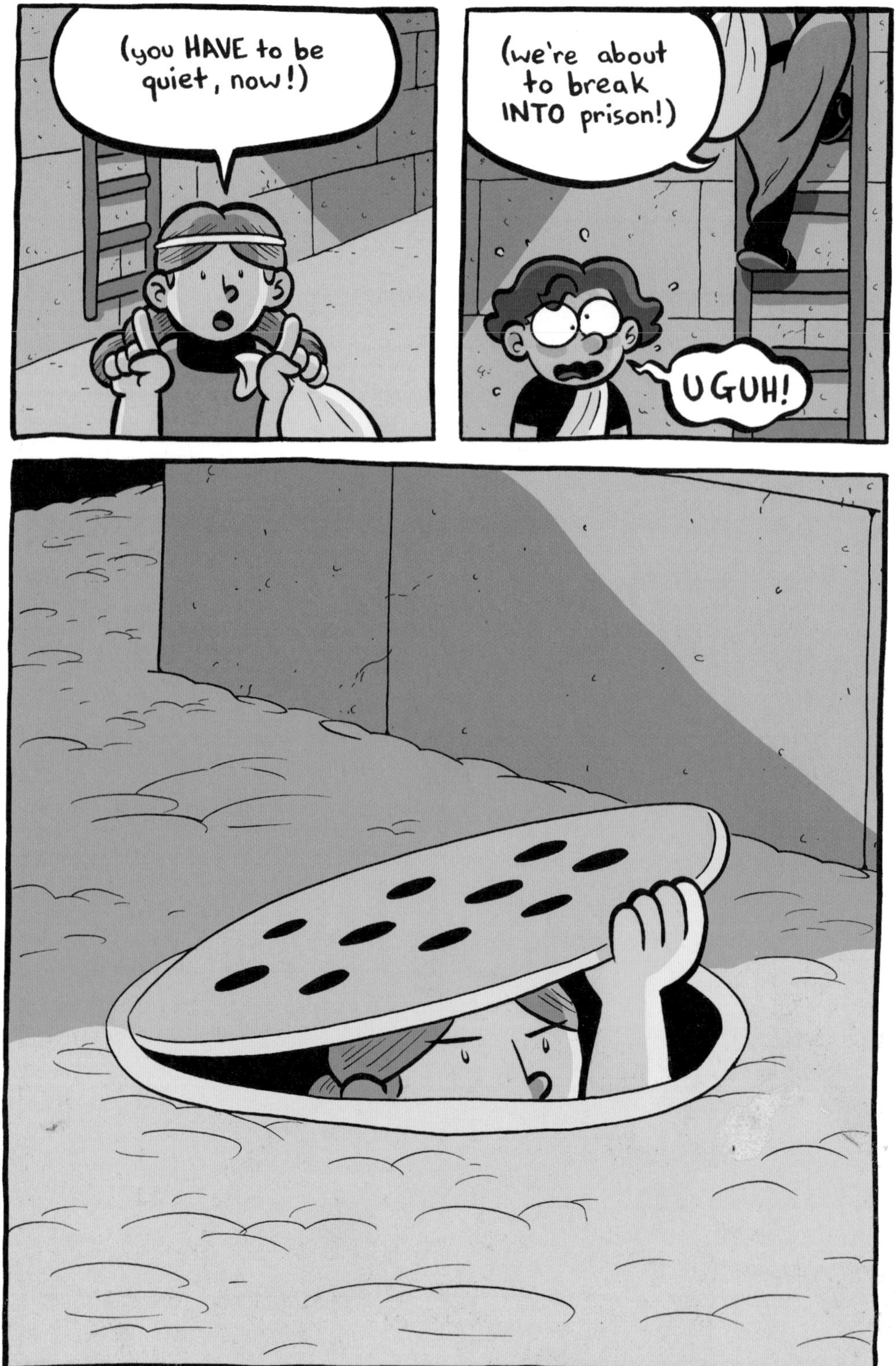
(you HAVE to be quiet, now!)
(we're about to break INTO prison!)
UGUH!

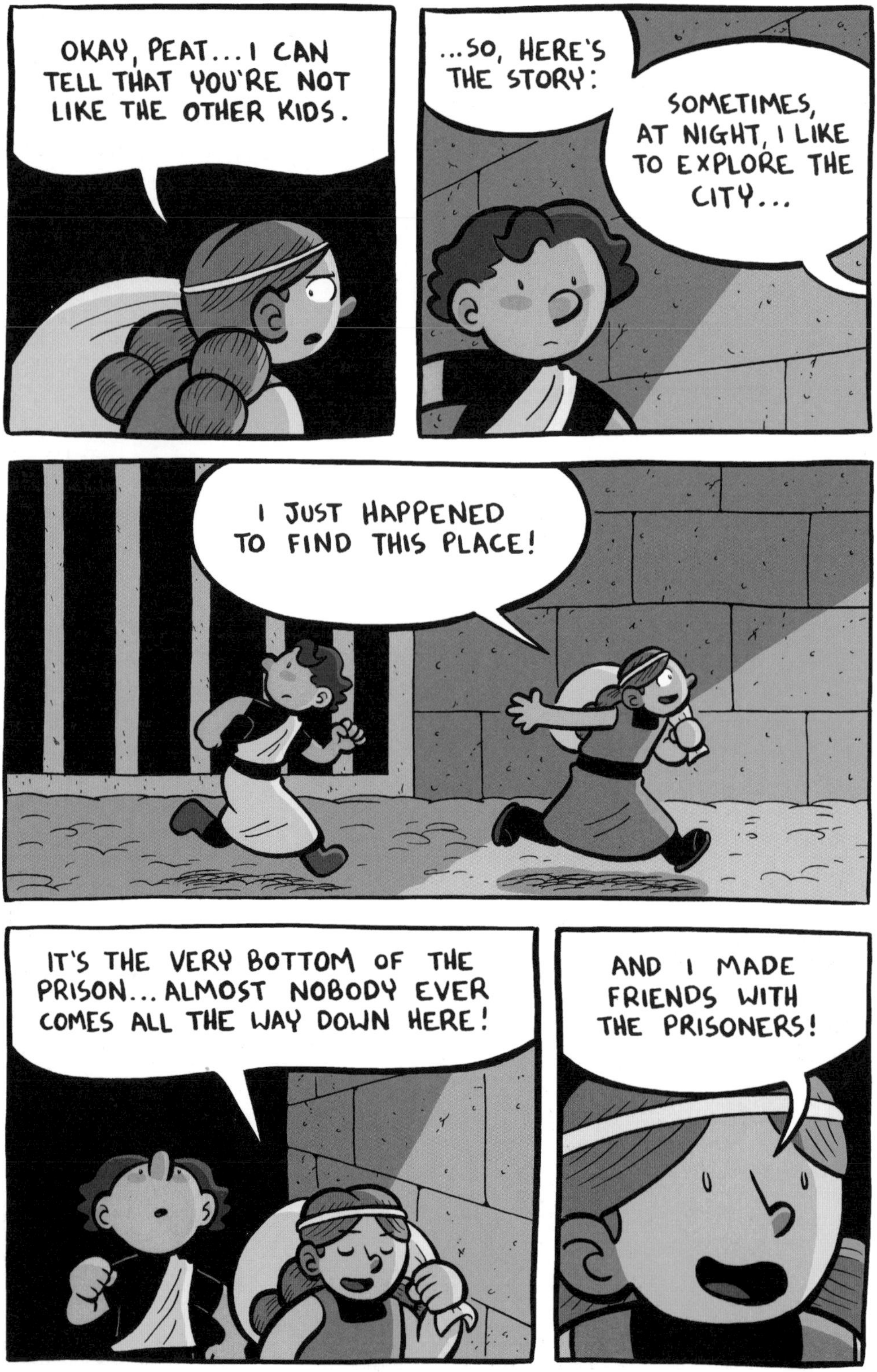
OKAY, PEAT... I CAN TELL THAT YOU'RE NOT LIKE THE OTHER KIDS.
...SO, HERE'S THE STORY:
SOMETIMES, AT NIGHT, I LIKE TO EXPLORE THE CITY...
I JUST HAPPENED TO FIND THIS PLACE!
IT'S THE VERY BOTTOM OF THE PRISON... ALMOST NOBODY EVER COMES ALL THE WAY DOWN HERE!
AND I MADE FRIENDS WITH THE PRISONERS!

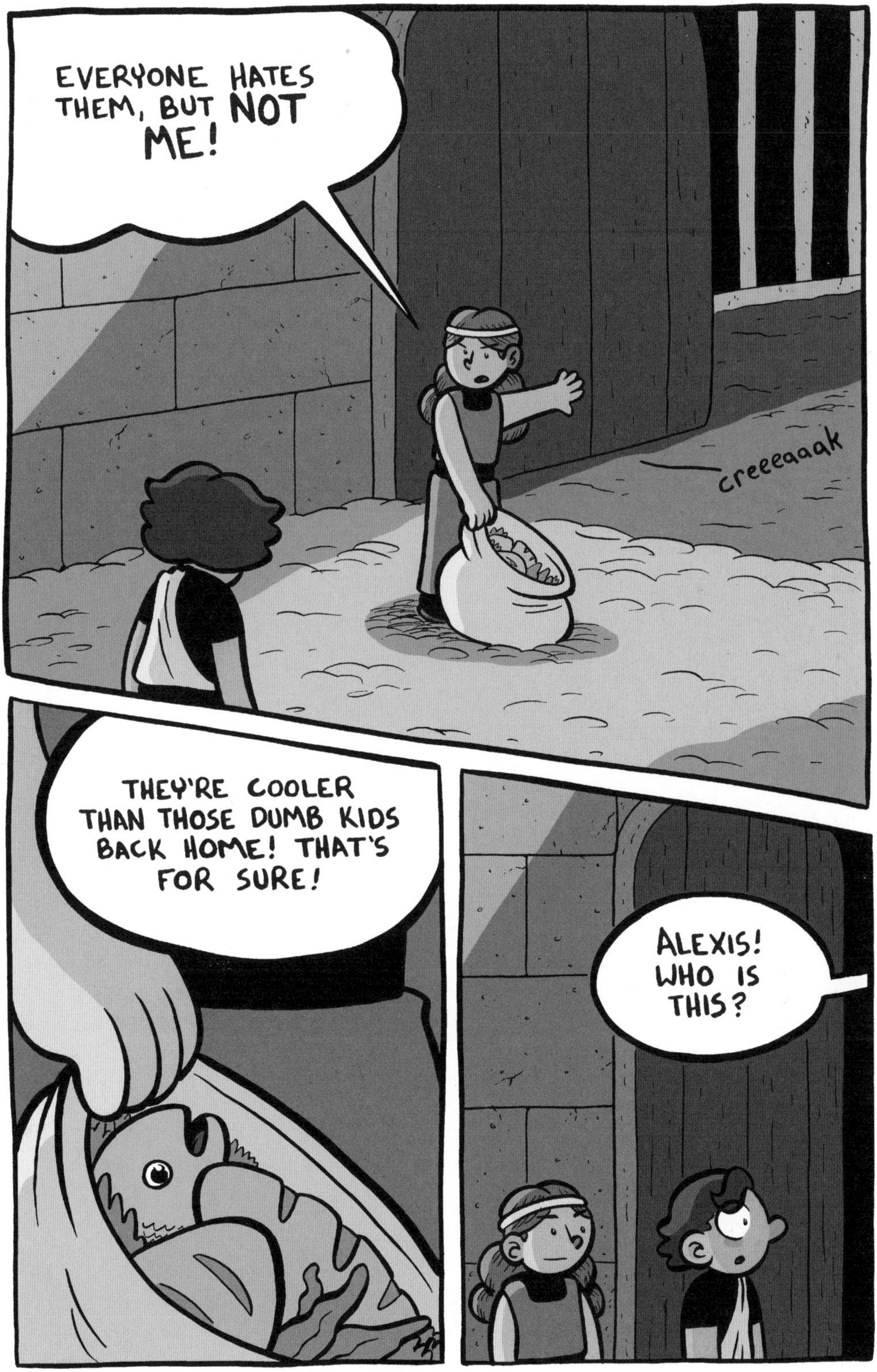
EVERYONE HATES THEM, BUT NOT ME!
creeeaaak
THEY'RE COOLER THAN THOSE DUMB KIDS BACK HOME! THAT'S FOR SURE!
ALEXIS! WHO IS THIS?

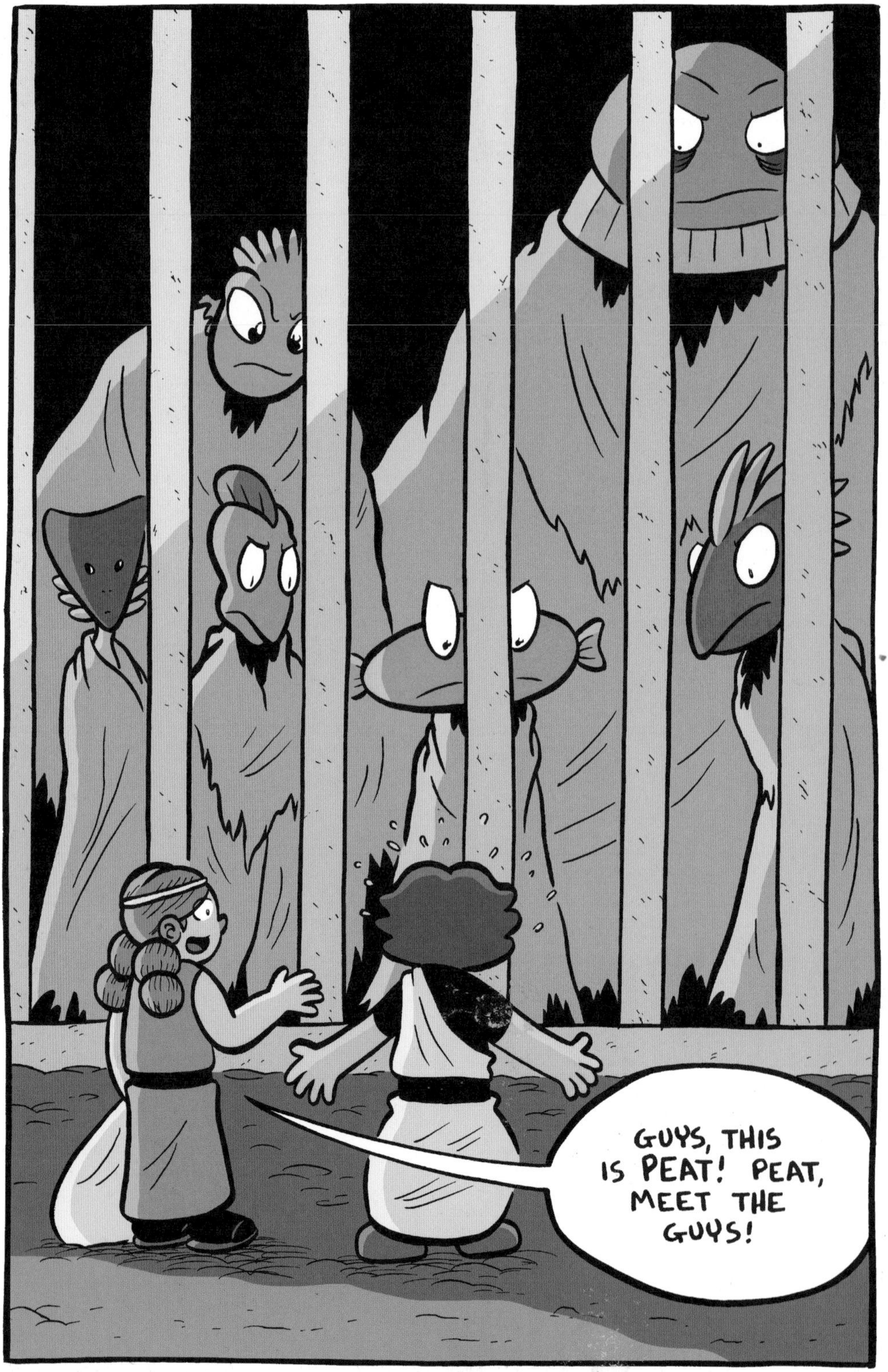
GUYS, THIS IS PEAT! PEAT, MEET THE GUYS!

CHAPTER FIVE

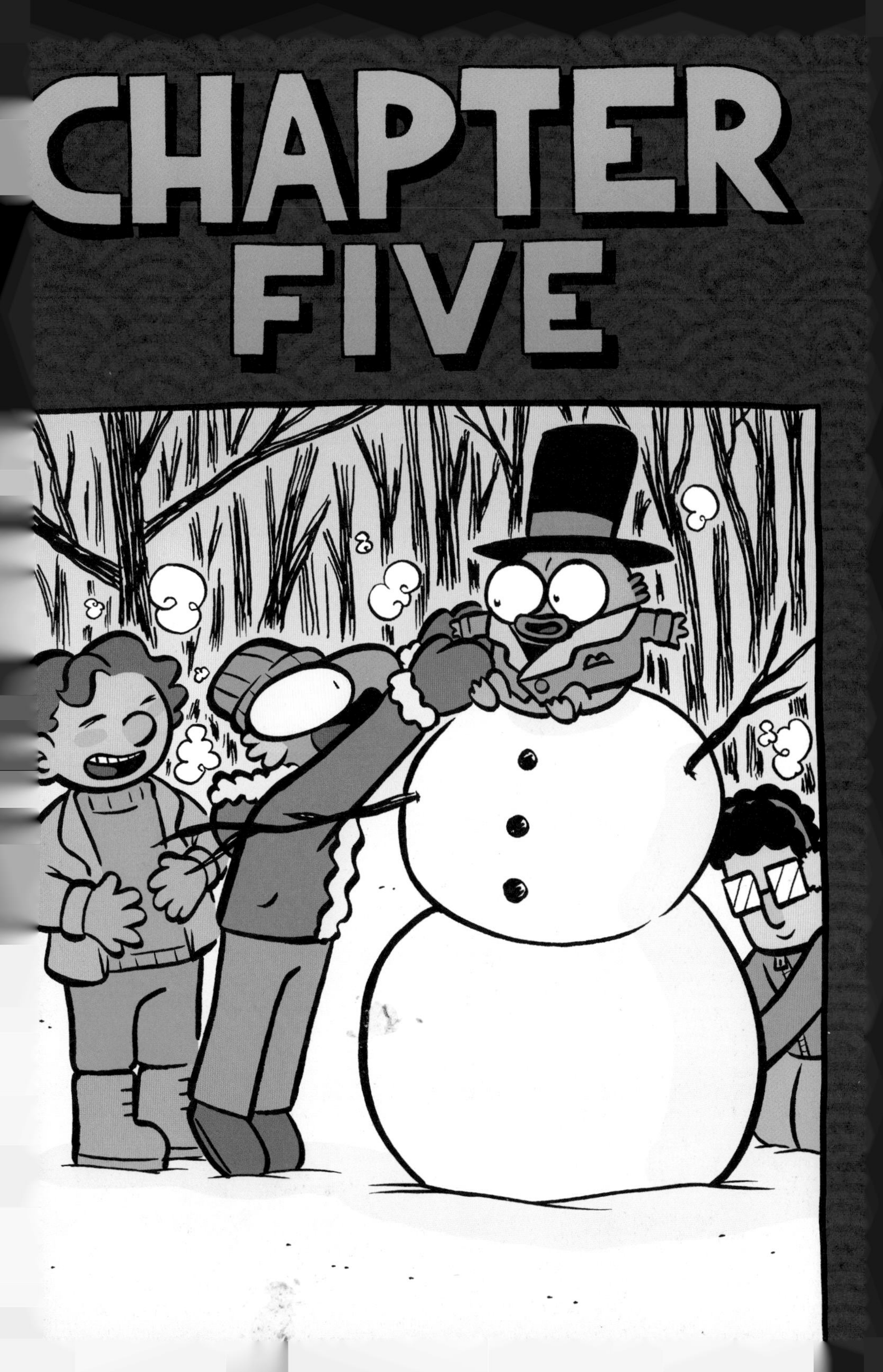

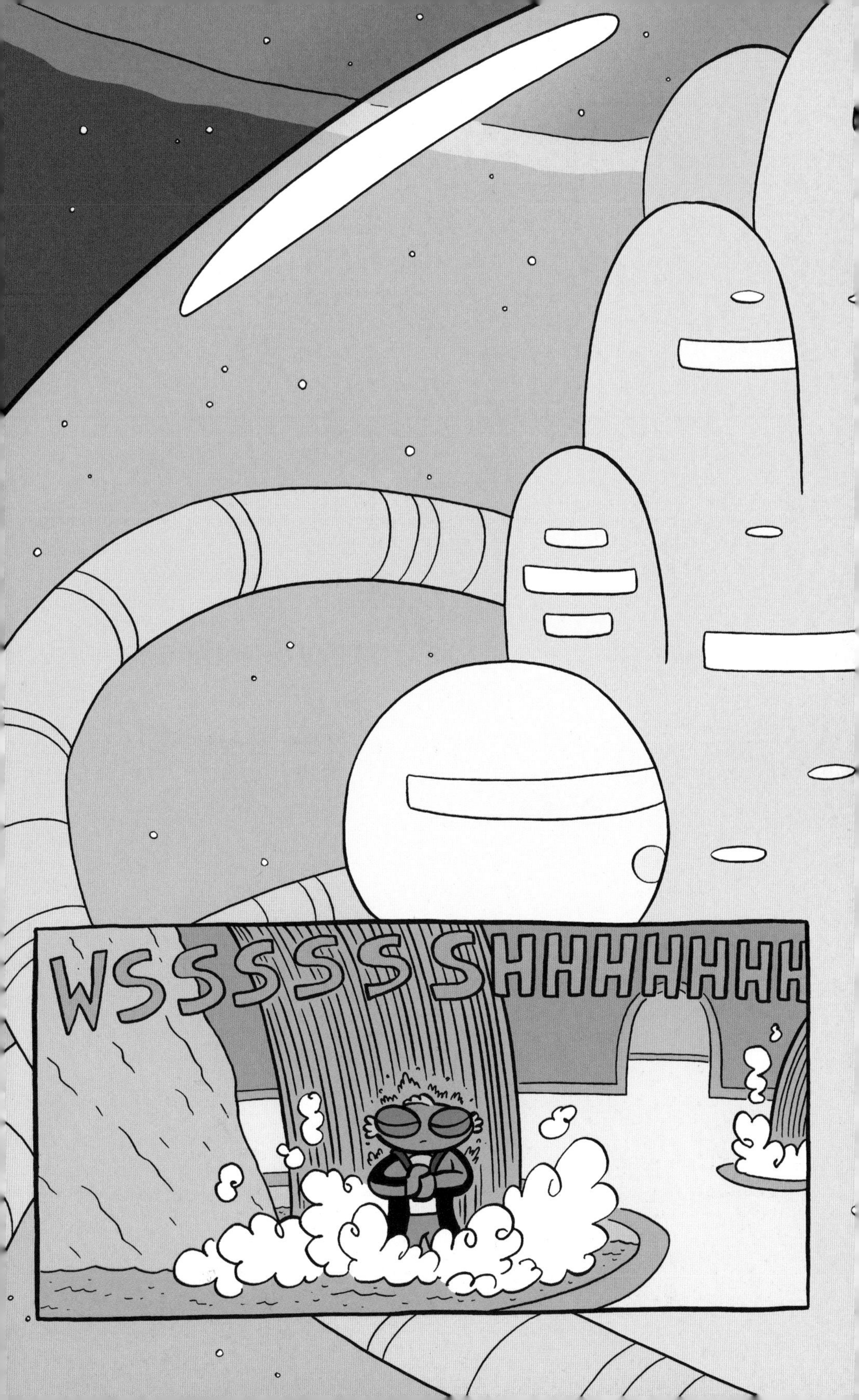
WSSSSSSHHHHHHH

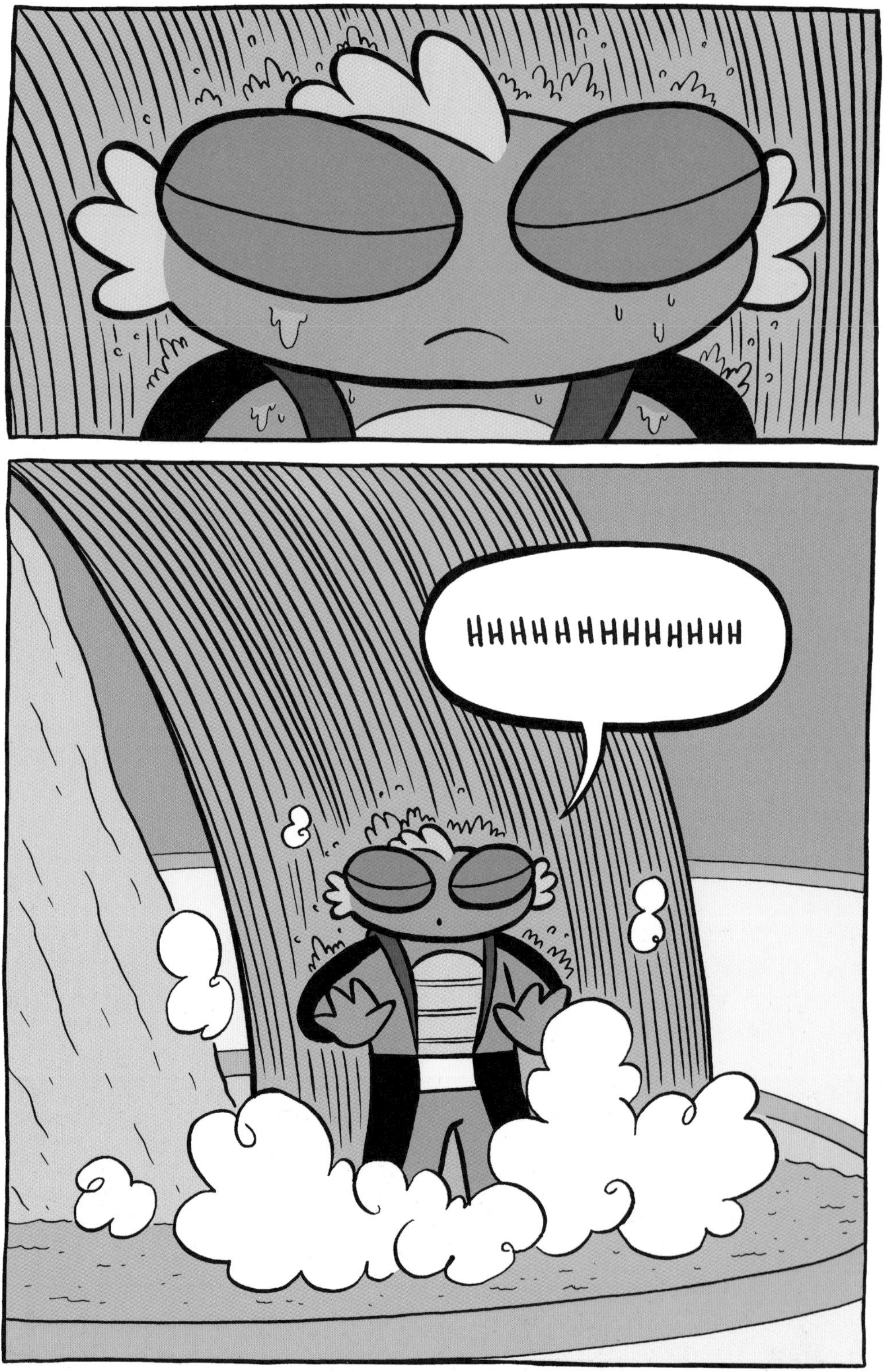
HHHHHHHHHHHHHH

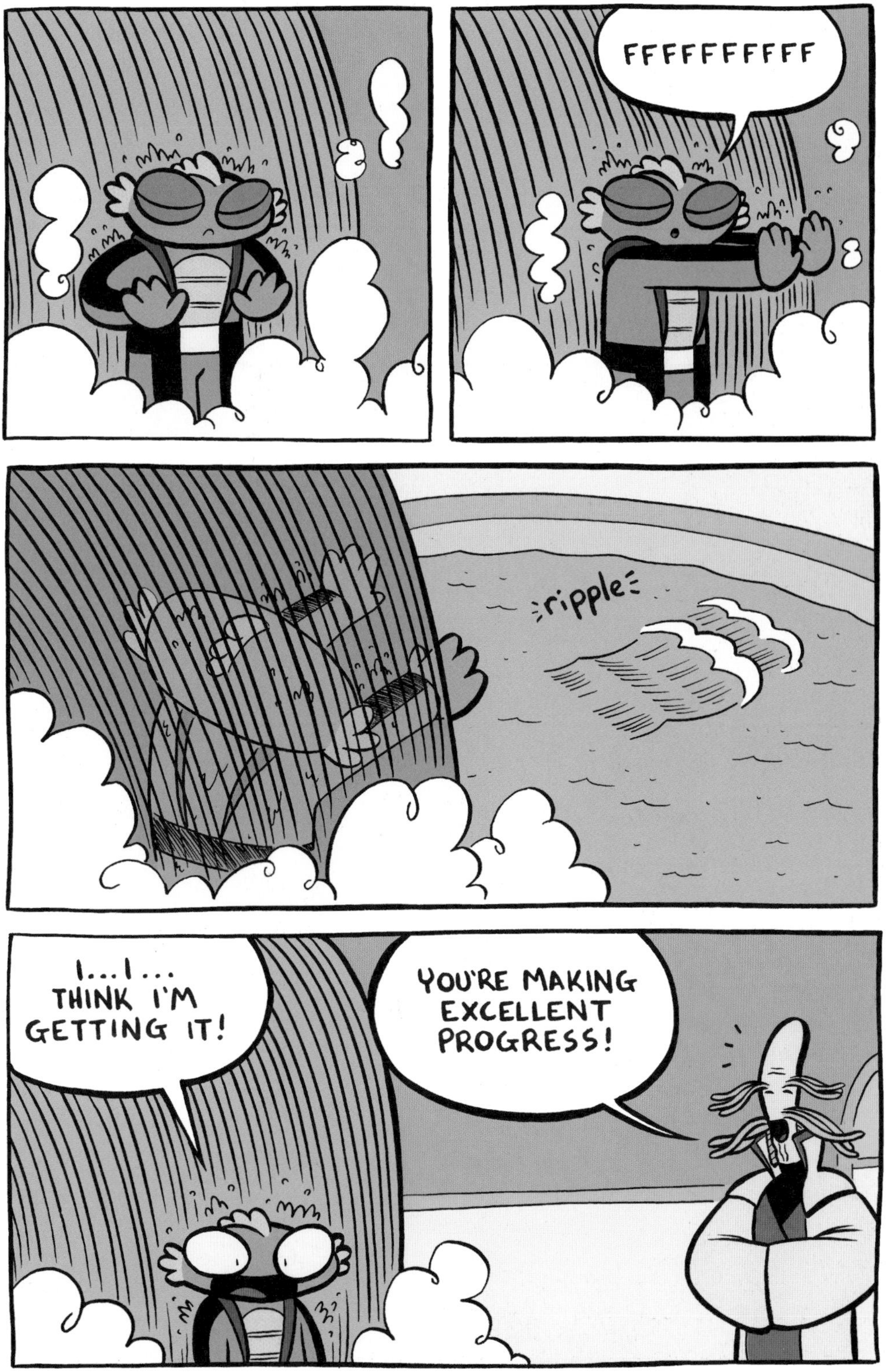
FFFFFFFFFF
ripple
I...I...
THINK I'M
GETTING IT!
YOU'RE MAKING
EXCELLENT
PROGRESS!

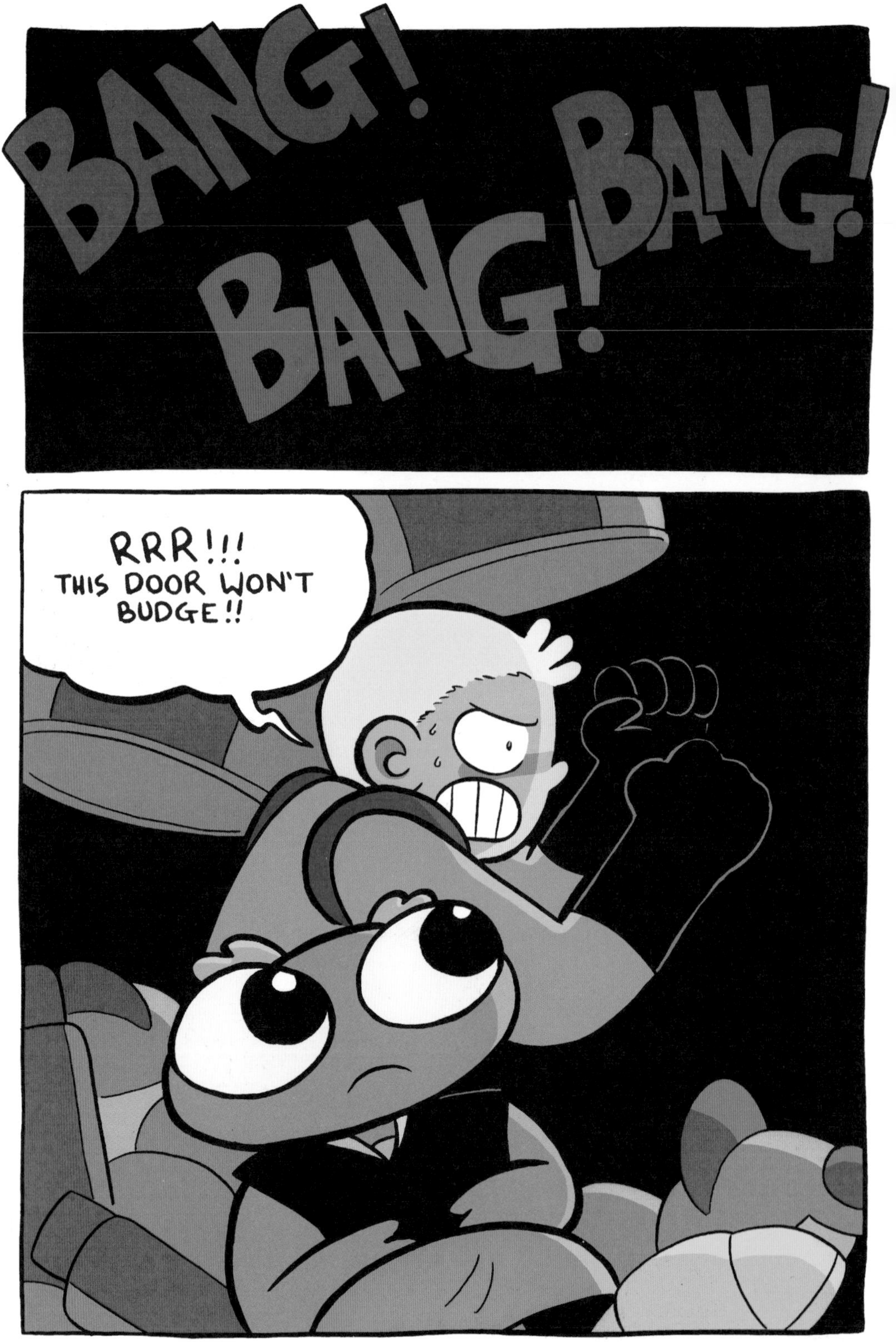
BANG!
BANG!
BANG!
RRR!!! THIS DOOR WON'T BUDGE!!

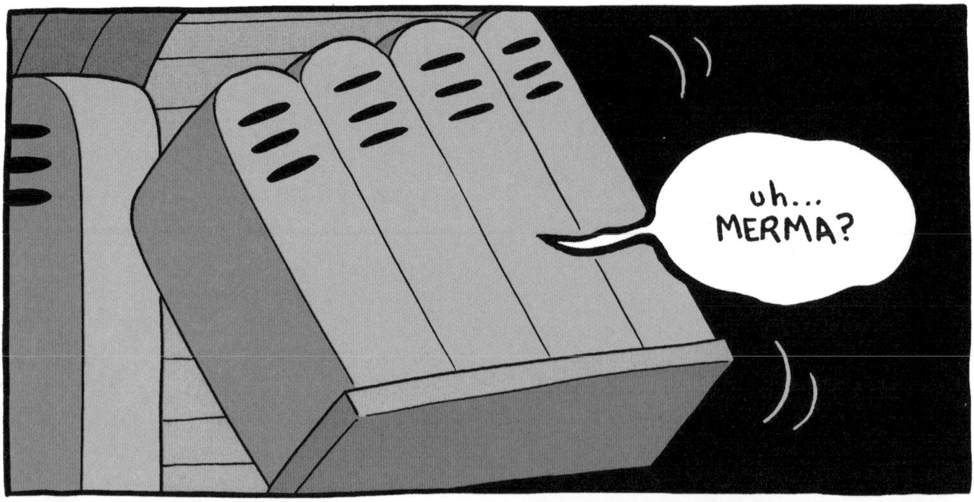
uh...
MERMA?

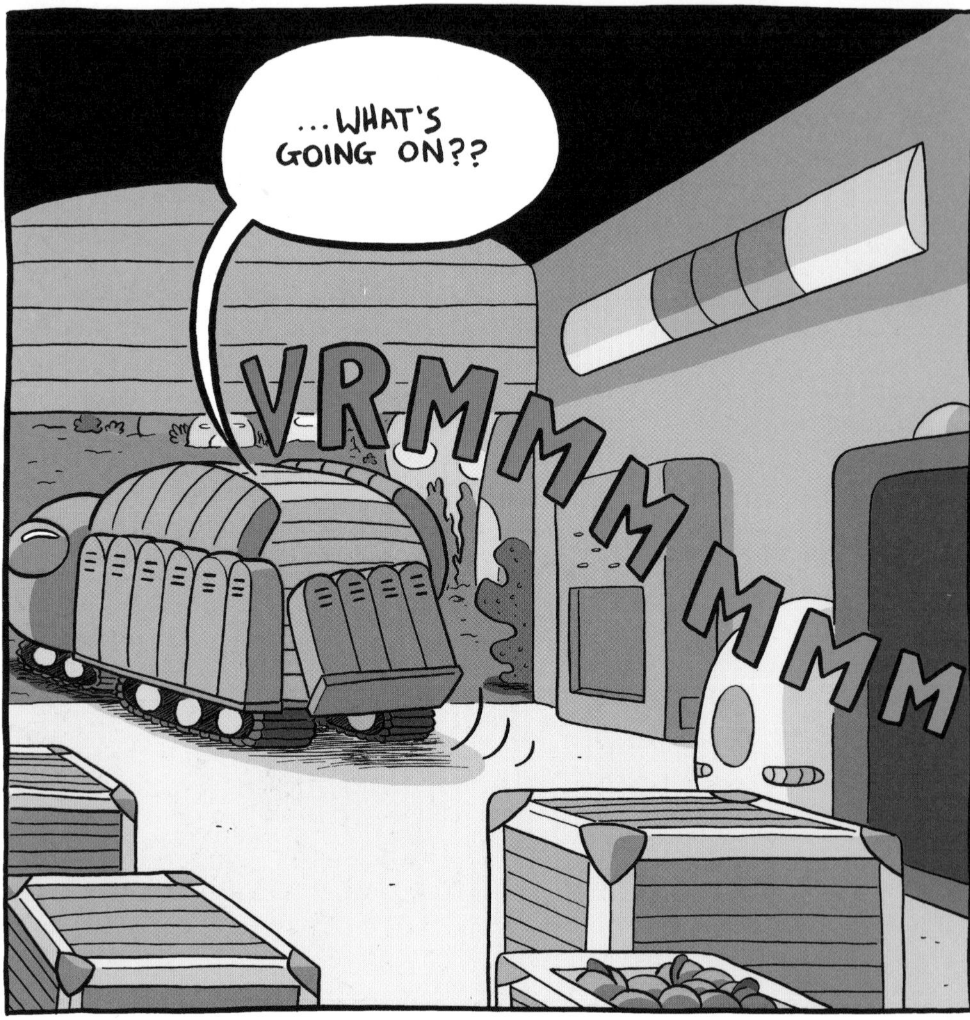
...WHAT'S
GOING ON??
VRMMMMMMMM

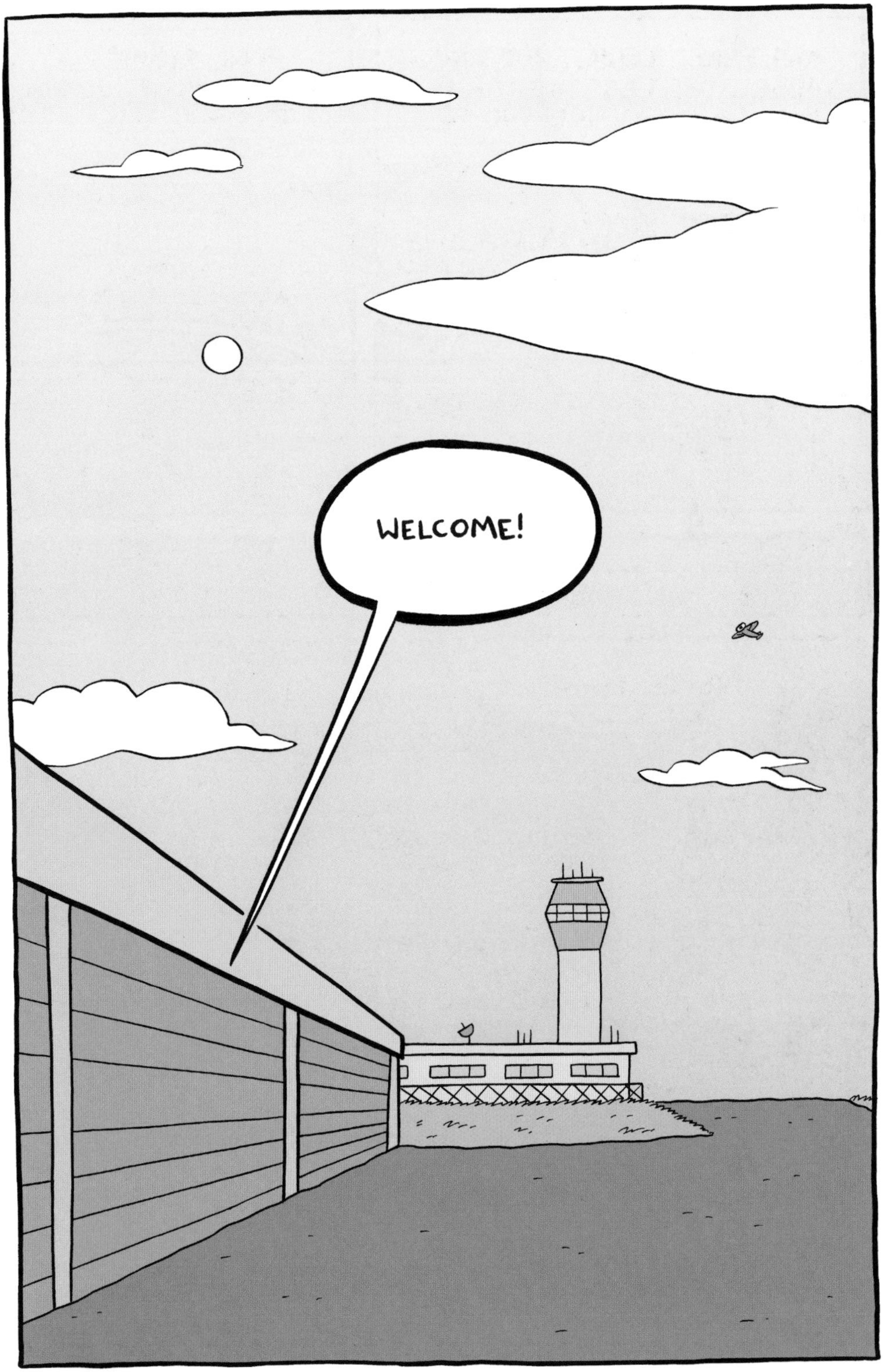
WELCOME!

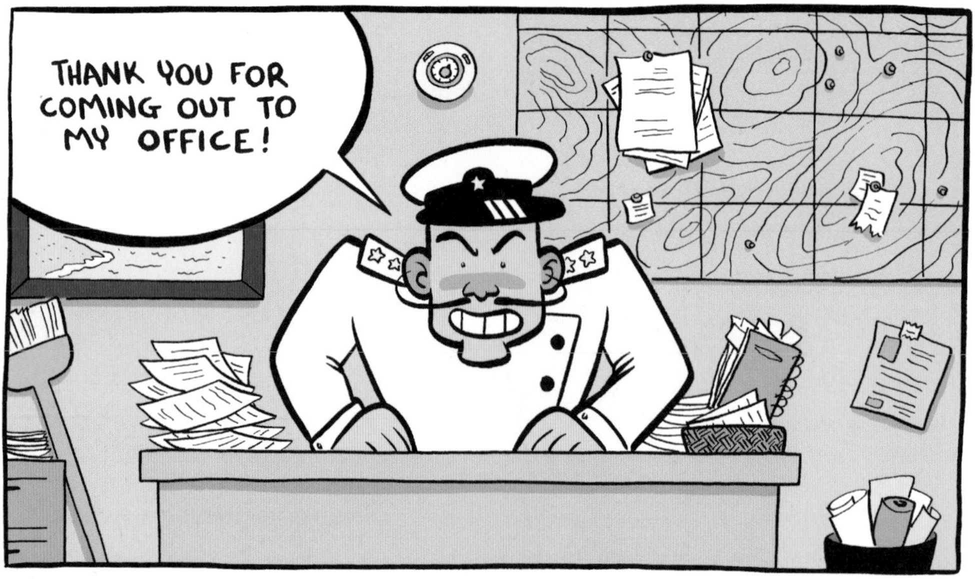
THANK YOU FOR COMING OUT TO MY OFFICE!

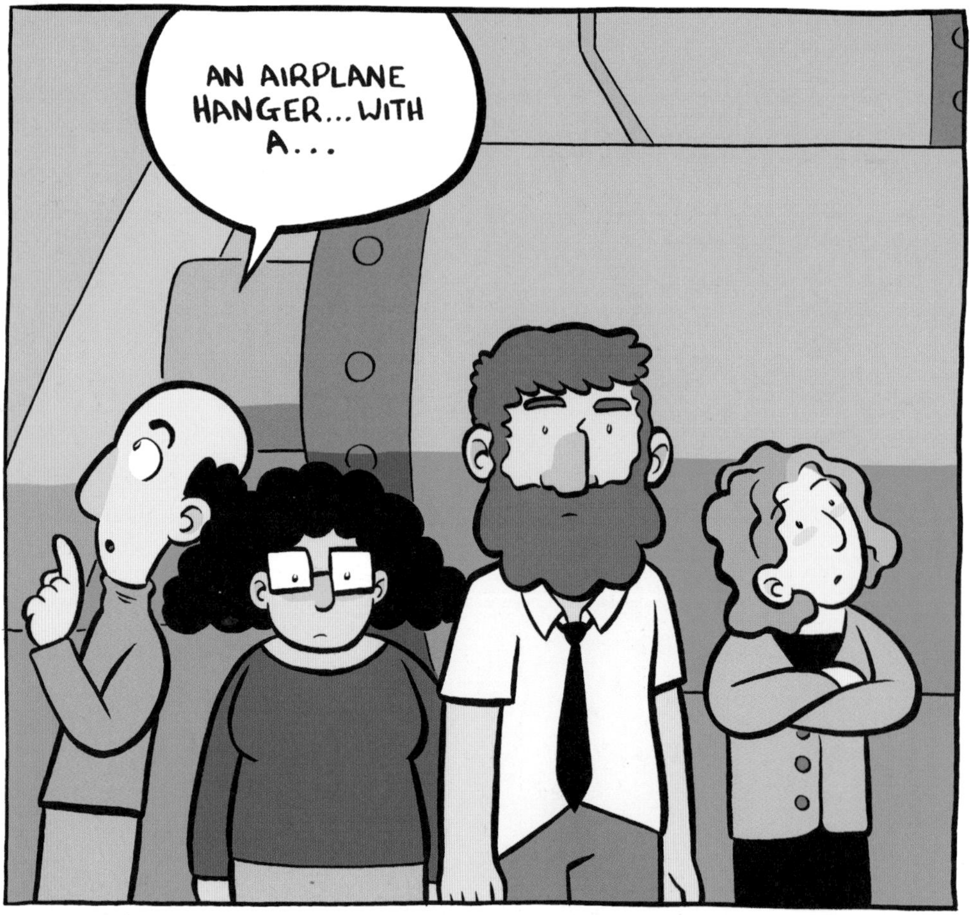
AN AIRPLANE HANGER... WITH A...

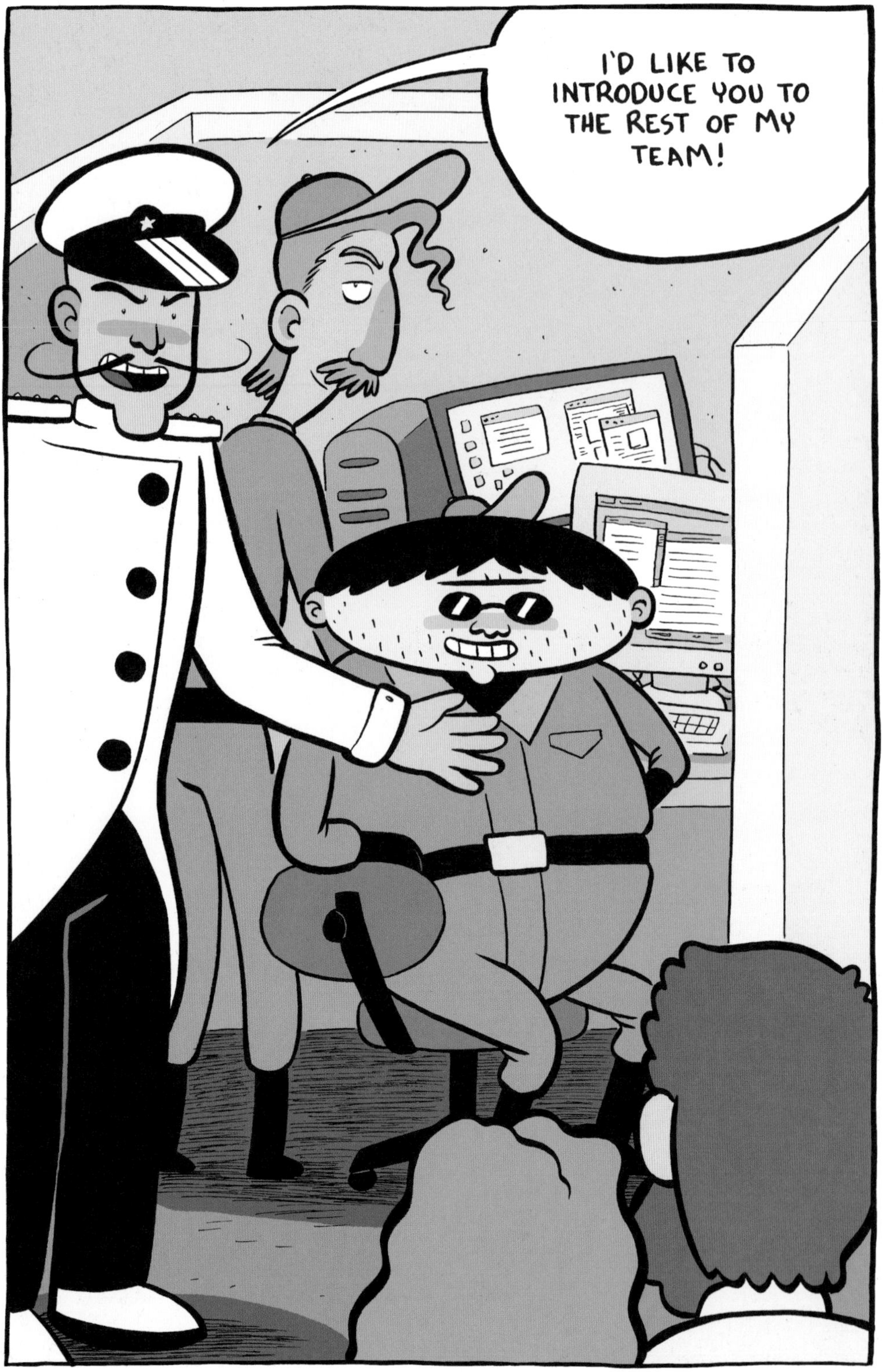
I'D LIKE TO INTRODUCE YOU TO THE REST OF MY TEAM!

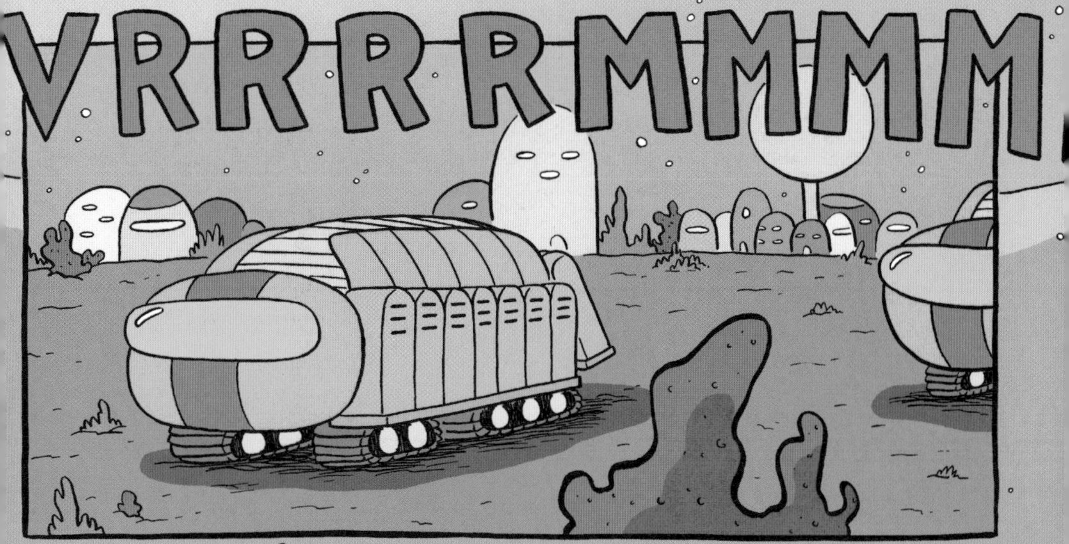
VRRRRMMMMM

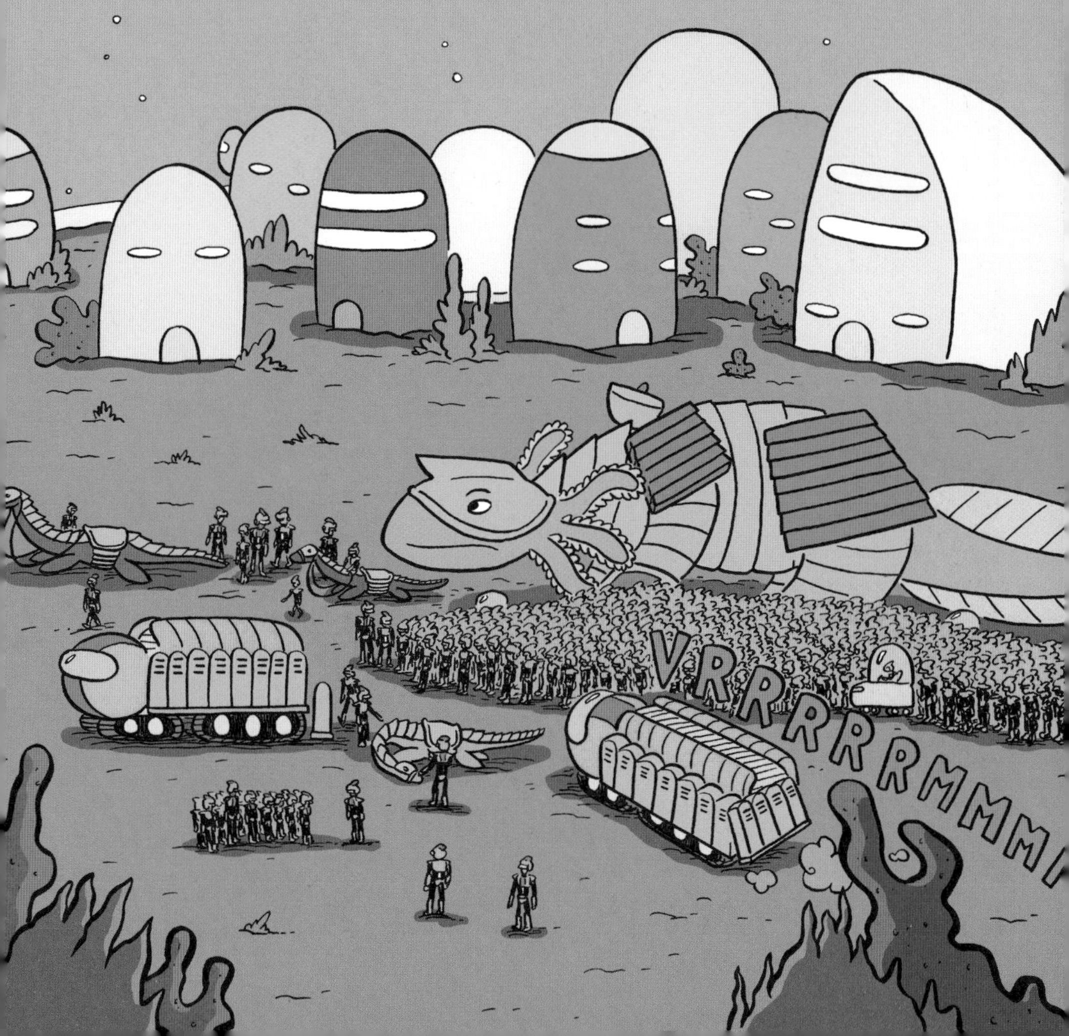
VRRRRRMMMM

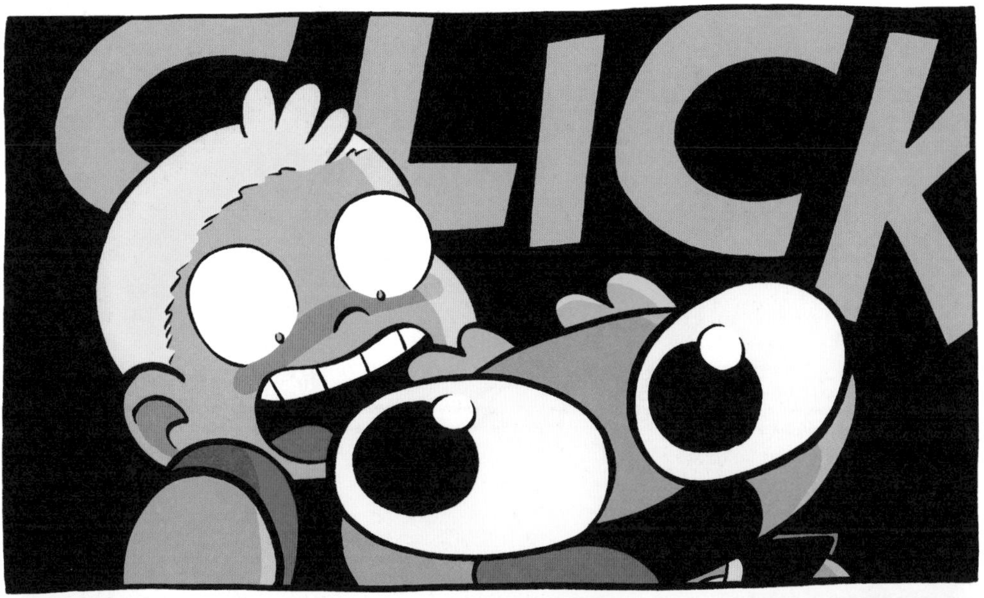
CLICK

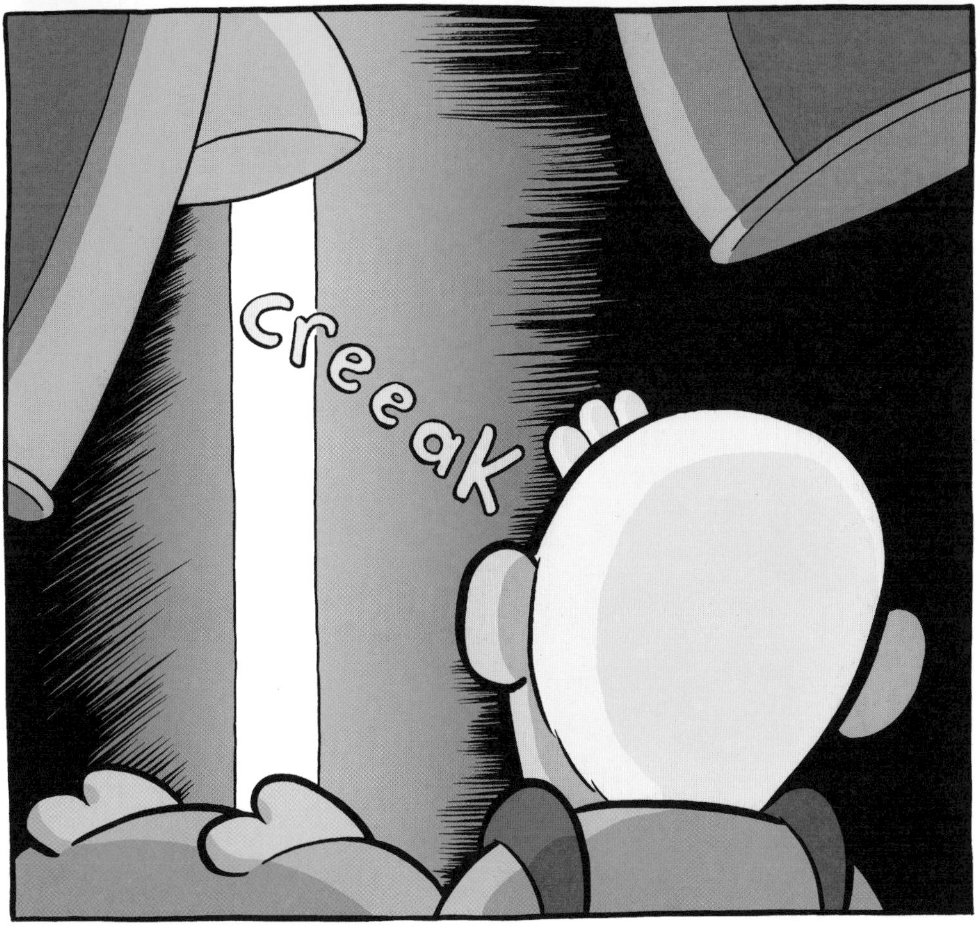
creeak

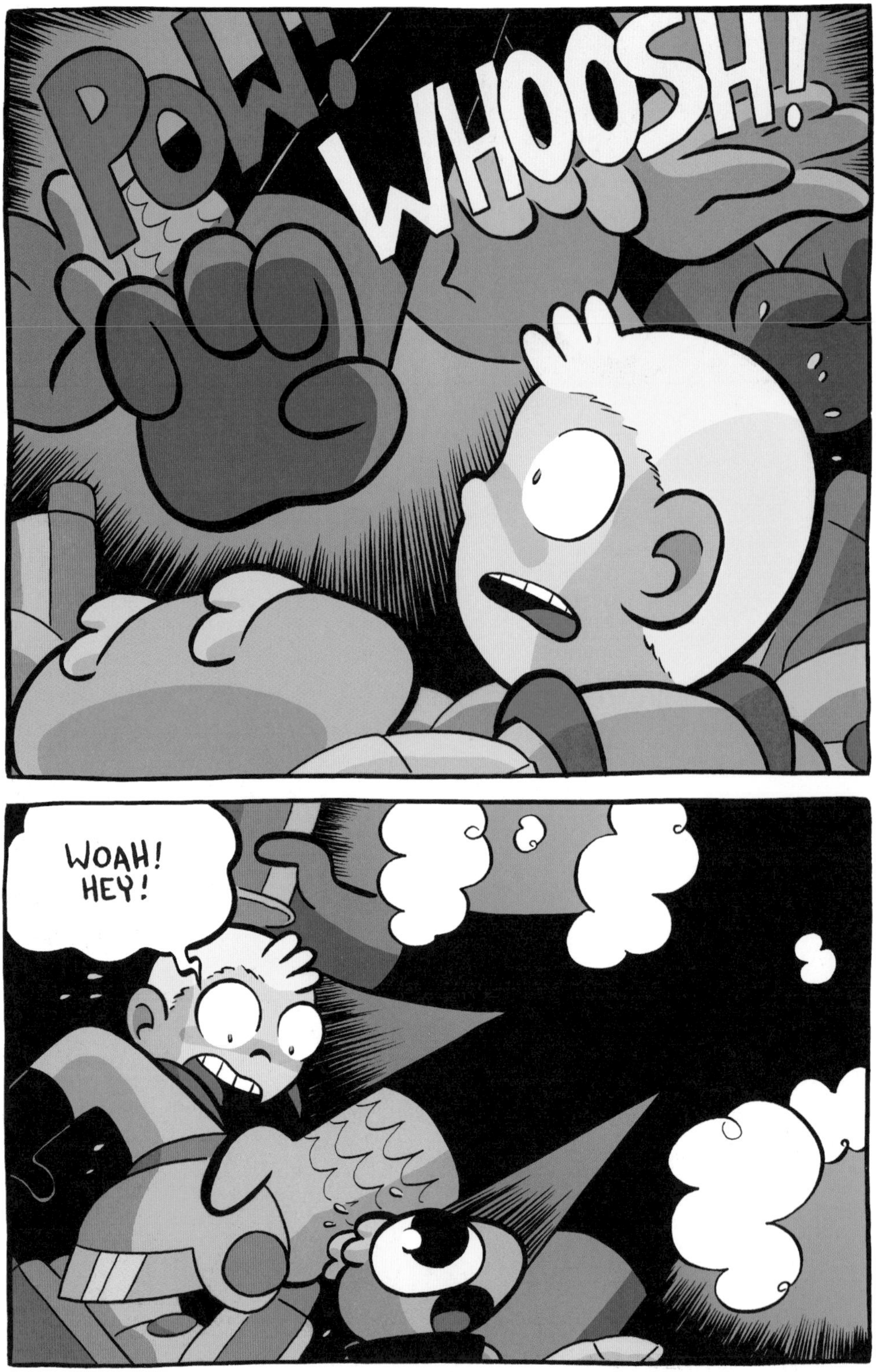
POW!
WHOOSH!
WOAH! HEY!

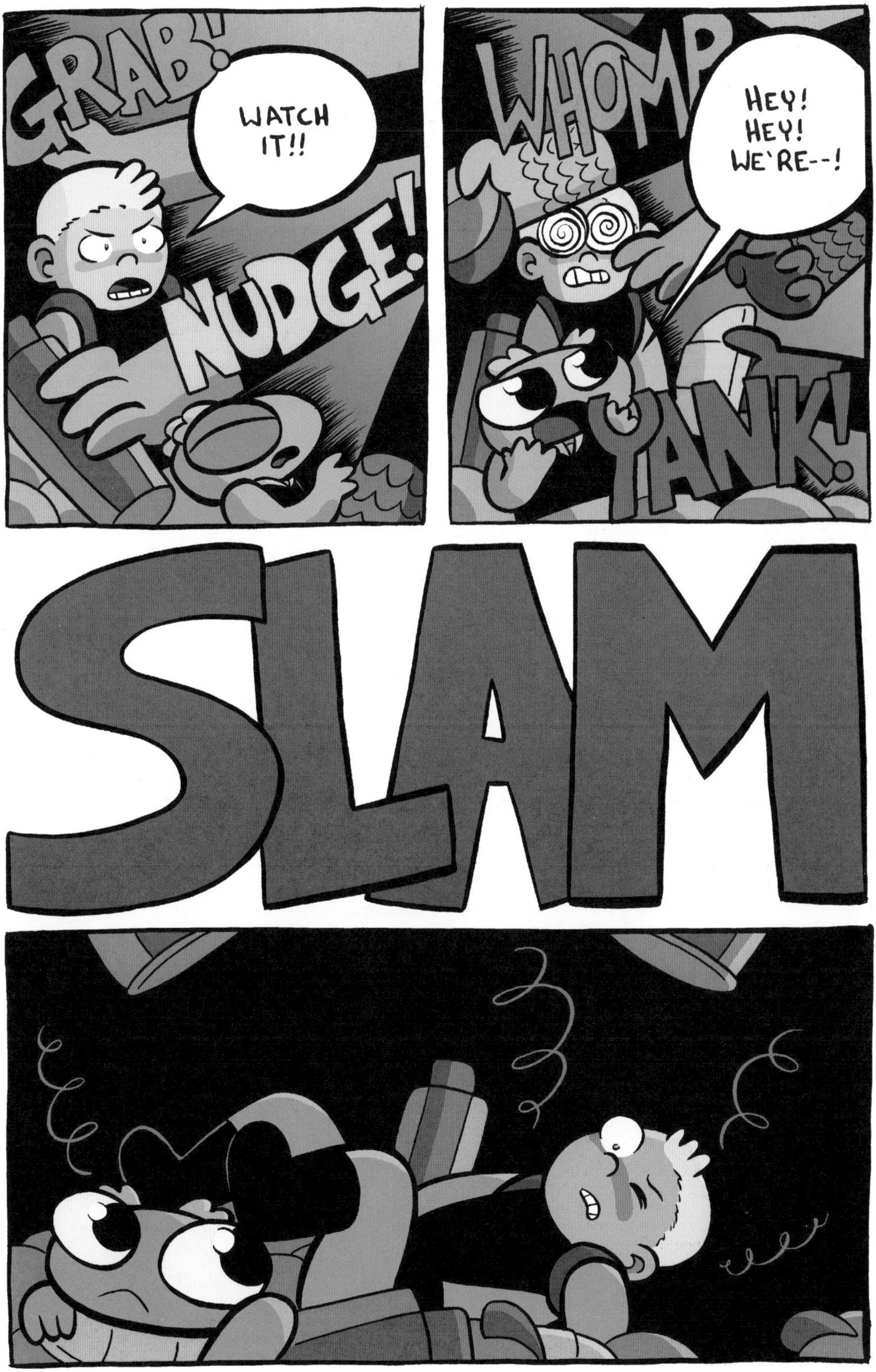
GRAB!
WATCH IT!!
NUDGE!
WHOMP
HEY! HEY! WE'RE--!
YANK!
SLAM

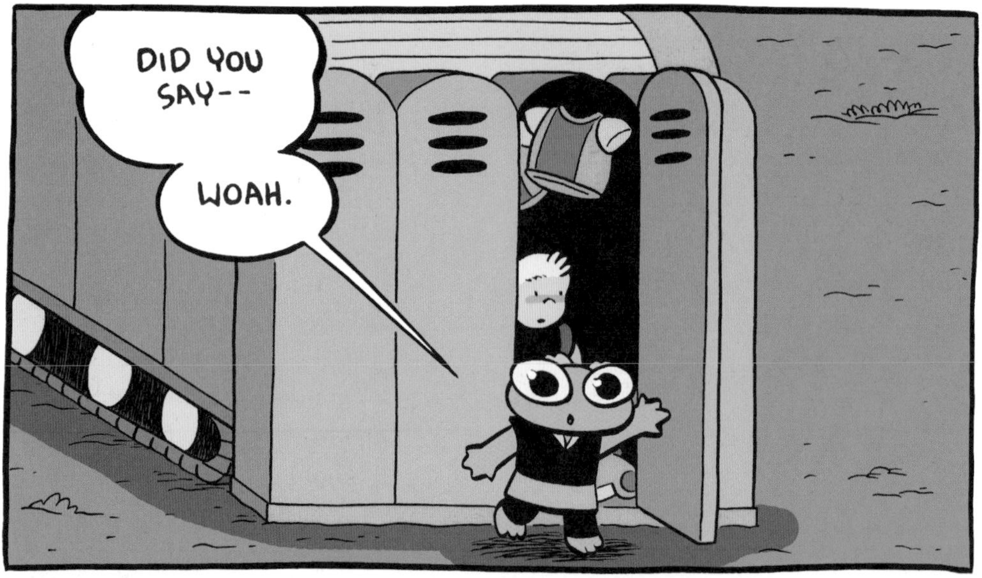
DID YOU SAY--
WOAH.

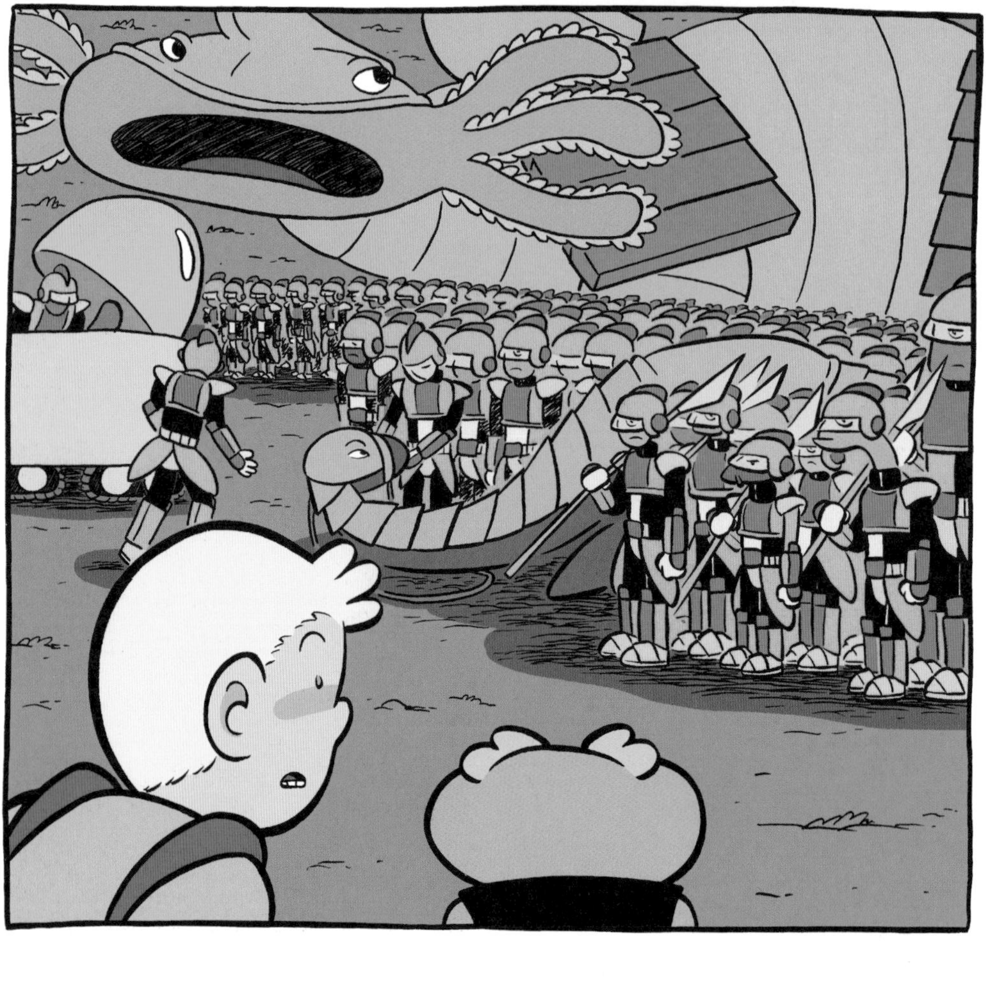

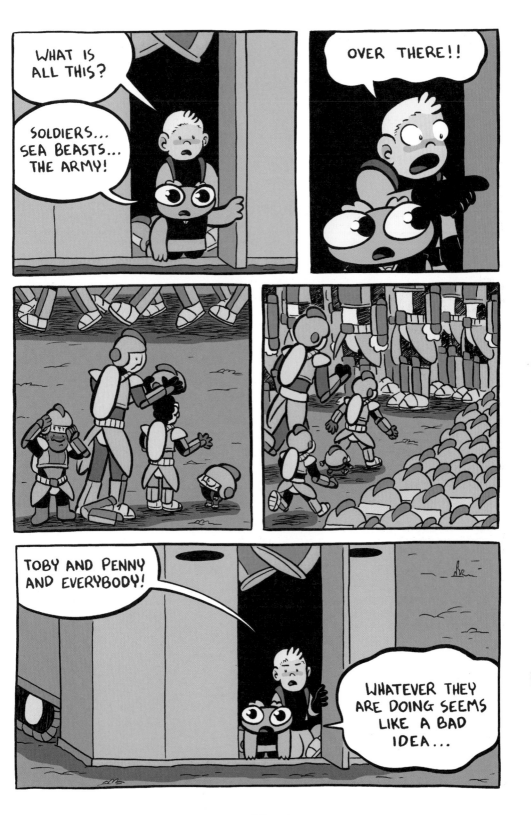

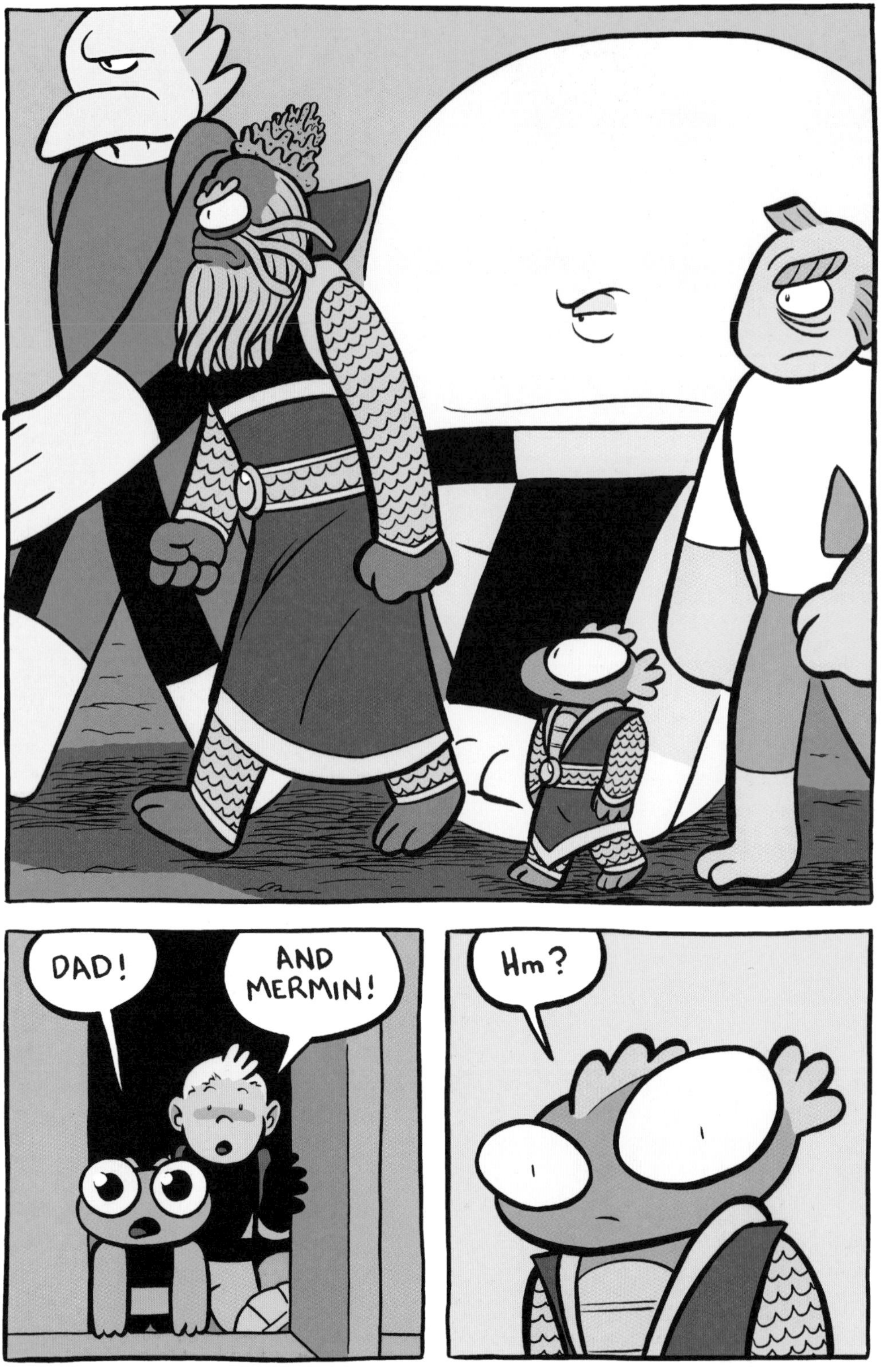
DAD!
AND MERMIN!
Hm?

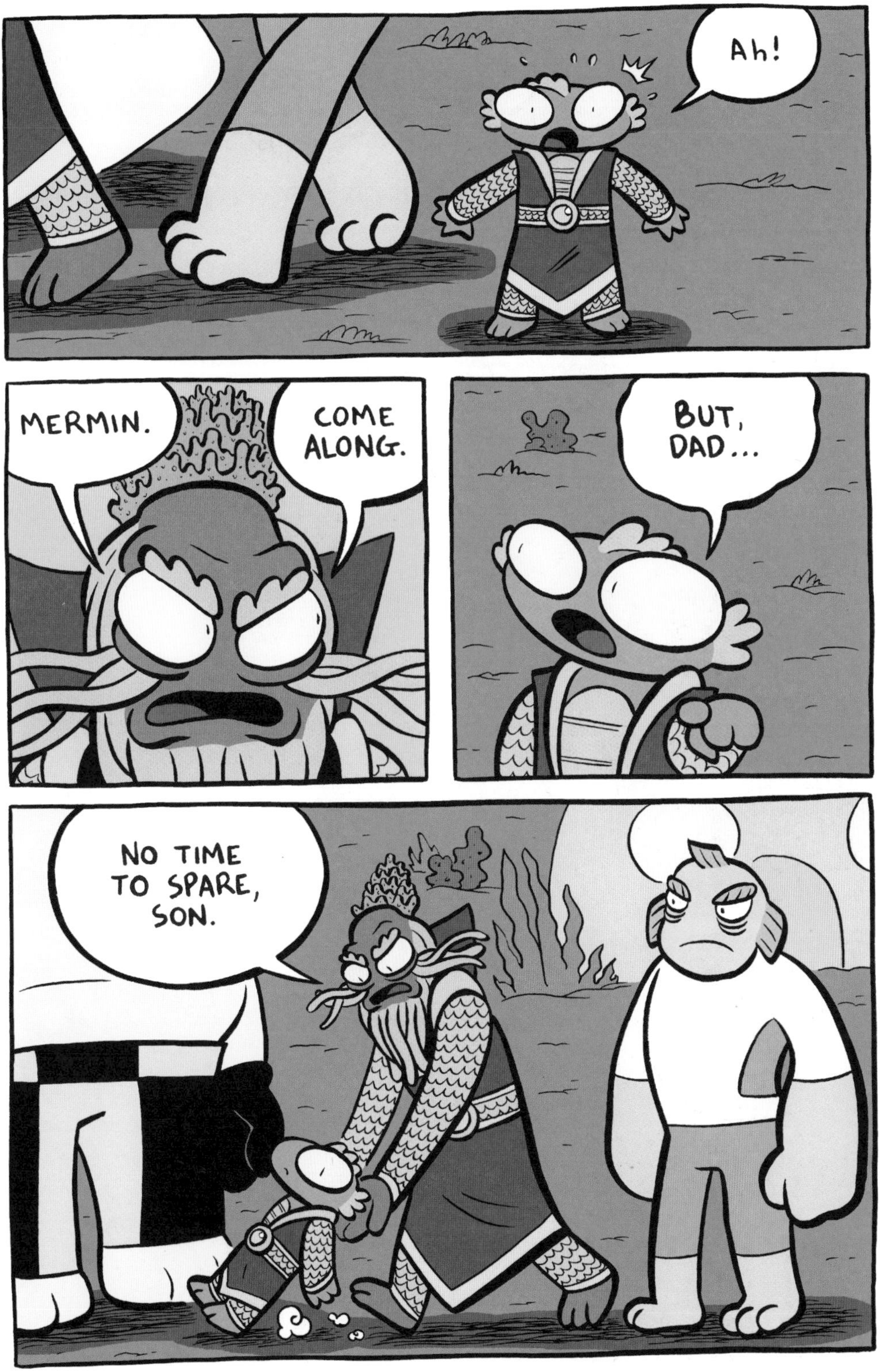
Ah!
MERMIN.
COME ALONG.
BUT, DAD...
NO TIME TO SPARE, SON.

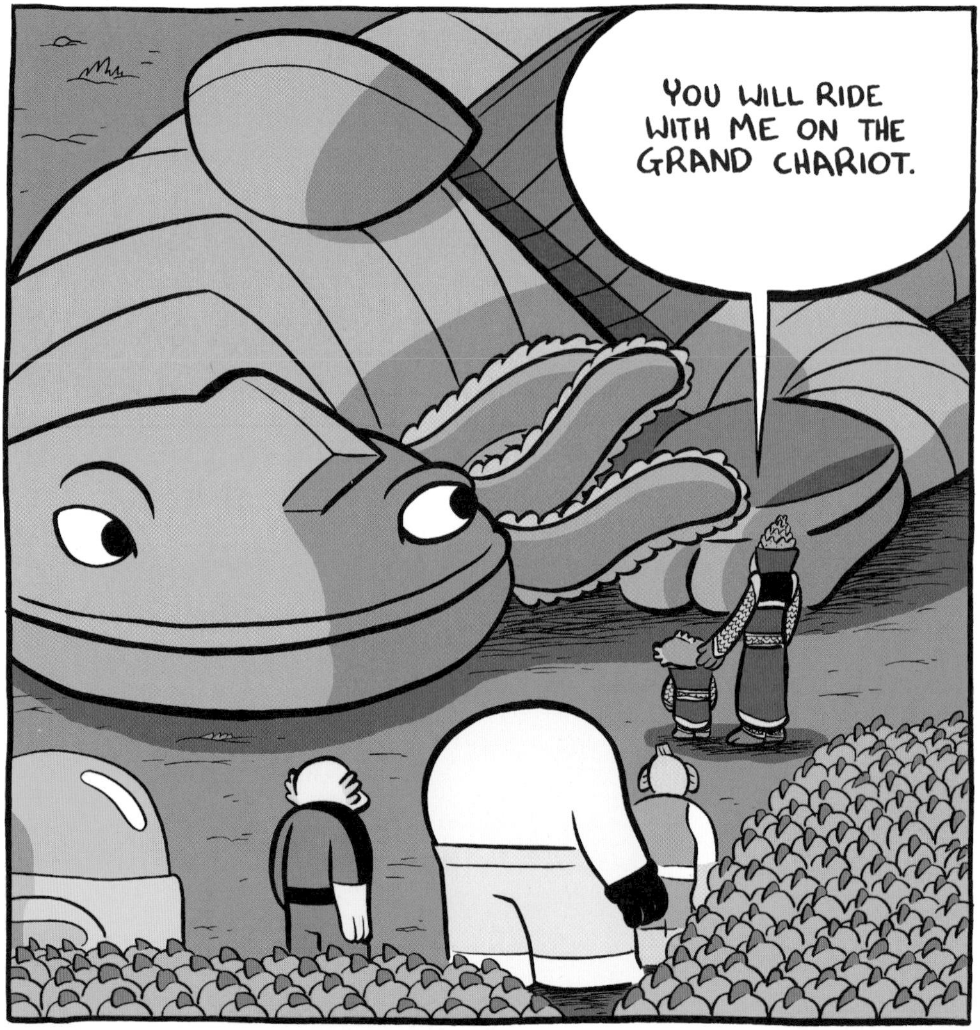
YOU WILL RIDE WITH ME ON THE GRAND CHARIOT.

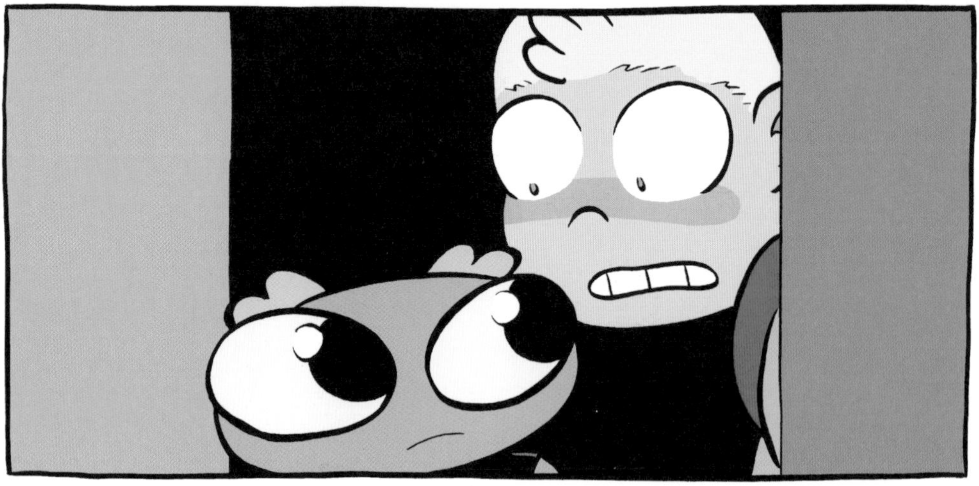

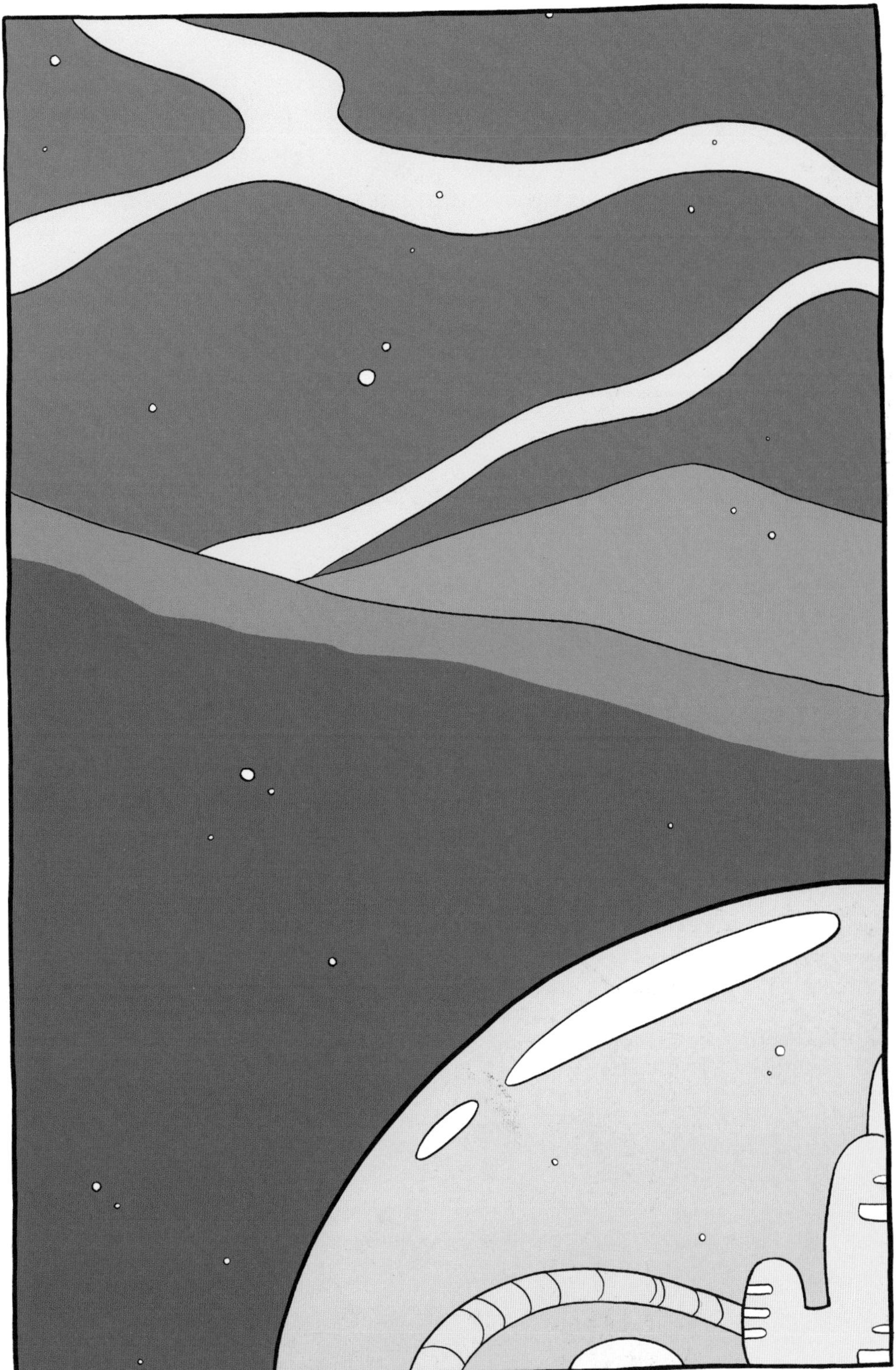

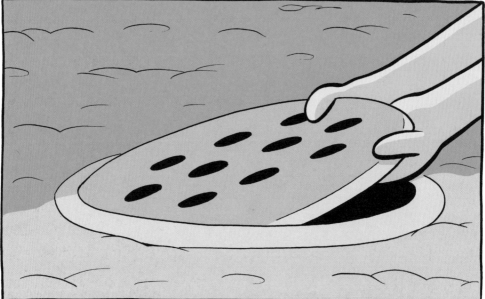

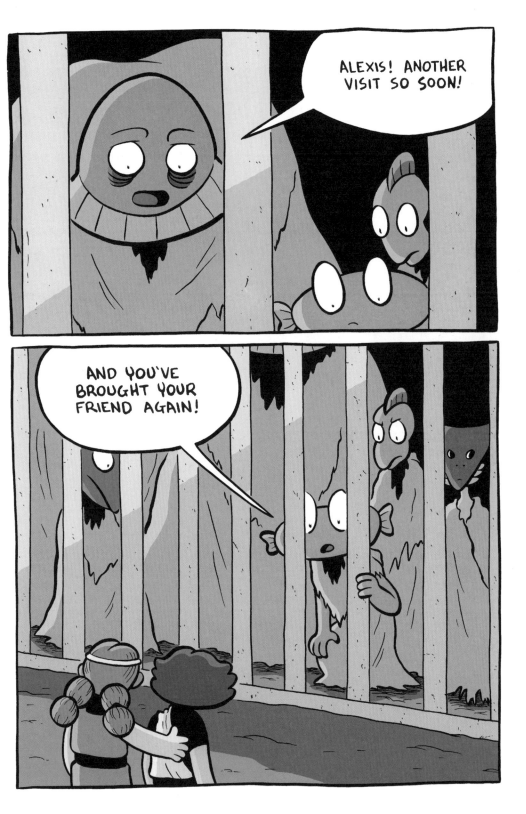

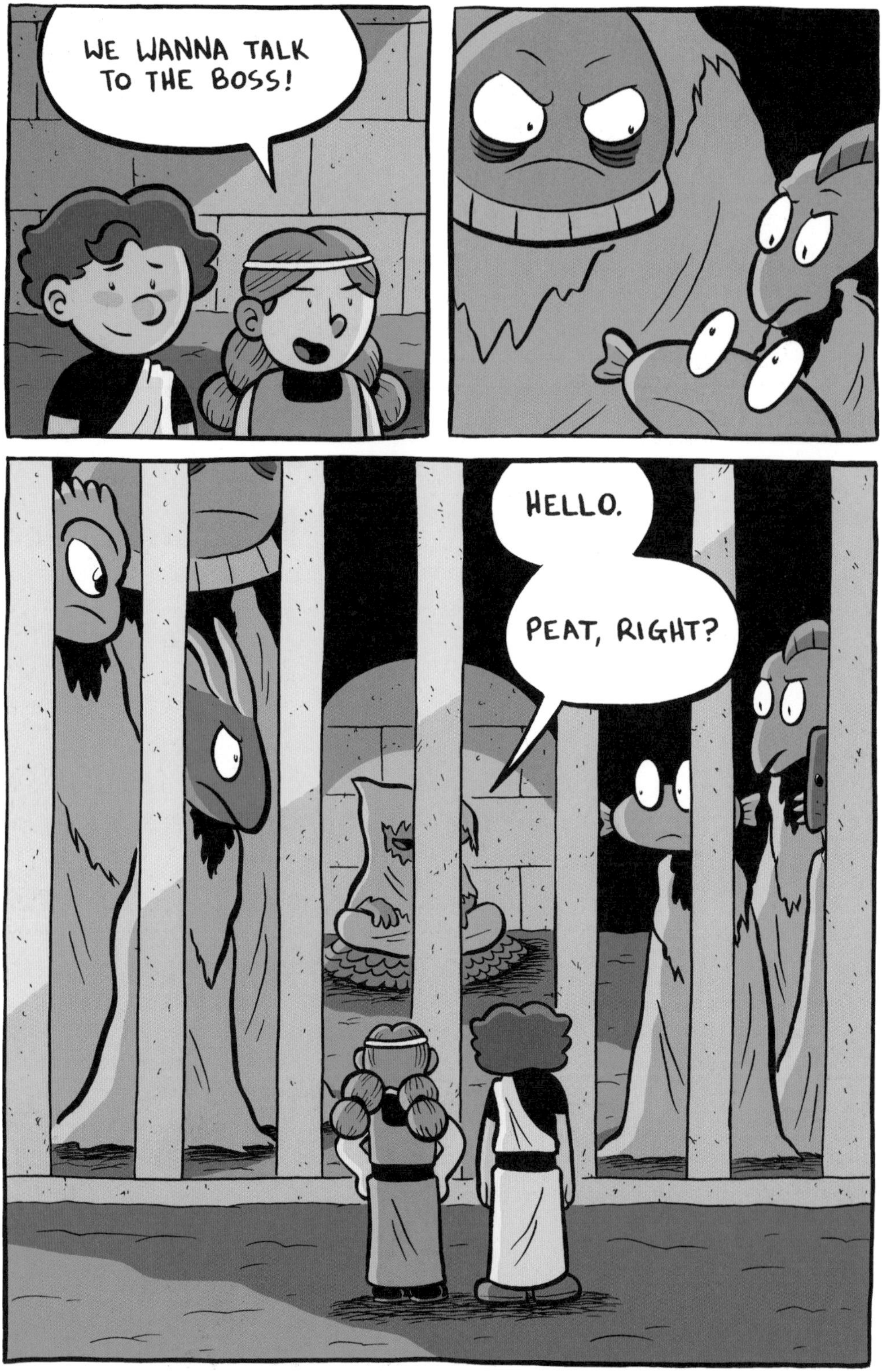
WE WANNA TALK TO THE BOSS!
HELLO.
PEAT, RIGHT?

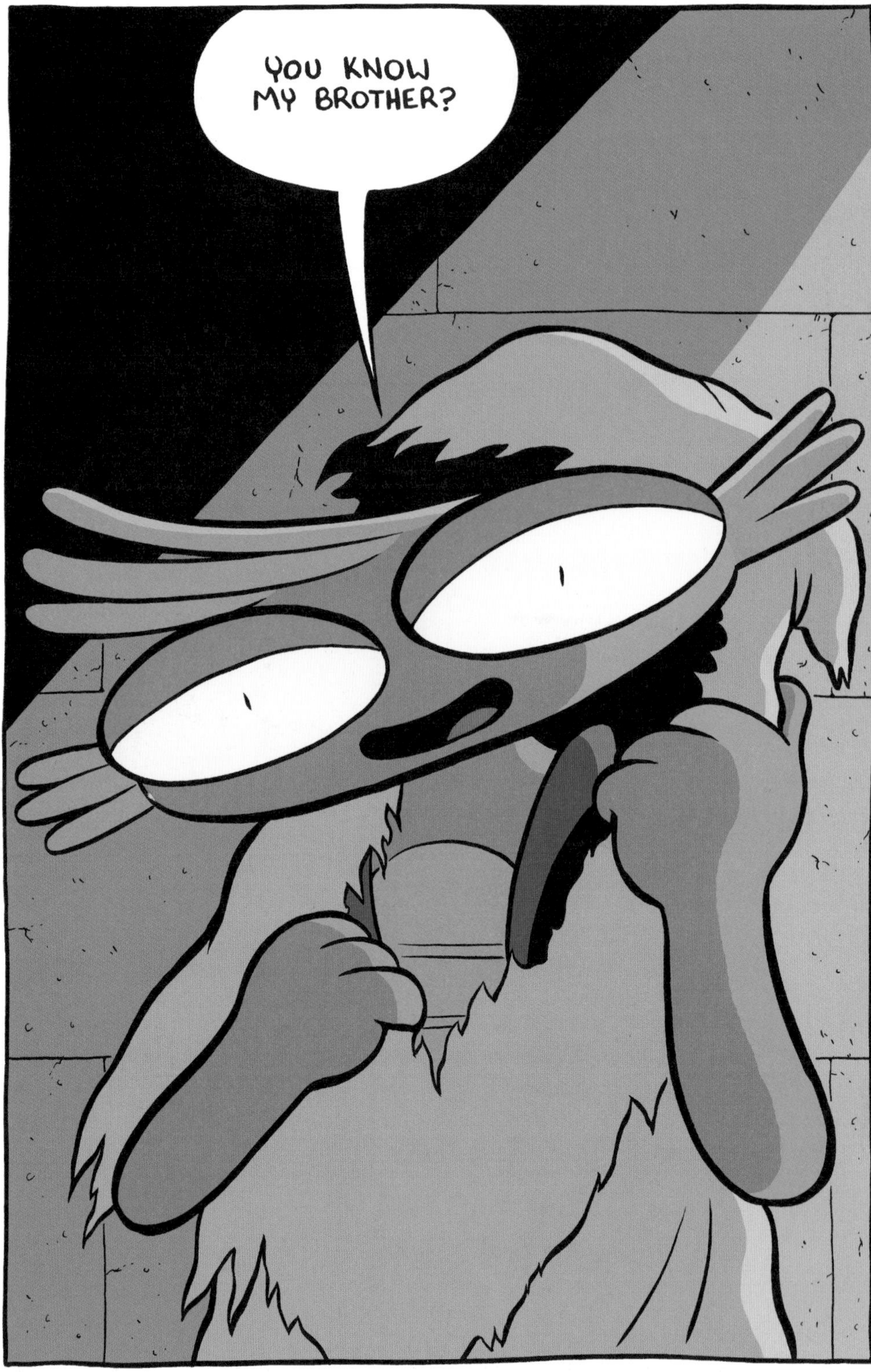
YOU KNOW MY BROTHER?

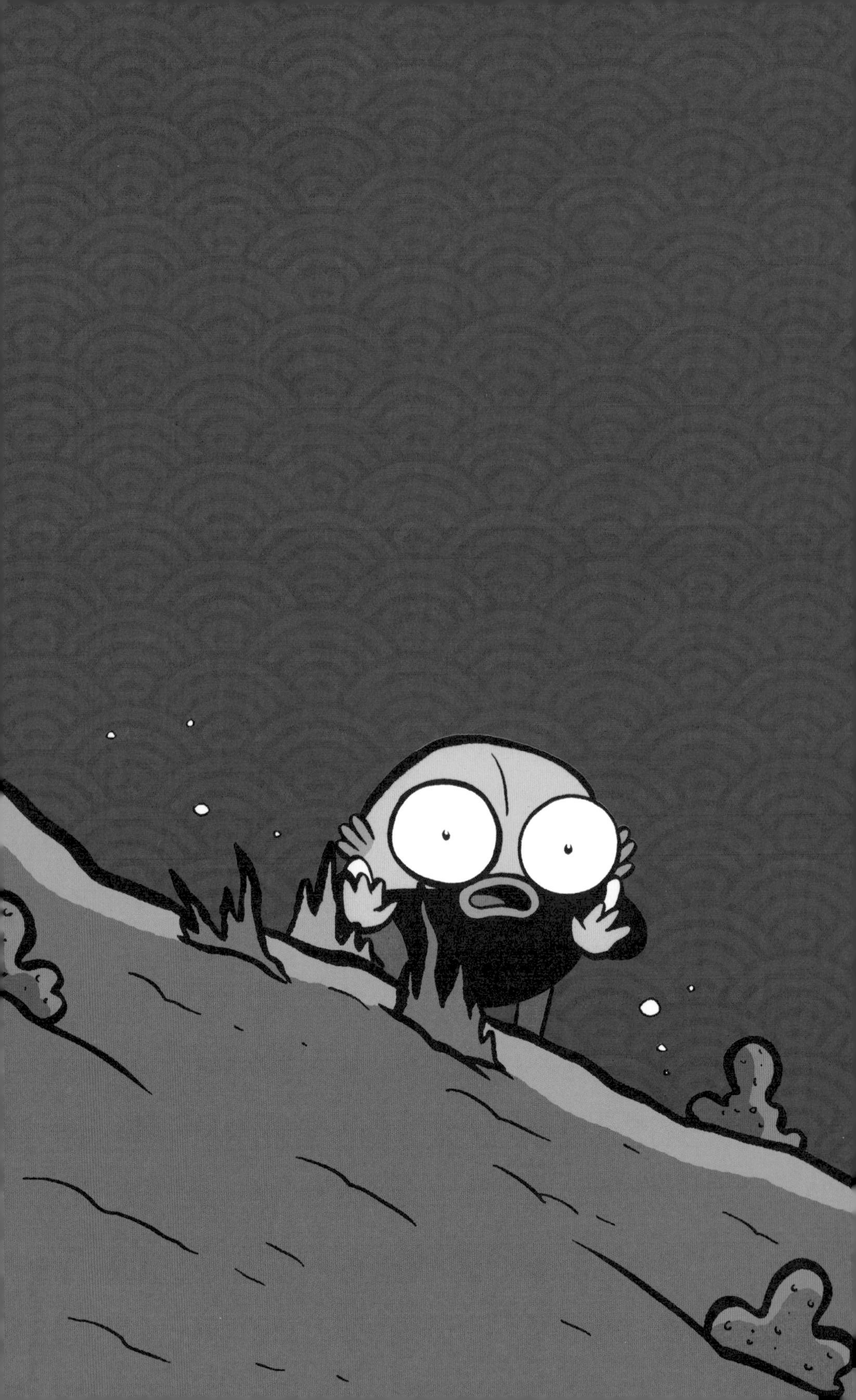

TURN THE PAGE FOR A BONUS MERMIN COMIC "A MERMIN HALLOWEEN!"

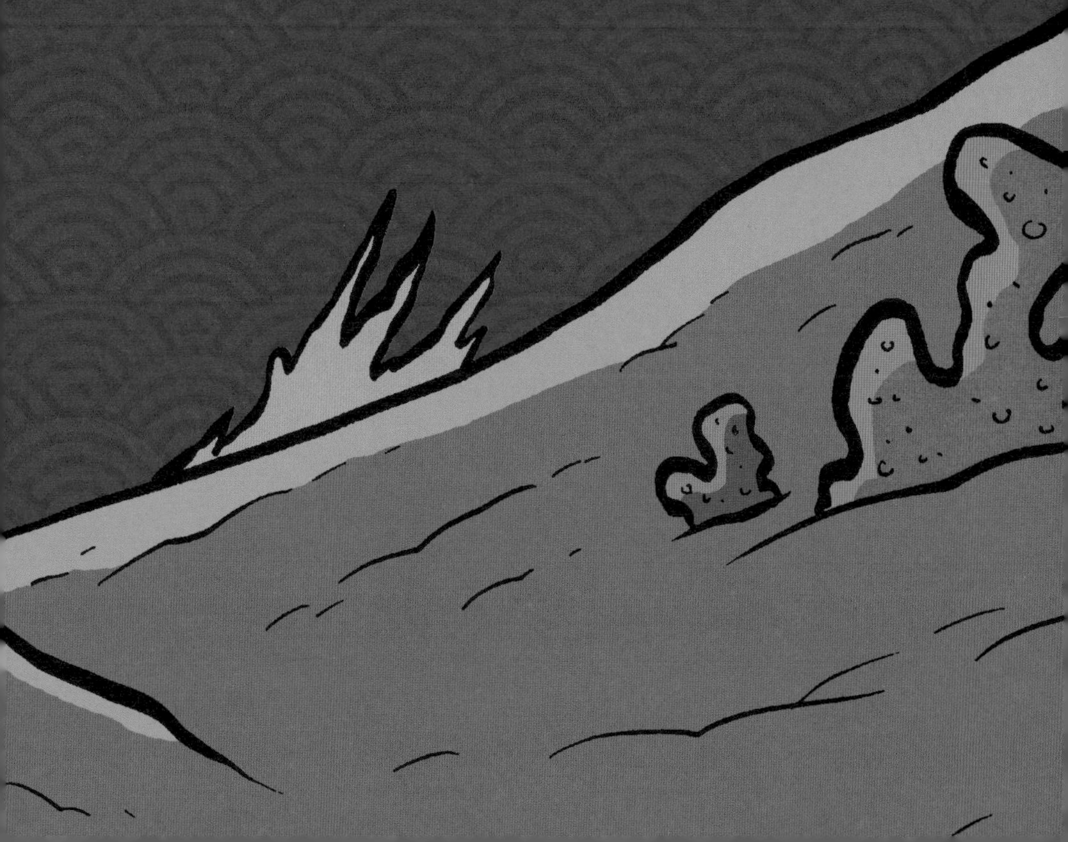

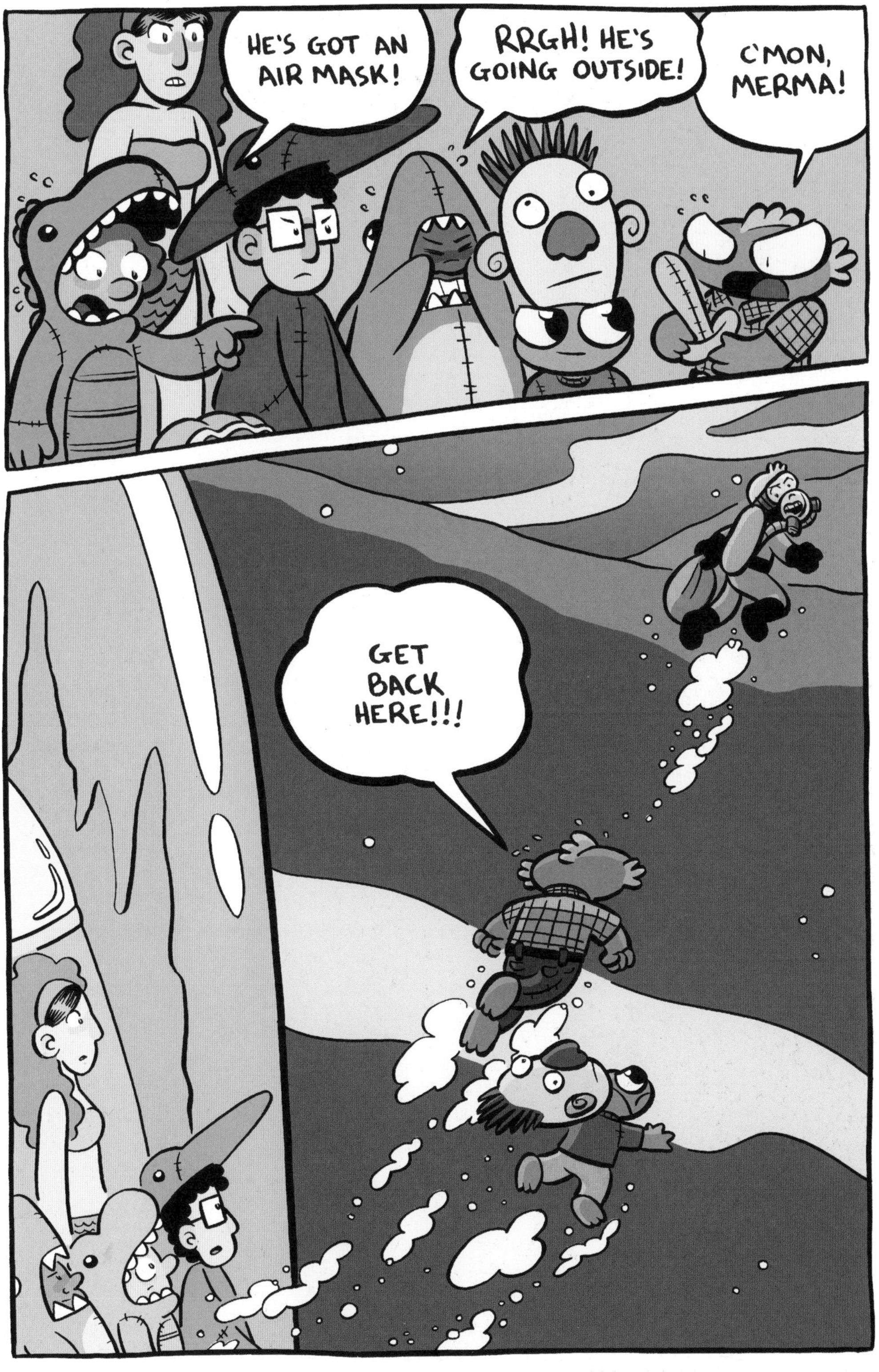
HE'S GOT AN AIR MASK!
RRGH! HE'S GOING OUTSIDE!
C'MON, MERMA!
GET BACK HERE!!!

144

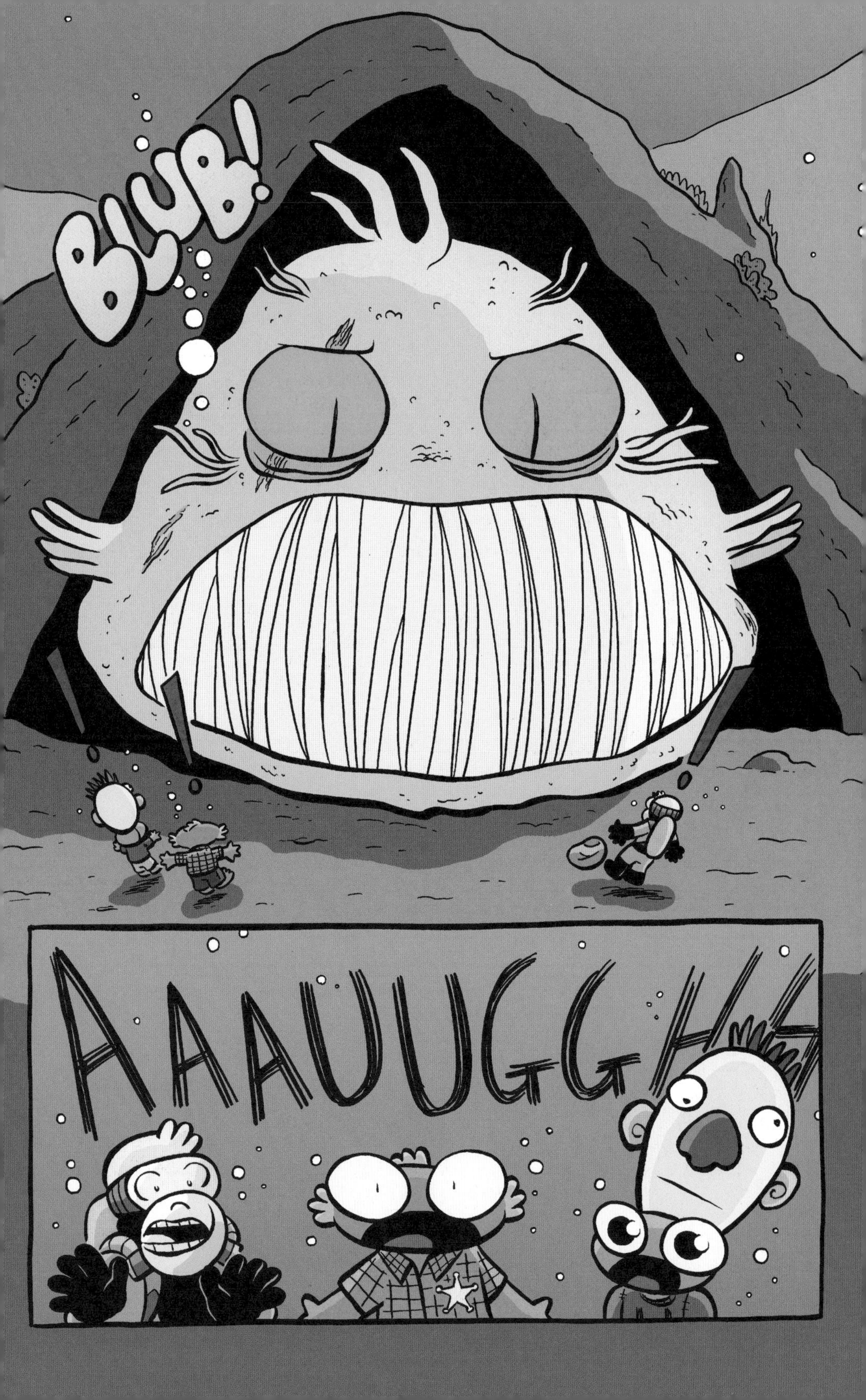
BLUB!
AAAUUGGHH

MERMIN™

SKETCHES

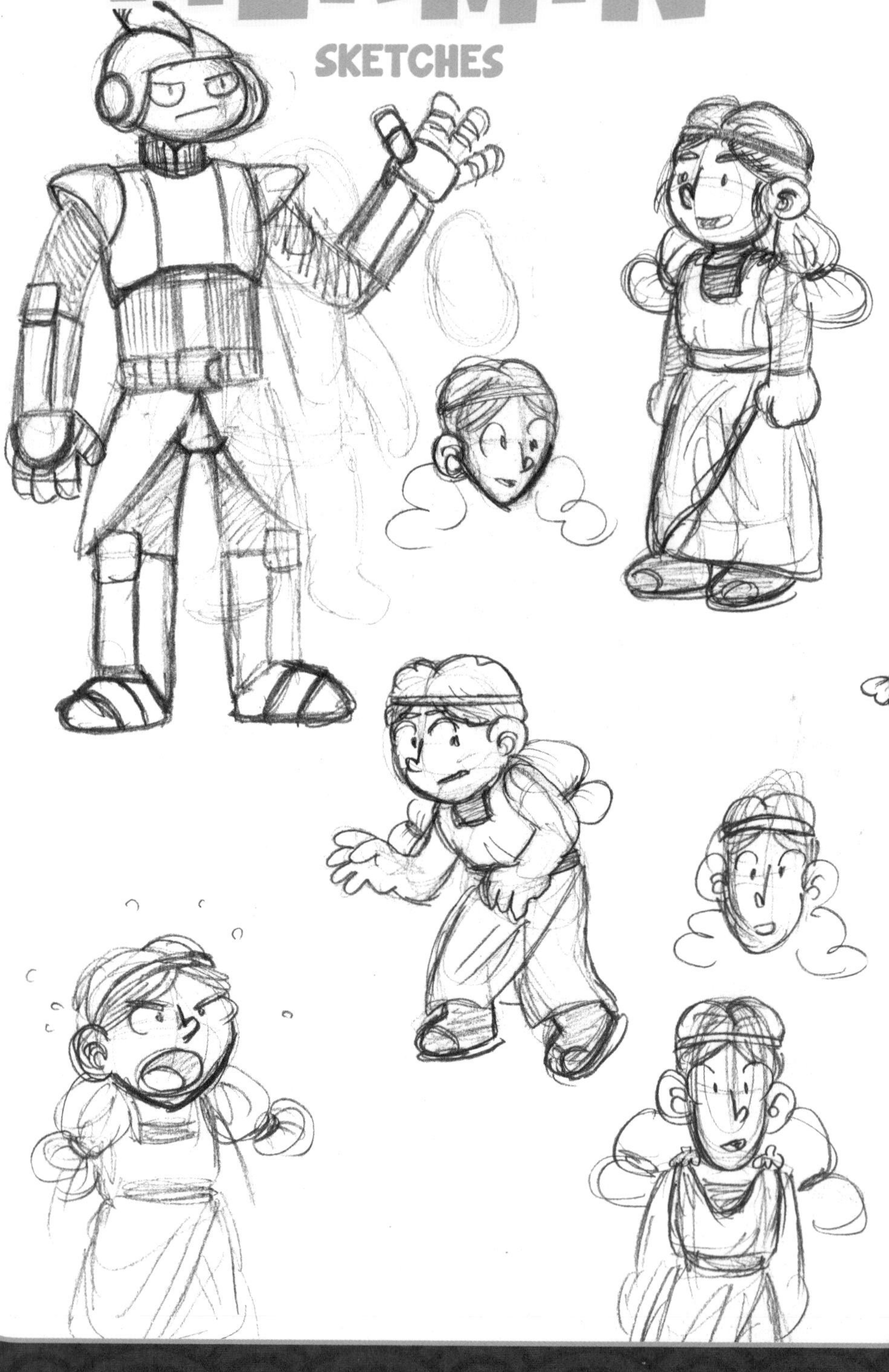

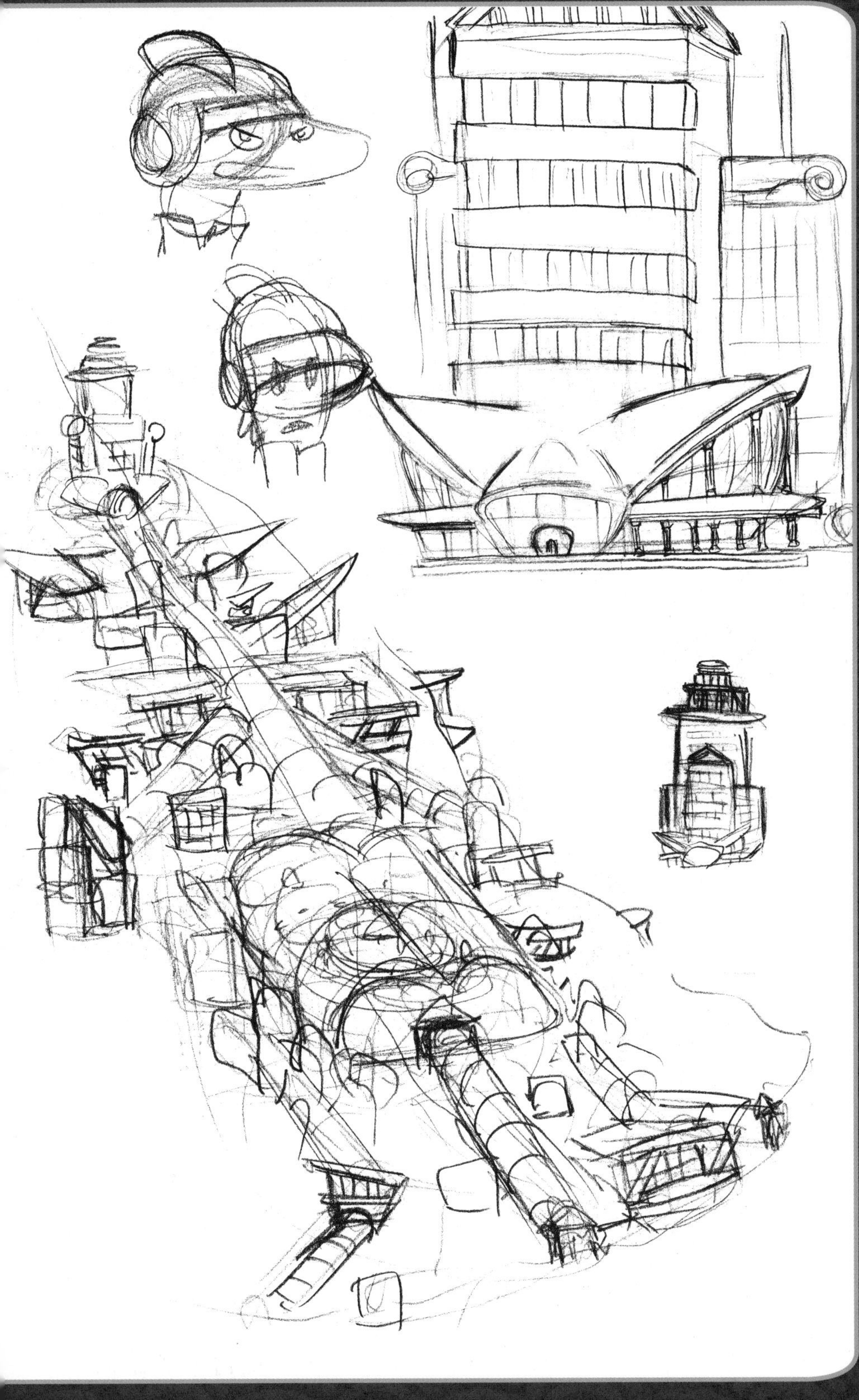

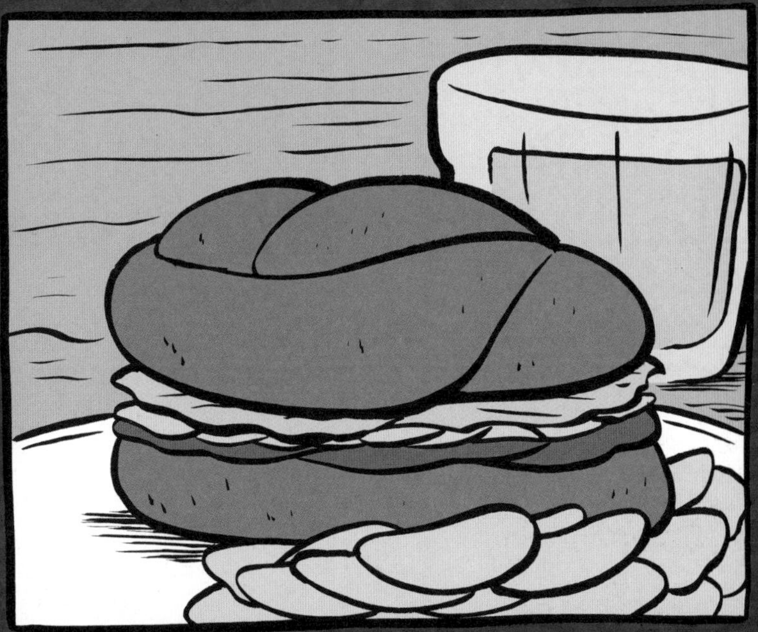

Joey Weiser's comics have appeared in several publications including *SpongeBob Comics* and the award-winning *Flight* series. His debut graphic novel, *The Ride Home*, was published in 2007 by AdHouse Books, and the *Mermin* graphic novels are currently being published through Oni Press. He is a graduate of the Savannah College of Art & Design, and he currently lives in Athens, Georgia.

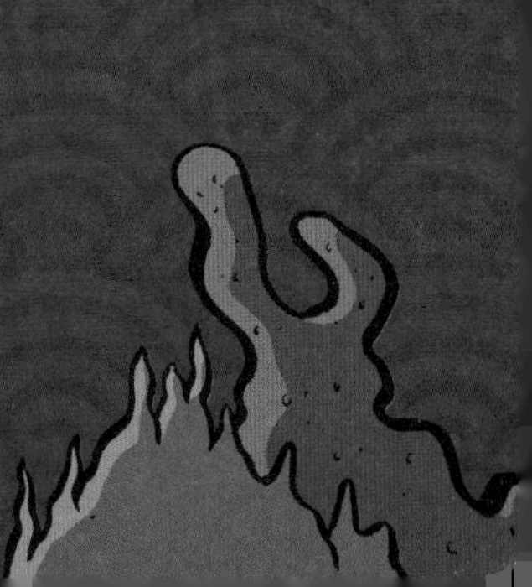

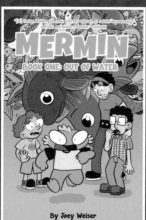